well - only opera is going even
more down the drain -

The approach is none professional
and less than mediocre - and
I have been so spoiled - so
to resume is really something
I'm not looking forward to -

Anyway we shall see -
If you want to write to me
I'll be in San Remo - C/o Pino
T. Di Stefano till the 2nd of
August then I'll probably be
travelling thru Spain to visit
George Moore & wife - then
San Remo or Paris - My
telephone in San Remo is
6012 -

I hope all goes for the
best and let me hear from
you -

All my affection &
friendship

Maria -

MARIA

Nadia Stancioff

MARIA
Callas Remembered

E. P. DUTTON  NEW YORK

Published in the United States by E. P. Dutton,
a division of NAL Penguin Inc.,
2 Park Avenue, New York, N.Y. 10016.

Published simultaneously in Canada by
Fitzhenry and Whiteside Limited, Toronto.

Library of Congress Cataloging-in-Publication Data

Stancioff, Nadia.
Maria.

1. Callas, Maria, 1923–1977.   2. Singers—Biography.
3. Stancioff, Nadia.   I. Title.
ML420.C18S68   1987   782.1'082'4 [B]   87-9195

ISBN: 0-525-24565-0

W

DESIGNED BY EARL TIDWELL

1 3 5 7 9 10 8 6 4 2

First Edition

For my mother,
the Petchenegs, and Jane Montant

"I do not like being called 'La Divina.' . . . I am Maria Callas. And I am only a woman."

—from an article by John Gruen
The New York Times
Sunday, October 31, 1971

Contents

Contents

Photo sections follow page 70 and 134.

Acknowledgments

My profoundest gratitude goes to my family and to those friends whose extraordinary generosity, support, and encouragement provided me with the strength to complete a project that at times seemed impossible: William Crawford, Jerret Engle, Adam Fremantle, Monique de Gravelaine Gadaud, Teresa and Sumner Gerard, Joel Honig, Anne Muheim, Alicia Paolozzi, Valeria Pedemonte, Edith and Karl Schönborn, Francis and Natalia Schell, Aimée Rachat Silverio and Feodora de Rosenzweig Diaz.

My grateful acknowledgments and thanks to the following for their help and faith: Andrea Anson, John Ardoin, Elena Balestri, Leslie and Rutgers Barclay, Joaquin Bernal, Giulia Cruise, Philippe Denis, Carole DeSanti, Luigi di Angioy, Dominick Dunne, Richard Fremantle, André Gadaud, Marina and Michael of Greece, Wendy Hanson, Norma Krause Herzfeld, Matteo Iacoviello, Carolina and Mario Laserna, Stevia

Lesher, Polyvios Marchand, Fiorella Mariani, Thiery Mille-rand, Gustav Ortner, Nicolas Pisaris, Henry Pleasants, Pierre-André Podbielski, Vivianne and Edmund Purdom, Lydia Redmond, Milava Riston, Cristina Sarafoff, Andreas and Ya-cinthy Stathopoulos, Rouben Ter-Arutunian, TPM Europe Inc., Caron Van Dyck, Eugenia Velez, Michael Willis, Richard Wincor, Joseph Wishy and Alexandra Zotos.

Space does not permit a separate listing of the names of those people who were kind enough to grant me their precious time for interviews. To them my heartfelt thanks.

Introduction

My friendship with Maria Callas began in 1969 during the filming of Pasolini's *Medea*. This book is, more than anything, about that friendship; for through it I came to know an intriguing and sensitive person who was often at odds with the diva the world knew and fans adored.

After Maria died in 1977, friends urged me to write an article in her memory. They felt I should share my personal view of the Maria Callas I had known during the last eight years of her life. And I had often promised Maria that I would help her tell her side of the story.

But an avalanche of articles and books on Callas followed her death. As she had always predicted, the "vultures" pillaged and exploited her memory. A few of the books and articles were well researched and scholarly, but most were repetitious gossip, written by self-appointed authorities on a woman they had never met. When I would mention my desire to add to the existing material, most people's reaction was: "What? Another book on Callas? Hasn't *everything* been said?"

One friend expressed it more brutally. "Why would you bother writing about such a dull woman?" he said. "No one cares about *her*. What we are interested in is Callas, *the voice*."

Such disparaging remarks annoyed me, but also made me more determined. I did intend to keep my word and write about Maria. But writing about her so soon after her death would have been comparable to sharing a very personal secret with a total stranger. The grief of her sudden death was too vivid. For a long while, I was very defensive about our friendship and concluded that the best way to pay her homage and prove my friendship was through silence. Eventually I moved from Rome, where I had been living for many years, back to New York, and there, the pressures of my new life and career seemed to promise to put the matter on the back burner indefinitely.

It had not been easy to leave Rome, a city that has always drawn me. My father, a Bulgarian diplomat, had been assigned there shortly before I was born, but I certainly cannot credit childhood memories for my attachment, as I was only two years old when we departed. I owed my return to Rome to my love for an Italian diplomat I'd met during my last year of college. The romance did not last, but, by then, I had fallen in love with the city.

After meeting Maria, Rome became even more important to me. I identified the city with our friendship. It was there that we worked together and really got to know each other. It was there, later, that she returned to look for comfort and to find cheer among new friends—many of them—whose youth and cultural diversity appealed to her. "With your friends," she once remarked to me, "I neither have to explain myself nor feel I am jeopardizing my image."

Rome became a haven from her growing solitude, a parenthesis to the disappointments and doubts brought on by her waning career. And yet, she rarely stayed longer than two weeks at a time. The hope of recording, the offer of a film role or a telephone call from Onassis, who had by that time reentered her life, would take her back to Paris.

Such globe hopping was a natural part of life for Maria. Having lived in many countries and traveled extensively, she had been exposed to a variety of customs and cultures she unconsciously made her own. She was very "exportable," adapting with ease to most situations and social spheres. Yet despite the gracious surface, she always remained "the foreigner," belonging to no country.

The very nature of Maria's life separated her from people. They were fascinated by the glamour and mystery but could not pigeonhole her within any particular culture or way of life. She wasn't French, after all, nor truly American. And she had lived in Greece for only eight years. Always outside those categories, Maria was seen as something of a singular commodity. Though this singularity was part of her allure, it had a dark side. It led to a sense of alienation that haunted her all her life. It constantly posed the question of "acceptance." It fueled her search for a sense of belonging, for a "country" to call her own.

I am familiar with that struggle. After sixteen years of work in film and public relations, I found myself, in 1978, exchanging the rewarding life Italy had offered me for the competitive world of New York City, where I was an unknown.

My life had gradually become a tug-of-war. The United States was where my family, for the most part, had settled after the upheaval of World War II. Being a naturalized American citizen, it seemed hypocritical to be living outside the country to which I had chosen allegiance. My decision to leave Rome and my own small but successful public relations business in the arts had been aided by the growing political unrest that swept Italy in the late seventies and the bureaucratic problems aliens were experiencing in obtaining work permits. It all spelled out: Go home! It seemed to be then or never.

Though I sometimes viewed Maria's choice of her Paris home as arbitrary, I told myself that I, on the other hand, belonged in New York. It was a difficult readjustment. The values of the big city bore little relation to those I had left abroad. Still, after the first year, I became somewhat accustomed to the pressures of my new life, and began to think of myself as a New Yorker and to accept the importance of the almighty dollar in the battle for survival. Then I was offered a job (as production coordinator and assistant to the producer) for the movie version of the *Fantasticks*. It was to be shot in Rome.

I jumped at the chance to return; I was ecstatic at the thought! Clearly, the umbilical cord had not been entirely severed.

Being bilingual, I was sent ahead to find a studio and recruit the best crew available. In four days I stuffed my personal belongings into overcrowded closets, handed the key of my newly found apartment to the friend who was to occupy it for the next six months and left a humid, airless Manhattan without regret.

In Rome, I worked diligently to convince some of Italy's most respected artists and technicians to put off their sacred summer vacation until the arrival of the *americani*. The *americani,* meanwhile, refused to believe that the "Hollywood of

Italy," let alone the entire country, could come to a standstill for three weeks during the Ferragosto holidays—or that Fellini could not be removed from Cinecittà's Teatro 5.

It had been a lean year in Italian cinema, but Fellini was at work shooting his latest extravaganza, *City of Women*. As is his custom, he had taken over the immense Teatro 5 and since he loathes working on location, he had a replica of a roller coaster built inside the studio. He was behind schedule. No one ever knew how long Fellini would occupy a studio. He didn't know himself, until he was satisfied with the material he had shot. But no one, not even his own producer, suggested that he rush, let alone leave.

"His contract is up," my American producer shouted over the phone. "He's just got to face it and clear out!"

Well, this was my job, after all; cross-cultural arbitration. I did my best. "Fellini is an institution in this country," I tried to explain. "I don't know anyone who would have the nerve to tell him to clear out."

"We've got to get in that studio! You tell him to take his roller coaster down."

"But in August the whole place is closed! Besides, contracts are adjustable when it comes to Fellini."

"Then what's the point of a contract? Go to Cinecittà and have a talk with him!"

And so, the following day, I set out for Cinecittà.

I had done some dubbing for Fellini, subsequently worked on his *Casanova* and had been totally won over by the genius and the man. To work with "the Maestro" is considered more an honor than a job in the Italian cinema. The notoriously tardy Italians report punctually when working on one of his productions, and when Fellini's voice calls for *silenzio,* a religious stillness descends on the set, an atmosphere foreign to

Italian productions, which are unaccustomed to using direct sound.

I was lucky. I arrived at Teatro 5 during a break. "Nadiona, *carissima*"—he loves using superlatives—"what a pleasant surprise!" he exclaimed, walking me out of the building. "Come along, I want to check the progress of next week's costumes. We can chat on the way."

"You'll be here next week?" I questioned timidly.

"Oh yes, we have a few more scenes to complete. If you'd like to come out and watch, you are most welcome. What brings you back to *bella Roma* this time? You seem to have difficulty in staying away for long."

I told him about the *Fantasticks* project.

"Where are you shooting?" he inquired.

"In the largest available studio in Rome."

He looked at me knowingly. A telephone call requested his presence on the set.

"You must come out next week. We have to catch up. Don't forget, we'll be in Teatro 5. *Ciao, carissima*."

Our meeting was ended. I had "spoken" with Fellini.

In the weeks that followed, there was more of the same, but rather than enjoying the cross-cultural roulette, I began to notice myself as the consistent loser on both sides of the Atlantic, as every phone call announced another delay in the Americans' arrival plans. Then, without explanation or apology, they called off the production completely.

Their unethical behavior infuriated me. Not only had I lost a job, but I had lost face with colleagues in the Italian film industry, a fate comparable to the firing squad in a country where *bella figura*, outward appearance, is terribly important. Returning to New York was out of the question. There would be no job opportunities in August and my apartment was sublet until November.

I called friends. No one was home. I tried to flee to Sardinia and better memories, but I could not get a reservation in the holiday rush of August.

Suddenly, I caught myself giving in to an incredible sense of loneliness. Why was I back in the country I had so painfully left a year earlier? What did I want? Where *did* I belong?

I remember looking out at the small park facing my window. Rome was still after the Ferragosto exodus. Only the footsteps of an occasional tourist interrupted the refreshing gurgle of the fountain. The deserted streets and absence of noisy traffic emphasized my predicament. In my loneliness I thought of Maria again.

Like my own, Maria's identity was closely linked to her concept of professionalism and to its accompanying sense of purpose and security. It reinforced who we were—without it, we felt vulnerable. That vulnerability and lack of control brought about the kind of loneliness I know Maria feared most: an isolating helplessness. While I at least had a devoted family (scattered all over the world) and close friends (somewhere), Maria's very isolation was sometimes the most striking thing about her. At such moments, it was Maria against the world.

Now I could hear her lecturing me in her northern Italian lilt.

"You are too trusting, my dear Nadia. There is no honesty or honor left in this world. Don't trust anyone, even those closest to you. Isn't it awful to have to live this way? We must always be on guard. They hit us harder because we are tall and imposing. We give the impression of strength. We are expected to land on our feet, without tears, without breaking down. Nobody consoles or feels sorry for us. It infuriates me! Why don't people realize that we big girls are as fragile as pocket-sized women? How I'd like to let myself go! Women's tears work wonders. I'm tired of picking up the pieces on my own, aren't you? I should have learned long ago how to cry effectively offstage."

"How true, Maria," I found myself thinking aloud. "How right you are."

The thought of her tenacity somehow shook me out of my listlessness. That's when I picked up pen and paper and began to write about Maria.

I had nothing else to do and no one to interrupt me. The work went quickly at first, then suddenly became laborious. What was the point? I asked myself. Who would care? Other questions arose. Should I reveal the private Maria? Could I portray her fairly—her defects as well as her virtues? Would I be betraying her confidence? As her friend, I knew how fiercely the woman had tried to separate the very mortal Maria from the public figure of Callas.

I soon discovered another stumbling block: I had only sparse information on her childhood and adolescence. Those were subjects she had touched on only fleetingly; in fact, she seemed to dislike discussing them. I was frustrated with myself for not having asked her questions during our holidays together. Yet I knew why I had not. Our friendship was based on a mutual respect that left certain things unsaid. I always felt I would come to share her secrets at the appropriate times. It never occurred to me that there was so little time; that I would be left with mostly an emotional story to tell. One with so many missing links.

As I set out to fill those gaps, my project steadily gained momentum over the next two years. As I worked, I began to realize how many aspects of Maria's life contained similarities to my own: the war, the roving existence, our love for the arts and our medley of languages. I also came to sense other Marias I had not known. Having met her at the end of her career, I felt I needed to add other people's impressions to my own. Now that I was fully committed to the project, I traveled extensively, interviewing Maria's friends and colleagues, determined to get a broader image of the woman and the artist. The results were fascinating, infuriating and mystifying.

The pages that follow are not an attempt at another biography. Maria's years of artistic achievement have been thoroughly documented elsewhere, and I am neither a musicologist nor an authority on Callas's career, in spite of my extensive research. Instead, my intent is to give an honest portrayal of a friend who also happened to be Maria Callas. As you will see through the personal and very different visions of those with whom I spoke, that woman had many sides. These points of view have added insight and have often been at odds with my memories of Maria and have helped me better understand the character and the life of a friend I cared a lot for. And this has also, oddly but somehow unavoidably, become a bit my story as well as hers.

It is difficult to give people their due, people who are memories, be they important or not. What matters is what they meant to us. One often says too much or too little. What I hope to present is the woman *I* knew.

MARIA

I

Prelude
Tragonissi, 1970

Ten years have passed since Maria Callas's death, yet it's hard for me to grasp that. For me the passage has not been measured by time but by emotion. I feel sudden, overwhelming moments of her presence, evoked by images and sounds; flashes take me back and forth between what is and what was. My memory recalls Maria as if seen in a film: in blurred, fleeting images, like those that guide our minds back to the vivid scenes and sensations of the past.

After so many years and the effort of compiling material for this memoir, my own memory intermingles with tableaux from conversations with those who knew, thought they knew, loved or hated Maria Callas. I knew Maria well; yet, when she was gone, I was astonished at how much I needed other people's testimonies to discover the Maria I had never met.

The first flashback occurred with the shock of Maria's death: sounds and images, a film played back at high speed.

Gradually the dizzy patterns crystallized, the incomprehensible noises became words. For me it was a warm sound, a voice with European inflections and cadence, its exact origin difficult to pinpoint.

"Isn't this place glorious? *Che bello!* Wouldn't it be perfect if we could stay forever? On second thought, no. Leisure would get on my nerves in the long run. I'd get impatient and want to be back to work."

As the image comes into focus, there is Maria Callas on the beach of an island where we spent a holiday sixteen years earlier; a slim figure in a two-piece bathing suit, long auburn hair loosely flowing around her shoulders, the Greek mainland a thin line on the horizon.

"If you think things would become tedious so quickly, consider what awaits us in heaven," I teased, "the sameness of it all. Hopping from cloud to cloud. What a bore."

"I hope it won't be quite like that, Nadia," Maria laughed. "To tell you the truth, I'm a little confused about my idea of an afterlife. I believe in God, but not in heaven and hell; I tend to believe in reincarnation. I think we pay for our actions on earth by returning and bettering ourselves each time. Do you believe in reincarnation?"

"Only when I find it convenient. I would hate to come back as a donkey or a rhinoceros. If you had a choice, Maria, what would you choose to come back as?"

"As a fish, I think."

"How about a sea gull? Wouldn't it be lovely to be a sun-basking Mediterranean sea gull? That way, you could enjoy both the sea and the air."

"I'm not sure I like that idea. Sea gulls have such ugly voices."

"Make a special request. Ask to be a sea gull with the voice of a nightingale."

"In that case, I accept. Think how wonderful it will be not to have to answer the phone, not to have to give interviews to journalists who change everything you say. I won't ever have to diet again or worry about my low blood pressure."

This lighthearted chitchat took place on the tiny island of Tragonissi, owned by Maria's friend and admirer Pericles Embiricos, who had invited us to spend a couple of weeks there. It was a fabulous day bathed in light and color. The Greek sea and sky were one. The scent of wild herbs, ripe peaches and oleanders reached us with the midday heat as we sunbathed by the shore. Three days away from Paris and Rome had transformed us. We were coddled in comfort and luxury, the most precious gift being the total privacy and peace the island offered. The only sound was the sea washing the burning sun off the pebbles and tumbling them back to the shore.

The sun and sea had smoothed Maria's drawn features. The anxious look was gone from her eyes. She glowed with contentment and health. She was in her element. She was Greek. She was home.

"If I should die before you," Maria continued, "I want you to tell people what I am *really* like. You know me better than most people."

"What are you talking about?" I interrupted. "Why should you die before me? You are only a few years older than I am and strong as an ox. Don't talk nonsense. Why are you trying to darken this perfect day?"

"I don't mean it that way, Nadia. I'm not being morbid. I just want to tell you something. What I mean is, people—my fans, the general public—have no idea who I am. This Callas myth! The Deee-va! 'The soprano of the century!' They haven't an inkling who Maria is. I just want to make sure someone *tells* them. Maybe I should write my autobiography . . . set the record straight. I'm the only one who's lived

[3]

it. Several magazines and publishing houses have asked me to tell my story. Well, I'll give it some thought when I get back to Paris. Maybe you'd like to do it with me, *cara*? How about helping me out this winter? I think it will be easier if we do it together. Your questions will revive my memory. What do you say? Oh, wait till that book comes out. A lot of people will wish me dead then." Exhilarated, Maria rubbed globs of suntan lotion on her legs with vigor.

"My funeral," she went on. "Can you imagine what my funeral will be like? Hundreds of people pushing and shoving, all saying they loved me and we were best of friends. I can see them now! Dressed in penguin suits, a handkerchief to their dry eyes, their main preoccupation the television cameras. I wonder how many people will be there who really love me? Four? Five? Anyway, *I'm* going to enjoy myself. I'll be hiding behind a column watching the performance." Orchestrator, audience and critic of her final performance—the reversal of roles delighted Maria.

"You know, I'm not afraid of coming to the end of the road. That is a natural part of being. What I'm afraid of is how the road ends. I just pray that God will take me before I'm old and disabled. I would find it terrible to be a burden to others. Besides, who will take care of me? Not my family! And I don't want to linger, suffering with some terrible disease, like those patients doctors and families keep alive for years; those poor devils in plastic tents, full of tubes. *Per carità!* If it should come to that, please, I beg you, pull the plug. I promise I'll do the same for you. Oh, while we are at it, remember Nadia, I don't want to be buried in one of those ghastly cemeteries on the way to the airport. I really want to be cremated and have my ashes scattered here, over the Aegean."

I reminded Maria that if she wanted to be cremated, she should state it in her will, as laws regarding cremation are different in each country and religion.

"I doubt that there would be any problem with the Greek Orthodox Church. Our church is very human. It's happier than the Catholic or Protestant religion. Even our funerals are happy. The church is filled with masses of flowers. The coffin is covered with them too. It gives one a spirit of hope and rebirth. That's the way I want it at my funeral. I want it to be joyful and full of flowers . . . please, none of those gloomy wreaths!"

An odd conversation for two women sunbathing on a beautiful island, yet we found it perfectly natural. Perhaps it was because we *had* left the world.

"I think I'll go for a swim before we are called in to lunch." Maria sprang to her feet, tied her auburn hair in a knot, donned flippers and goggles, strapped a large knife to her upper leg and dove into the clear water.

From the shore I watched her descent with amazement. Her movements were youthful and agile. Except for her heavy legs, her figure in no way hinted that she had ever weighed 250 pounds, nor did it betray her forty-six years. I had never thought of her as athletic. She'd always complained about walking, asking to be driven whenever possible. The aquatic Maria was a revelation.

Joined by Pixie and Djedda, Maria's toy poodles, I waited for her to surface. Ages went by, but there was no Maria. The dogs looked at me questioningly, then set off in a high-pitched concert as they ran to and fro at the water's edge. I was beginning to question my impression of Maria's swimming capability when a hand clutching a broken terra-cotta urn rose out of the water and the other came up with a large shell.

MARIA

Back on the beach Maria triumphantly displayed her trophies. My ohs and ahs were genuine (perhaps just a trace obligatory) as I admired her salvaging skills before returning to my reading.

But in midsentence, I was screaming, drenched book in hand. Maria, now doubled up with laughter, had just given me a cooling-off with an urnful of sea water.

Gathering my wet belongings, I followed the still giggling Maria through the flowered garden up to the house to change for lunch. It was one o'clock and time for another *cordon bleu* feast prepared by the French chef. These wonderful meals were our only commitment and, for those two idyllic weeks, our only timetable.

2

Flashback
A Job with Callas

As with most good things in my life, meeting and working with Maria Callas happened by chance.

It was spring of 1969. Rome was packed with Easter-week pilgrims, and the warm weather had brought the Romans out of winter confinement and back into their outdoor living rooms: the piazzas designed by Bramante, Michelangelo and Bernini. In crowded sidewalk cafés, people gossiped, discussed politics or just relaxed while scrutinizing the parade of beautiful women and the varied fauna of tourists.

I was engrossed in the spectacle at Piazza di Spagna when I suddenly saw an old friend, the film producer Franco Rossellini, director Roberto Rossellini's handsome nephew. We hadn't seen each other for over a year. During our conversation, Franco mentioned his next film project.

"I'm planning to do a film version of *Medea*. Pier Paolo Pasolini will direct it and . . . guess who is going to play Medea?"

I suggested Anna Magnani and Irene Papas.

"No, the star is going to be Maria Callas. How about that for a great coup! It will be her first film—and she'll be acting in it, not singing. Listen—seeing you has given me an idea. Why don't you do the public relations for us? Would you be interested? You could help Matteo Spinola with the foreign press when we get to Turkey."

Typical Italian approach to a job, I thought. This would never happen at home. Yet, what strikes me now was that I found it a perfectly natural way to conduct business. I had become a true Roman.

But work with Callas? In Turkey? During my career I had worked with a number of difficult celebrities, at times in uncomfortable circumstances, but Callas and Turkey seemed too much to contend with simultaneously. Her press coverage over the years was anything but encouraging. Most of the unflattering adjectives in any language seemed to have been applied to her. She was depicted as temperamental, ill-humored, demanding, spoiled—in short, an egocentric *monstre sacré*. Would I willingly tie myself down to several months of shooting in an inaccessible area of Turkey with such an impossible woman?

"Thank you for thinking of me, Franco," I answered, "but I'll be working at the Spoleto Festival in May and June as usual, after which I must be around to keep an eye on my P.R. accounts, which are doing very well. I can't just drop everything and vanish for three months even for Maria Callas. Anyway, she's not going to sing, so what's the interest?"

"Nadia, you don't seem to realize the unique opportunity I am offering you. Listen, after this job with Callas, your accounts will double. Besides, think of the exotic places you will have a chance to visit—Ankara, Istanbul . . . the fascinating Turkish men," he added with a wink. "What more do you want out of a job?" Franco argued that the shooting would take place in late summer, when business was slow in Rome. "You know as well as I do that there isn't a soul around in the summer. This town is a *tomba* until September."

He had a point, but I had additional doubts when I thought of Callas's reputation for last-minute cancellations. The film, I felt, had a strong chance of remaining an idea. And what about my vacation plans in the Dolomites? The time I'd set aside to spend with my beau, to relax, picnic in the woods and read? Why should I give that up for the "tigress," as the press had nicknamed her?

"You see," Franco explained, "this is a prestige job. I can't just hire anyone. It has to be someone with your experience and savoir faire. I can't think of anyone who could do this job as well as you. I'll tell our administrator that you'll be by to sign the contract. Okay? That's wonderful!"

Franco, like many Italians, can convince one of just about anything with his charm alone. I had to admit, the project intrigued me even though the thought of disrupting my summer was unsettling.

The following week we met at Piazza del Popolo's Caffè Canova. "Well, Franco," I told him, "your proposal is titillating, but there is a 'however.' I won't sign a contract until I've spent two working weeks with Callas. If I don't like her, I'll feel free to leave. I'm not going to work with her if she's a monster."

Franco was laughing. "Listen to the way you are carrying on. One would think *you* were the diva!" We baptized my unsigned contract with a Campari soda in the Roman sun.

*

"Do you remember how scared you were about working with her?" said Franco Rossellini, one of the first people I interviewed after I started to write about Maria. We spoke of *Medea* over a lunch of mozzarella and spinach (without oil or dressing). Franco, once rail-thin, had become portly in ten years and was now very determinedly dieting.

"Remember," he continued, "how you didn't want to commit yourself? Well, now I can tell you something. Callas was so insecure that she didn't sign her contract until we were halfway through the film. Incredible, no? I prayed and kept my fingers crossed. What could I do? I knew I had to be patient. With someone like Maria, if you are not patient you don't make the film."

My first encounter with Callas occurred on an evening in May. She was expected in Rome for costume fittings and screen tests. Rossellini and I went to the airport to meet her in a chauffeur-driven Cadillac hired for the occasion. The production office had obtained permission for Franco to greet Callas on the runway, before the press descended on her. I watched him disappear into the air terminal clutching an immense bouquet of red roses and speculated on what was to follow.

The wait in the car seemed endless. The driver embarked on a run-of-the-mill questionnaire regarding my private life and job status. I was annoyed I hadn't brought a book along.

Suddenly, without warning, an untidy group of screaming paparazzi materialized from nowhere. Shoving each other and shouting, they ran backward so as not to lose sight of their prey for an instant.

Intrigued by the clamor, I stepped out of the car. Only by standing on tiptoe was I able to see the Diva in the midst of this frenzied knot of people. Her image appeared and disappeared, her features a chalk mask under the flash of lights.

Eyes open, mouth shut. Eyes smiling, mouth open. Profile. Full-face, pouting. The battle and the voices grew more intense as they approached the car. They had little time left.

"Signora Callas, is it true you are here to make a musical?"

"Hey, Maria, give me a smile. Over here, Maria. Look over here!"

"Have you seen Onassis since he got married? How come he left you for that American?"

"When are you going to come back to sing at La Scala?"

"*Signori, basta, basta.* That's enough, now. Thank you all for coming, but the Signora is tired."

With great patience and ability, Franco waved his long arms to separate the crowd of newsmen and stepped out of the group with Callas at his side.

First of all, she was taller and slimmer than I expected. She wore a navy blue pantsuit with gold buttons down the front and on the pockets and cuffs, and matching gold earrings. I remember thinking, Biki (Maria's favorite high-fashion designer and longtime friend) has gone wild with the gold buttons! Her hair was brushed away from her face, knotted in a thick double chignon. Her features were too pronounced and heavy to be considered pretty or beautiful. She was handsome. She had style, presence and great nobility of carriage. Her dark eyes were her striking feature. They were questioning and penetrating, yet a certain reserve made it difficult to tell what lay behind them. Of course I could not have a fresh opinion, influenced as I was by the many articles and photographs I had seen. I had come prepared to dislike her, but my animosity was replaced by a sense of curiosity and perhaps a touch of clemency.

During the drive into town, Callas chatted with Franco about her life in Paris and the various friends they had in common. She had not addressed me since the initial introduction at the airport. Once or twice I caught her looking at me through oversized horn-rimmed glasses, which she'd put on the minute the paparazzi were out of sight. Seeing that I noticed her glances, she smiled faintly and turned to resume her conversation with Franco. She talked endlessly and besieged Franco with questions regarding the professional appointments planned in the days that were to follow. Her chatter exasperated me. If she's always like this, I thought, she'll drive me around the bend in no time.

"Franco," she said, turning to face me, "my secretary, Signora Stancioff, is very quiet. By the way, why wasn't she allowed to enter the inner sanctum of the airport with you? Don't tell me you waited in the car all this time, Signora Stancioff?"

Franco laughed uncomfortably and mumbled something about my not minding, and changed the subject. Her concern surprised me, but I found it strange that she had addressed me as her secretary. I gave the incident little weight. After all, I knew that I'd been hired to do public relations.

The arrival at the Grand Hotel was perfectly timed. We were met by the hotel manager, Natale Rusconi. Madame Callas seemed flattered by his welcome, appreciative of the proficiency of one of Europe's great hoteliers. He had chosen a spacious top-floor suite to assure her privacy. The apartment was furnished with antiques and decorated with precious silks. The Empire furniture was set off by the soft hues of Aubusson carpets. Above a sideboard, flanked by ornamental vases, the dazzle of the crystal chandelier was reflected in a period mirror. There were flowers everywhere, mostly roses and gardenias, which I was soon to learn were Maria's favorite. Friends and admirers had filled the room with fragrance.

Callas was visibly pleased with her accommodations. She walked around from room to room inspecting cupboards and admiring knicknacks. Having finished her tour, she turned to the manager and asked, "And where is Bruna sleeping?"

Rusconi looked puzzled. "Bruna?" he repeated.

"Bruna Lupoli, my maid. She always has a room near me when I travel . . . and what about my chauffeur, Ferruccio?"

"Oh, of course, of course," Rusconi broke in, "we have taken care of their rooms, Madame Callas."

"Could I see them?" Callas asked.

"See the servants' quarters?" Rusconi said incredulously, deep color rising to his cheeks.

"Yes, I'd like to see them now." She spoke gently, but her gloved hand waved impatiently in the direction of the door.

We left the elevator at the attic level and walked up a flight. On either side of a narrow corridor was a row of small mansarded rooms. Each had an iron bed, a rudimentary table and chair and a glorious view of Rome's rooftops. Though clearly not to be compared with the apartment from which we had just come, the rooms were functional and cozy.

Callas's graceful hand movements abruptly became robotlike, chopping the air as she pointed at the furniture. She turned on the manager, her eyes flashing. Rusconi blushed again. He placed his right hand inside the jacket of his dark suit, à la Napoleon. Having worked with him in the past, I knew that gesture well. It accompanied the blush whenever he was ill at ease.

"You expect my servants to sleep up here?" Callas exclaimed. "Where is the bathroom? . . . And look at this tiny bed! My servants are to get the same treatment I do."

"The production company assured us these rooms would be fine," Rusconi ventured. "These are the only rooms we have at the price they are willing to pay. Many of our guests have their staff stay in these quarters."

"I'm not interested," Callas snapped. "The film company will have to make up the difference. I want my maid and chauffeur on my floor. They are to have comfortable rooms with a private bath. Kindly call the accounting department and inform them of the change." Her voice had risen slightly to underline her point. Her eyelids narrowed. The meeting was over. She opened her bag and her hand impatiently searched for her glasses. Unable to locate them, head lowered, blindly groping for the next step, she stomped down the stairs in her high-heeled shoes.

As we followed in silent Indian file, avoiding further discussion, I surmised that my new boss was as difficult as she had been made out to be. It was not the time to dwell on my doubts, however. Other arrangements had to be made.

I was not present for the follow-up of the story and only learned it years later, when I told Rusconi I was writing about Callas.

"I didn't tell you? Oh, you must add that to your book, Nadia. The day after our 'eventful meeting,' I was in my office signing the afternoon correspondence, sipping a cappuccino. There was a knock at the door. '*Avanti,*' I said without looking up.

" 'I'm sorry to disturb you,' Callas said from across the desk. 'I want to thank you for the servants' new rooms.'

"There was Callas, rested and smiling, all dressed in turquoise. I jumped to attention, coffee cup in hand. The cappuccino splashed out all over my trousers. It was boiling! The penetrating heat took me back to a sitting position. Again, I tried to get up but only made it halfway. I could feel the spot spreading, so I bent my knees and tugged at my jacket in the hope that the desk would hide the increasing damage. Her visit was so unexpected, I couldn't think straight. What a sight I must have been: a beet-red jack-in-the-box with coffee dripping down my leg! I can tell you it didn't do much for my dignity. You know what? Callas solved my predicament. She grabbed a wad of Kleenex and, with care, dried me off. By then we were both laughing at the absurdity of the situation. We became good friends after that episode and she always stayed with us, at the Grand, whenever she visited Rome."

The rest of my first evening with Callas was occupied by the splendid champagne party Franco Rossellini and Pier Paolo Pasolini had organized in her suite. In terms of such affairs, it was slightly out of the ordinary for two reasons. First, it was to be the introduction of a great opera singer to the film world. But for Callas herself, the event also marked a reconciliation with Rome and the Roman press.

The scandal was common knowledge. On January 2, 1958, during a gala performance of *Norma* at the Rome Opera in the presence of Giovanni Gronchi, president of the republic, Callas refused to continue singing after the first act. She said she had a high fever and a throat infection, but the press and her fans were unconvinced. She was violently attacked for her "unprofessional" and "capricious" behavior. The incident caused a political ruckus and brought about a lawsuit that lasted thirteen years. For her part, Callas had at one point sworn she would never sing in Rome again.

Now she was back in a new guise. As eight o'clock approached, she retired to her room to prepare herself for the party. "I'll be ready in twenty minutes," she said. She looked flushed and nervous.

The guests began to arrive. An interesting mixture of celebrities, government officials, a few personal friends of Maria's and a half dozen handpicked journalists crowded into Maria's suite. Italian actors and directors such as Anna Magnani, Gina Lollobrigida, Mauro Bolognini, Federico Fellini and Michelangelo Antonioni had come to pay their respects to their new colleague.

Three quarters of an hour passed before an apprehensive and beautiful Callas in a simple black silk dress and costume jewelry made her entrance. She was immediately flanked by Rossellini and Pasolini. The warm and outgoing Rossellini made the introductions while Pasolini, who was known for his reserve, filled her in on who was who.

After a tense beginning, the beneficial effects of the champagne were felt. I walked around the crowded, smoke-filled room curious to discover the guests' reaction to Callas's new career.

"Pasolini and Callas! What a combination. I can't see it working, can you?" . . . "She's desperate, poor thing. She lost her voice and now she's lost Onassis." . . . "But what makes her think she can become a movie star overnight? Opera singer one day, movie star the next? Just like that? . . . You've got to hand it to her, she's got guts." . . . "Give her a chance." . . . "I can see the headline now: THE RETURN OF THE PRODIGAL DIVA." . . . "Well, from what I've read, she brought most of her troubles on herself."

Meanwhile, Franco Rossellini and Matteo Spinola mingled among the guests, ignoring the negative comments and promoting the success of the project.

Aside from the press, those most interested in Callas were the ladies. Their eyes were glued to her. I could hear the fashion-conscious Romans commenting on her dress, which was conspicuously long and severe for the miniskirt era. They also disapproved of her costume jewelry.

During most of the evening, Pier Paolo Pasolini stayed by Maria's side. He was very protective of her. His low, soothing voice seemed to reassure her. One felt she was at ease in his company, and he in hers. Although Maria was visibly weary toward the end of the evening, her performance was flawless. I was pleased to note that she greeted everyone graciously, took time to answer often repetitious questions and acknowledged the endless "good luck" toasts for her new career. Still, I was exhausted and relieved when I saw that the last guests were leaving.

Maria accompanied her director and producer to the door. In typical Roman style, they kissed each other repeatedly on the cheeks and said endless good-byes. They were to meet for dinner an hour later.

I was preparing to leave when I found myself face-to-face with Maria Callas. We looked at each other and smiled, but we were both silent. The room, saturated with gardenia perfume and smoke, was stifling. The embarrassment increased. Someone had to say something. I took the initiative.

"Could I open the window?"

"Of course," said Callas, ". . . and . . . do sit down, Signora Stancioff. By the way, when I receive flowers, I like to thank those who were kind enough to send them, as soon as possible. Could you please collect all the cards and make a list of the names? When you come in tomorrow, I will dictate a few notes—you do take shorthand, of course—and then I will sign them in the afternoon."

Before I could utter my surprise, she had vanished into the bedroom, still talking. I was no longer listening, but thinking about this new predicament. I seemed to be involved in a situation of mistaken identity.

Callas reappeared with a handful of letters and sales slips. "This is something I would like you to take care of to-morrow. Look these over and make sure everything is clear, just in case I am still asleep when you come in the morning. I wake up quite late."

"Madame Callas, I believe there must be some misunderstanding. Franco Rossellini hired me in a public relations capacity. I'm not a secretary. I don't even know how to type"—a white lie. "If you are in need of a secretary, I'm sure the production office will find you a good bilingual assistant. I'm afraid I do not fit the requirements."

It was now Callas's turn to be astonished. "My contract calls for a maid, a chauffeur, a hairdresser and a secretary. I asked Franco to find me a secretary. I *must* have a secretary. This is ridiculous. Had I known, I would have brought one with me from Paris. Please call Franco at once. I must speak with him."

She didn't raise her voice, but her annoyance was evident. When I got Franco on the phone, he seemed unperturbed.

"What are you going on about! What difference does it make if she calls you her secretary or her public relations agent? It's just a matter of terminology. What do you care? A job with Callas is not an everyday occurrence. You'll see, it will all work itself out. Just be patient and keep Maria happy. She's very nervous about the venture she has embarked on, so don't upset her."

For once Franco's nonchalance and Latin charm did not touch me. I felt I'd been duped and had no intention of wasting my time any further. I was furious.

"Listen, Franco, Madame Callas wants and needs a secretary. Since that is what she wants, that is what she should get. I won't—"

Callas took the phone out of my hand. She was calm but firm. She informed Franco of her displeasure. It was an unfortunate and unprofessional beginning, she said, and was sorry she had turned down the secretary Mr. Gorlinsky, her agent, had offered her.

"Have the production office send me a choice of girls for interviews. I am indignant at the way I am being treated." She replaced the receiver and slowly walked up and down the room. Her walk was regal, her expression tense and distant. She was the diva I had so often seen in photographs.

"You realize, don't you, that you are talking yourself out of a job with Maria Callas?"

"I do," I replied, "but I very much doubt that Maria Callas would put up with a bad secretary. Being as professional as she is, it wouldn't take her long to discover my inadequacies in that domain. I think she'd be happier if she picked one out herself. I too am professional, Madame Callas. That's why I'm bowing out. Besides, I'm not always comfortable working with women."

"You don't like women?" Callas asked with surprise.

"Of course I like them. Don't misunderstand me, but given the choice in a work situation, I prefer men."

Callas looked me over very carefully. "I think you have a point there . . . I really do too."

She poured two glasses of champagne.

"*Cin cin*. To our good health."

The tension had vanished. The reserve was still apparent, but her voice had lost its authoritarian edge. She questioned me about my life in Rome, my work, my friends. Having lost the job, or rather, never having had it, I sipped my champagne and relaxed.

"Since our business relationship has ended, do you mind if I call you Nadia?" She didn't wait for my reply. "Could you do me a great favor, Nadia? Could you stay a few days to help me choose a secretary? I really would appreciate it. Just a few days. . . . Okay?"

The telephone rang. The concierge announced Pasolini's and Rossellini's return.

On the way home, I wondered why I had agreed to do a favor for someone I hardly knew. Was it the champagne?

The days that followed brought a stream of terrified secretaries in their Sunday best. During the interviews, their voices were hardly audible and their fingers froze at the type-writer. Since they had been screened by the best secretarial agency in town, there was no reason to doubt their capabilities, but their awe of the great Diva was such that their talents and personalities would forever remain unknown.

By the fourth day, Maria had lost interest. "Let's forget it, Nadia. None of these girls will do. They'd bore me to tears. Anyway, they are terrified of me. I couldn't work with some-one who is frightened of me. Do I frighten people? What about you? Why aren't you frightened of me like the others? You know, I don't really *need* a secretary," she said with an impish smile. "I insisted on this point with the production people because they promised me that I would have a secre-tary. It was a matter of principle. I hate having wool pulled over my eyes and I loathe unprofessionalism.

"You see, what I really need is someone to help me out with the public relations and foreign press, and I understand Matteo Spinola won't always be with us when we are on location. So, in Turkey it will be your job to keep the jour-nalists at a safe distance while I'm working. I'm told you speak several languages; besides, I think you understand me and can be a friend." Maria was laughing. "I know you don't want to work with me, but please come to Turkey with us. You'll see. Callas is not the tigress she is made out to be."

That afternoon I called Franco Rossellini and signed my contract.

3

On to Turkey

We sat in the director's office at Ankara airport awaiting news of Maria's and Bruna's lost luggage. One of Maria's suitcases, loaded with her sheet music and personal effects, and the one containing all of Bruna's belongings were nowhere in sight. Maria was confident and good humored.

"They'll turn up! Anyway, Pixie and Djedda's suitcase with their biscuits and toys got here. That's more important. I won't have much time for my music, so that takes care of that."

Apologies in broken French and English were accompanied by endless cups of Turkish coffee and smiles befitting the occasion. Bureaucracy is irritating the world over, but not being able to understand the language made the ordeal unbearable. A continuous parade of airport personnel were our messengers of hope but the same man never returned twice.

After the first hour, Maria began to get edgy. She was not used to waiting.

"Nadia, *cara,* would you please see if you can find an English paper? It would help pass the time."

She looked pleased when I returned—after a considerable search that had taken me all over the airport—with the *Rome Daily American.* She glanced at the headlines, then flipped the pages in rapid succession.

"Ah, here we are. November-December, Sagittarius. Listen to this: 'You have overspent your emotions. You feel confined but autonomy and strength will return with a sense of magic. Best days, ninth and thirteenth.' Good. Three, six and nine are my lucky numbers. It's amazing how accurate these horoscopes can be," she added, as if it were written for her personally. "What are you, Nadia?"

"I'm an Aries."

"That's a good sign too. Loyal, headstrong people. Here," she said, offering me the paper, "would you like to look at it? I've finished."

I couldn't believe it. All the trouble I'd gone to for a silly horoscope! I hid my annoyance behind the newspaper. I'd barely finished the first column when Maria interrupted.

"How much longer do you think they'll keep us? This is ridiculous. I'm going to write to the president of the airline. Matteo, find out his name for me, won't you? . . . Nadia, is that the paper published for the English-speaking colony of Rome? Anything interesting? What's the temperature in Paris?" But my answer fell on deaf ears: her attention had turned to her miniature poodles. "Bruna, please take the little ones for a breath of air. Thank you."

Dusk slipped into darkness, the pitch of voices rose and the polite smiles became scowls and yawns. We were exhausted. Our thoughts turned to a hot bath and a comforting meal. We couldn't wait to get to the Ankara Intercontinental Hotel, where we were booked.

The day had started early for Maria and Bruna, who had traveled from Paris, joining Matteo Spinola and myself on the Turkish Airline plane in Rome. Maria was in first class with Pixie and Djedda. They were jet-propelled poodles used to following their mistress's moves. Perfectly trained and blasé about world travel, they never made their presence known unless ordered by Maria. They huddled quietly at her feet in a blue cloth bag. The ever-present bag would follow us up and down the hills of Cappadocia, the shores of Grado and studios of Cinecittà, and was soon christened the *"Wagon-Lit."*

We had not been airborne more than fifteen minutes before Maria appeared in tourist class, a bottle of champagne in hand. Alone and bored by herself in first class, she had asked Bruna to exchange seats with her. Maria, Matteo and I sipped champagne as Maria chatted with the passengers, to the delight of the young stewardess and the dismay of her first-class colleagues.

At last, after hours of negotiations, it was agreed that Turkish Airlines would be responsible for the delivery of the lost luggage to the village of Goreme, the film location in the heart of Cappadocia. We were relieved, although, in fact, the luggage never did arrive. Maria's bag turned up in Paris six months later in a rather sorry state, but the contents were intact. Bruna's suitcase was never seen again.

At 9:00 P.M. Turkish time, we piled into a ratty, two-tone, third-hand Cadillac taxi. We would travel in a number of these during our stay, all the better to experience the uncanny manner in which the Turks drive.

This driver attacked the inky road as if it were an enemy. He darted into Ankara as we rocked and rattled, clinging to each other and to what was left of a broken strap above the window. Our desperate pleas for him to slow down had no effect, so we tried patting him on the shoulder in slow motion. His mustache nodded at us in the mirror. "Yes, yes," he said. He spoke English! Reassured, Maria reminded him of the safety code of the road—in English, of course. He smiled broadly and his foot again went down on the accelerator. A herd of sheep was attempting to cross the road but, blinded by the headlights, most of them didn't make it. We were moving at such speed that the driver plowed through the herd without making any attempt to stop. We turned in horror to look out the back window. A number of fluffy creatures lay on the road, while the transfixed figure of their shepherd held his head in a mute cry of despair.

The following day around noon, Matteo and I went to Maria's suite to invite her to join us on a tour of Ankara's citadel.

"Thank you, but I'm not a great sightseer. I've been to Turkey before, you know. Not to Ankara, but I've seen Istanbul. You go ahead. My ankles are swollen from the trip; I have very poor circulation." Sitting in an armchair, her legs propped up on the bed, Maria was "looking over"—as she always put it—her favorite magazine, the *Reader's Digest*.

"And Nadia, while you are out, could you get me a few things to replace the stuff that got lost with the suitcases?"

The list read: insect repellent, toilet paper, glucose tablets, feather pillow, foam-rubber mattress.

Most of our afternoon was spent in bazaars attending to Maria's shopping list. At the time we felt her requests were a bit capricious, but the objects proved to be precious necessities in the wilds of Cappadocia. Although I was to learn that Maria was generous in spirit and in life's more important circumstances, her reputation for being tight about lesser matters was confirmed that day. A dozen times she said, "Remind me to reimburse you." But she never did.

As we returned to the hotel, Pixie, who had joined the outing, started whining. To my horror I discovered she was limping! I massaged her thin leg but to no avail. She took on a suffering, self-pitying look and hopped back to the hotel on three legs. Knowing Maria's adoration for the animal, I was terrified to face her. Had I caught Pixie's leg in the revolving door on the way out of the hotel? Was it broken? How could I tell Maria Callas that her dog was maimed? I knew that if anything serious had happened to Pixie, Maria would without hesitation fly back to Paris.

The minute Pixie entered Maria's apartment, she put her leg down and walked normally (watching me sheepishly, I thought). Relieved, I explained my fears to Maria. She laughed and proudly hugged her poodle. "What a clever girl you are, Pixie. She wants to win your attention. She does that with new people. She's an actress like her mother. Now, let's show Matteo and Nadia what else you and Djedda can do."

Maria clutched the miniature poodles between her knees and proceeded to vocalize. The dogs' eyes were alert and their ears pointed upward. In a matter of seconds, they produced sounds that were extraordinarily human. After repeating the exercise several times—this was only a warm-up—Maria started on an aria from *La Bohème*. Although their rendition was less successful, the pathetic efforts made by the little creatures filled Maria with pride. It was strange to witness "the voice of the century" taking part in this weird circus act. The dogs were rewarded with lumps of sugar and our perfunctory clapping. These somewhat depressing exhibitions were repeated a number of times for the benefit of the film staff and crew.

On June 2, we left Ankara at 6:00 A.M., and reached Goreme, our destination in Cappadocia, at midnight. The negative events of that journey overlap: motor problems, a picnic lunch left behind at the hotel in Ankara and an endless wait by the roadside under the scorching sun while our driver extracted the wheels of our two-tone Cadillac from a muddy pothole.

By comparison with those of the cast and crew, our accommodations were grand. Maria, Bruna and I were privileged. We were put up at the brand-new Club Méditerranée in Uchisar. The hotel, constructed around natural rock formations, was very attractive. We were its first guests and work was still in progress. The hallway smelled of fresh whitewash, the bathrooms were being completed and the kidney-shaped pool was bone dry. The aroma from the kitchen heralded fried brains for our inaugural midnight dinner, not everyone's favorite.

Maria was given a vast and airy room at the end of the hall, away from noise and curious eyes. The bed was situated in a rock niche carved out by Mother Nature. The newly tiled bathroom was equally impressive, but a turn of the tap produced running sand. Though this was not always so, frequently after a hot, exhausting day on location, our bodies caked in reddish sand, we'd get back to find that there wasn't a drop of water. The most dependable source of water was the constant trickle down the rock wall in Maria's niche. At first she welcomed the coolness and humidity, saying it was "good for the voice," but when rheumatic pains set in, she asked to have her bed moved to a drier side of the room. She was a good sport. She gave no indication that she missed the comfort she was used to in her Parisian home and to which she'd become accustomed during the lavish years spent with one of the world's richest men. We were all astonished.

Goreme and Uchisar, the villages in the heart of Cappadocia, where we spent four weeks, dominate a lunar landscape the likes of which I had never seen. It kindled the imagination: the hand of a child or a neurotic sculptor could have created the strange rock formations that seemed to grow in the parched valley. Cappadocia is a realm governed by the wind and sun, a voyage into the remote past of mankind.

On June 4, the eve of the first take, the telephone rang in Maria's room. The operator announced, "The United States calling. Mr. Lupoli on the line." Knowing Bruna's last name was Lupoli, I handed her the receiver.

"It must be one of your relatives, Bruna. A Mr. Lupoli."

Hearing the name, Maria remained motionless. Her expression hardened. Between clenched teeth she uttered a slow determined "*No!* I will not take that call. The call is for me, Nadia, but tell Mr. Lupoli that Madame Callas does not wish to accept the call."

I complied and replaced the receiver, mystified. Bruna's *sotto-voce* explanation was interrupted by another ring. The overseas operator was insistent, as was a husky male voice that interrupted her at intervals.

By now Maria was extremely agitated. Bruna managed to make me understand that the caller was none other than Aristotle Onassis, who often used her last name so as to discourage eavesdropping telephone operators.

Overhearing our conversation, Maria flew into a rage. "Yes, it's that dirty little Greek. That pig of an Onassis. Why doesn't that old man leave me alone? He's got what he wanted. He got the social status he was itching for. What more does he want? He's not happy? Bored with the First Lady? That's too bad. One pays for everything in life. The gods will make sure he pays."

Before our eyes Onassis' call had transformed Maria— the charmer and good sport—into a preview of Medea.

It was past midnight. Maria had to be on the set at nine the following morning, which meant rising at six to be coiffed and made up. It was evident that the telephone call had prepared her for a sleepless night. She was worked up and wanted an audience. Bruna made some camomile tea, in which she took no interest. Instead, as we watched, she paced up and down the room calling upon the "gods" to punish the "dirty little Greek."

The lateness of the hour aggravated the situation. By 2:30 A.M., a sleeping pill seemed the only answer. Frustrated and exhausted, Bruna and I finally said good-night.

"You are going to abandon me now? You are just like him. None of you care!" she yelled.

As we still made our way to the door a frightened voice pleaded. "Stay a little longer. Please don't go . . . not yet. . . . *Vi prego.*"

"Maria," I finally said firmly, "tomorrow is your first day. You need your sleep. You have to look beautiful. Come on, drink your camomile and take your pill. We must get some sleep too." I realized I might be stepping out of line. My bossy behavior might threaten our relationship, but I also knew that indulging her now could not be to her benefit.

I expected another outburst, but to my surprise she obediently took her pill and bid us good-night.

"Does she often get into such a state?" I asked Bruna as we made our way to our rooms.

"The Signora is highly strung. She has a sensitive character," said Bruna, choosing her words carefully. "Mr. Onassis' marriage has been a terrible shock to her. She is often irritable these days."

"You are a saint to put up with it. I wouldn't. How long have you been with her?"

"A long time. Sixteen, eighteen years. . . . I'm used to it now. In the past, when it got bad, I sometimes thought of going back to my village in Italy, but now I know I couldn't leave her. She is like my family. She is difficult because she is so talented, so extraordinary. But you know, she is kind."

Maria's recuperative capacities and professionalism were astonishing. The following morning, a beautiful and regal Maria in full costume and makeup was ready on location at 8:45. The rage of the night before was replaced by evident tension at meeting the cast and technicians, professionals in a field she knew nothing about. What she was unaware of was that most of the actors and crew were equally awed by her.

"Here she comes. God help us!" whispered a grip as Callas, the legend, walked past.

A silent semicircle formed around her. Pasolini introduced Giuseppe Gentile, who was to play Jason, and called out everyone's name in an informal introduction.

"Where is the champagne? Bring the champagne!" Franco cried out. "Even if we are in the wilds of Turkey, we must have the traditional champagne christening for good luck."

Corks popped. Franco and Pier Paolo raised their glasses. "A toast to success and good health. To Maria. To *Medea*."

Everyone joined in. "*Cin cin. Auguri.* To *Medea!*"

"All right everyone, *al lavoro!*"

Pasolini took Maria aside. "Let me explain what I'd like you to do in the first scene. As Medea drives by in a cart with her brother, she sees Jason, her future lover and husband, for the first time. This priestess, sorceress, is instantly smitten. The impact of that encounter changes her life. I want you to show what Medea feels, just with your eyes, your expression. *Va bene?* Let's try it."

The clapper boy announced, "*Medea,* scene one, take one."

"Camera, action," said Pasolini.

We all held our breath. In a matter of seconds, Maria's features were transformed. Her expression was that of a wild animal until she saw Jason. As she observed him, her eyes reflected a startling range of emotions: freedom, pride, strength and sensuality.

"Cut. Good," said Pasolini almost inaudibly.

No one moved. All at once, spontaneous applause broke out. Maria had completed the scene in one take, quite a feat for a newcomer.

Filming in Cappadocia was arduous. The stifling heat, shortage of water and indigestible food made for uneven tempers. Ninety-eight percent of us suffered from chronic stomach problems, but Maria carried on without a rumble. I marveled at her physical resistance.

"The reason you are all sick," she said, "is because you eat that exotic Turkish food. I eat only yogurt, apricots, and drink a bit of vodka to kill the bacteria."

At every meal Maria announced she wasn't hungry, but before I'd finished helping myself she was already scrutinizing the contents of my plate.

"What's that? It looks good. Could I try it? Just a bite, *posso?*" and before I knew it, her fork was in my plate. This habit had apparently stayed with her since her rigorous dieting days.

To protect Maria from the severe heat, occasional sandstorms, and to save her energy, the production staff built a special *portantina* like those used by the doges in Venice. It was quite a sight to watch her being transported over the hills, a black Turkish scarf wrapped around her head to prevent her makeup from melting, clutching her cassette recorder on her lap. As we moved from place to place, Maria listened to taped music. She sang along with the Beatles, Frank Sinatra, or harmonized to Mexican ballads. Her favorite songs were "Stormy Weather" and "Hernando's Hideaway." The latter became the *Medea* theme song. We became so accustomed to her impromptu concerts that we forgot it was Callas singing.

Most of the costume changes and hairdressing on location took place in rock caverns hollowed out by the inhabitants of ancient settlements. They had once been the hideouts and churches of early Christians. A number of them were adorned with breathtaking wall paintings dating from the ninth to the fourteenth century. Cool, beautiful, but not the Ritz. Maria didn't complain; she thought it adventurous and fun.

"After all we'd read and heard, we expected a capricious prima donna," production director Ferdinando Franchi commented years later to an Italian magazine. "Instead, she was like a lamb. She crawled in and out of the narrow cavern openings sometimes on hands and knees, wearing heavy robes and five kilos of jewelry without complaining. She caught us off guard. We were totally unprepared."

Knowing of my project, Roman friends sent me a copy of Franchi's interview. It was difficult after years of friendship to remember just how I had seen Maria during these early days of filming when we were just getting to know each other. But as I read Franchi's words I suddenly felt the revelation and relief of those first weeks with Maria all over again.

During breaks, Maria clung to Franco and to me. As we relaxed in the cool caverns, the conversation would revolve around Maria's Medea. "Franco, how did I do? Was that gesture too much? Tell me, Nadia, did you watch the scene? Was my makeup all right?" After she had asked us, she would turn to Bruna and get her opinion as well. She needed constant reassurance. When it wasn't shoptalk, the general gist was love and food. She greatly enjoyed discussing everyone's romantic life and could talk about a plate of pasta (even someone else's plate) with more passion than any Italian chef. Aside from her outburst the night of Onassis' call, however, she hardly mentioned her own private life.

Filming was progressing. Pier Paolo was pleased with his newly created movie star, and Maria was growing more relaxed and confident. But in spite of the uncomfortable working conditions, she would not allow a stand-in. No one had understudied Callas at the height of her career. She saw no need for someone now.

"Even at a distance," she said, "the understudy looks and moves differently from me."

"You have low blood pressure and anemia," argued Pier Paolo and Franco. "Be reasonable. You still have two months of hard work ahead of you in Italy."

Hardheaded as she was, she was finally convinced.

Throughout the shoot, Maria followed every scene of the film, even those she was not involved in, in order to maintain a sense of continuity. On one of her days off, she wanted to watch the "fire scene" the newly hired stand-in was going to act in. During this ritual, Medea crosses through fire and comes out unharmed because of her occult gifts. The cameras were placed on a hill, and two fires were built with a passage between them wide enough for the stand-in to pass through without danger. The scene was announced, followed by the familiar sound of the clapboard. As instructed, the stand-in rushed between the fires screaming and shielding her face against the flames.

"Once more, please," Pasolini called from the hilltop.

The girl positioned herself for the second take. *Clack.* "Action!"

As she reached the heart of the fire, she tripped on her long muslin gown. She swayed for a second and went down screaming.

"That's not bad acting," said Maria approvingly.

From where we were watching, none of us grasped the seriousness of what had taken place until the Turkish extras started to gesture frantically. The girl's gown had caught fire. Paralyzed with panic, she remained crouched in the flames, screaming. By the time one of the technicians reached her, her hands were severely burned. Our efforts to apply first-aid ointment on her burns were rebuffed. Between screams and sobs, she explained that she belonged to an Oriental sect that does not believe in doctors or medication. She finally consented to fresh tomato pulp suggested by the peasants, which seemed to relieve her pain if not our concern.

Although no press or photographers—with the exception of our official set photographer, Mario Tursi—were allowed to be present while we were shooting, somehow news of the "burnt Callas" spread rapidly. A blurred photograph of the accident even made the front pages of several Turkish and foreign papers. The articles stated that Maria Callas had been seriously burned. We were mystified as to how this rumor had spread and who had taken the photograph.

It turned out that an ingenious Turkish reporter dressed as a veiled peasant woman had snapped the falling figure from an adjacent hill. He had evidently been unaware that the burned Medea was the stand-in.

The following day Maria received a telegram from her mother and sister in Athens inquiring about the accident: Was Maria badly burned? Maimed?

Maria was livid.

"I haven't heard from them in years! All they are interested in is my money. They want to make sure I can still sign their monthly check because they know that when I die, that's it—no more. My mother, sister and ex-husband have had all they are going to get during my lifetime. And what's wrong with my sister Jackie? Why can't she work?"

"Oh, come on, Maria," I stammered, "they can't be that bad. Now, be fair."

Maria was determined. "My mother *never* loved me. When I was born, she refused to see me for four days. She wanted a boy, because Vasily, my little brother, had died; in fact, that's why my parents moved to America. Do you know, my mother doesn't even remember the date of my birth! Once it's December 3, the next time it's the fourth. If you don't believe me, read the book she wrote about me. She made things up to suit herself. It's a humiliating pack of lies."

I tried to quiet Maria. It was my job, after all, to keep her calm. I still find it hard to believe that throughout the subsequent years of our friendship, only rarely did we discuss her family. The subject was obviously so painful that I had felt it wrong to pry. I could not have imagined then that years later I'd be back in New York struggling to find answers to the questions I could have asked that night in Turkey.

4

Beginnings

A telegram? Mother did send
Mary a telegram? That's very interesting. Tell me. Tell me,
Nadia. I remember Mother talking about an accident during
the filming in Turkey . . . that Mary had been hurt. She was
worried about Mary and wanted to contact her. 'Why do it?'
I said. 'Why send a telegram to someone you haven't received
a postcard from in fifteen years?' I wouldn't have done it. I'm
too proud. So, my name was on the telegram too? I learn of
this only now. You were with her when she opened it?"

"Yes, and she really was furious."

"Why? My mother was concerned. What mother wouldn't
be? In spite of everything, she loved her."

Seventeen years after the fact, over an elegant dinner in
Athens, I was finally listening to Maria's sister, Jackie Kalogeropoulos tell her version of the Turkish telegram incident.

Dr. Polyvios Marchand, author of a scholarly study of Callas's early career in Greece, had been instrumental in bringing us together. We dined at the Atheneum Restaurant in the fashionable Kolonaki neighborhood. Amber candlelight enhanced the red-and-gold brocade curtains, marble columns, and wood-paneled bar, lending the Atheneum a gracious and sophisticated atmosphere. Despite the soothing surroundings, I was not relaxed. I asked myself, would Jackie be reluctant to discuss personal matters with a stranger? Fulfilling my promise to Maria had become increasingly demanding. I knew that her life had not been dealt with clearly, and I was faced with the problem of whom to turn to for the facts behind the vague, opinionated references that Maria had volunteered about her family. Maria's repeated complaints about her ambitious mother and her sister's life of comfort and leisure were not really helpful, since she had never clarified her comments with any concrete insights or actual proof. To my mind, those declarations were a shield for a more vulnerable, childish Maria, a woman who, it was becoming evident, never came to terms with her true feelings about her family during her life.

So what was I to do? My endeavor was made more complex by her mother's conflicting declarations in her book, *My Daughter Maria Callas*. I soon became convinced the only person who could shed light on the matter was Jackie, Maria's older sister and the only surviving family witness. To my knowledge, Jackie had never been interviewed for any of the major books on Maria.

Having heard that Jackie had moved from Athens to London, I asked my mother, who lives there, to investigate, but the two Kalogeropouloses she found led to a dead end.

Then, after several false starts, friends arranged for me to meet Vasso Devetzi, president of the Paris-based Maria

Callas Foundation. She would help, they assured me: she apparently was closely associated with the Kalogeropoulos family. After Maria's death, they had appointed her to represent the *droit moral* of the Callas estate.

The prospective meeting sounded so promising I postponed my work in Rome and traveled to Paris with high hopes. But the scheduled meetings never took place. On two occasions, Miss Devetzi vanished at the last minute with no explanation. My only—or last—hope was to find Jackie. Rumor now had it that she was very much alive.

More clues had finally led me back to Athens, where Jackie has lived since 1936. Now I sat at the Atheneum Restaurant, my head filled with the conflicting stories I hoped Jackie might help me sort through. This muddle was aggravated by apprehension—and a bad case of jet lag.

When the maître d'hôtel announced the guests of honor, I was truly startled. Jackie was slight, her fine features framed by honey-colored hair. The light-brown eyes were clear and lively with hardly any wrinkles around them. A diamond necklace sparkled at her smooth neck. She approached our table, her youthful figure accentuated by her ankle-length chiffon dress. Had I not known that she was six years older than Maria (which made her sixty-nine), I would have guessed she was a well-preserved fifty.

The younger man with her was of medium height with a round cheerful face and dark hair. He introduced himself as her husband, Dr. Andreas Stathopoulos, pathologist.

"I have brought you a little surprise," he said, handing me a cassette. "My wife sings on one side of this tape and Maria on the other." Beaming, he turned to Jackie. "You will see what a lovely voice Jackie has."

Neither Jackie's youthful husband nor her singing voice was a total surprise, as Dr. Marchand had briefed me. It seemed

Jackie and the forty-three-year-old Andreas had met when they were studying voice with the same teacher. The romance had led to marriage three years later. Their glances and entwined hands during dinner confirmed they were very much in love. Later, while listening to the tape, I was astonished by Jackie's voice, which, she told me had been recorded after only two years of study. Had her formal training started earlier—who knows, she might have embarked on a professional career.

"Your ring is beautiful," I said hesitantly to Jackie, admiring the slender, perfectly groomed hands that resembled Maria's. "What stone is that?"

"Thank you. You are very kind. It's an amethyst," she answered, twisting the large pink stone set with diamonds. "My former fiancé, Milton Embiricos, gave it to me. He has been dead for many years, but I still treasure it."

Her smile had Maria's magnetic charm, but it was gentler and more trusting. The similarity in their manner of speech was uncanny. Jackie's voice was lighter, but the cadence and idiom were remarkably similar. The occasional awkwardness of her speech reminded me that she, like Maria, had only spent a few years in the United States. To stress a point, she repeated words, such as "tell me, tell me, Nadia. . . ." If I shut my eyes it was Maria speaking.

"Your smile and speech remind me of Maria," I ventured. She looked at me quizzically.

"Really? You think so? Well, we *are* sisters," she answered softly.

I started in cautiously. "What was your sister like when she was little?"

Jackie sipped her ouzo pensively. "She was a nervous child—though not so much as they say," she added quickly. "But she was difficult. She blew up sometimes. She had a very pretty face but she was fat. I think that made her very unhappy.

She was studious even then—the truth is the truth—but from twelve, thirteen years old she was very fat and had many pimples. At sixteen she was very fat, *very* fat. She wanted to be slim like my mother and me, and this made a complex inside her. I think it played a great role in her soul. 'Mother,' she would say, 'why have you given me such big ears that stick out, such a big nose and these awful, fat legs!'

"When I was becoming a young girl and an admirer would visit me, Maria would burst into the living room and sit between us. She would pour down her long, beautiful hair—she had gorgeous hair—making a curtain, to block our vision and interrupt our conversation."

"Your mother says she was first aware of Maria's vocal gifts when she was four years old. Isn't that unusually young?"

"Well, Mary had a lovely voice from a small girl—but maybe ten years old."

"Did your mother want you both to have musical careers?"

"Maybe yes. For me she wanted piano, although Maria studied piano too. But I never opened my mouth when I was a child. I didn't know I had a voice then. I accompanied Maria, that's all."

"Maria said that she hardly had any friends because your mother made her practice all the time."

"Now come on, Nadia. You believe that? Why did Mary say such things? How could she have studied and practiced all the time when she didn't even have a teacher when we were in America? A piano teacher, yes. But not voice. Of course we had some friendships. But Mother would come to pick us up at school because she was afraid for us in a city like New York. She was a good mother. Why did Mary say she had no childhood? That's not true."

Jackie's comments, Maria's version of her childhood and my own thoughts slowly converged in confusion. If Maria had not been pushed, then what about the tape author and music critic John Ardoin had found? He reports that Maria told him she sang on the "Major Bowes Amateur Hour" when she was thirteen. Yet when I listened to the deep, resonant voice it seemed mature for an eighth-grader. In addition to complaining that her mother pushed her relentlessly, Maria had, in fact, told me about a singing contest. We were swapping tales of times we'd made up names for ourselves. I mentioned that whenever strangers bothered me at parties or on trips, I kept my anonymity by calling myself Mimosa Dubois.

Maria was amused. "When I was a kid," she told me, "I took part in a singing competition. My father didn't like the idea because I was too young. In fact, my mother raised my age to sixteen so that I could qualify. I called myself Anita Duval. That way my father wouldn't find out. Afterwards I switched to Nina Foresti. I thought that sounded more like an opera singer!"

When I told John this, he remarked, "Maria always denied that she had ever sung under any name than her own, but still, I firmly believe that the voice on the tape was hers."

Ardoin also discovered a letter dated March 13, 1935 addressed in care of Foresti, 549 West 144 Street, which corresponds to the address where the Kalogeropoulos family lived at the time. The letter, probably written by the thirteen-year-old Miss Foresti's mother, requests an audition for the radio program:

> My musical studies were begun when I was four years old. I studied piano many years but as my family was in very comfortable circumstances, my

music was not considered seriously. I was sent to finishing school, studied languages and singing all as social accomplishments only. One day in 1930, upon our return from a cruise, we found our "comfortable circumstances" had vanished so I have been giving piano instruction. However, I always loved to sing so I continued my vocal studies and have sung in concerts and made my debut as Nedda, in *Pagliacci,* but as an amateur. My voice is admired but opportunities are so few and I find that corner—from amateur to professional—a very difficult one to turn.

(Marginal notes, scribbled by a judge at the auditions, indicate that the "red-haired" Nina Foresti, had sung "Un bel dì" and that she had 'faint possibility for future.")

"But Jackie," I persisted, "what about the 'Major Bowes Amateur Hour' contest? Didn't your mother push Maria into that?"

Jackie perused the menu. She raised her eyes and gave her order to the waiter in Greek. "No, Nadia. From a small girl Mary loved music and wanted to be an opera singer."

"Maria told me she wanted to be a dentist."

"No. *I'm* the one who wanted to be the dentist." Jackie returned the menu.

". . . You see, we read in the paper that there was going to be this contest for children. So my mother said to Mary, 'Why don't you sing that nice little song you know?' And my mother wrote and they said, 'Come and sing.' "

"So, your mother wrote the letter and signed it Anita Duval. And then Maria called herself Nina Foresti when she tried out at the competition?"

"Nina Foresti? Who is Nina Foresti? Oh, that's Mary's fantasy again. I taught her the song and I accompanied her. It was "A Heart That's Free," a Jeannette MacDonald song. She was ten years old, she was a small girl."

Perhaps the singing competition Jackie referred to was not the "Major Bowes Amateur Hour" but a children's show in Chicago hosted by Jack Benny where Ardoin assures us Maria did indeed sing "A Heart That's Free." It's also possible that Jackie accompanied Maria singing that song for the Major Bowes audition on March 28, 1935, then, on the day of the broadcast 'Nina Foresti' sang "Un bel Dì." The contradictions do not stop here.

"And what did your father think of the audition?" I asked.

"He didn't mind. He was pleased. It was just a children's contest!" Jackie exclaimed.

Throughout the evening Jackie's rose-colored view of their youth would not match her sister's, and yet meeting Jackie had made Maria's animosity and envy somewhat clearer to me. It was easy to imagine how the charm and glamour of the beautiful woman I was dining with had won her numerous admirers. Meanwhile, her little sister fought complexes and weight problems.

"The only explanation I can give for the problems was that Maria was fat and suffered from that when she was young," said Jackie. "And my mother and Maria had similar characters. They could not agree. One wanted to dominate the other."

Jackie turned to her husband and placed her hand on his.

"Oh Andreas, what a pity we didn't meet Nadia sooner. She really was a friend of Maria's."

Andreas excitedly answered in Greek, but Jackie broke in. "Excuse me for interrupting, dear, but we had better tell

Nadia all that another time. We must see each other again, Nadia. I have many things I wish to discuss with you."

"I only wish it hadn't taken so long to trace you, Jackie."

"Perhaps some people got between us because they didn't want you to find me," she said, glancing knowingly at Andreas.

"Well, since you had vanished, I had to do a bit of investigating about your childhood on my own. I looked up Maria's godfather, Dr. Lantzounis, and a lady who had been to school with Maria," I said. "But there seems to be so much that no one knows."

"So now I will tell you as much as I can, Nadia. We will meet again while you are here. You will see, you will see."

At first it seemed important to get the facts straight. I had started my research in New York, helped by a friend with a true enthusiasm for such endeavors. We discovered Maria's birth certificate after plowing through hundreds of records at the Bureau of Vital Statistics. No wonder it had never been found: it was under Kalos. Most likely, Kalogeropoulos was abbreviated by someone on Manhattan's Fifth Avenue Hospital staff who found it difficult to record—let alone pronounce—a foreign name. On the birth certificate, even Evangelia Demetroadis, Maria's mother's maiden name, had been shortened to Litza Demes. What struck me was the date of birth: December 2, 1923 (her mother's book had said December 4; Maria herself had often mentioned the third). It was the first of many inaccuracies I would find in Evangelia Kalogeropoulos's book about her daughter. The baby registered as Sophie Cecilia Kalos was not born during the violent snowstorm that her mother so vividly described. Weather reports for that week indicate no snowstorms in New York City.

Finding the certificate of business for George Kalogeropoulos's drugstore, the Splendid Pharmacy (a name probably chosen by his wife), increased my obsession for data. But after weeks of zealous work, the mass of records and documents covering my desk only made me recognize that the missing ingredient here was human truth. The facts of Maria's life, I was quickly realizing, would often be intermingled with make-believe, a phenomenon not always discouraged by Maria herself.

There was one man whom Maria had always spoken of with affection and esteem: her godfather, Leonidas Lantzounis. I set out to find him, in the hope that he could bridge the gap between Litza's fabrications and what was perhaps a more pedestrian reality.

Leo Lantzounis was not listed in the Manhattan phone book, so I contacted the first Lantzounis I found, Pericles Lantzounis. He turned out to be Leonidas's cousin. We met at the Greek Orthodox Cathedral of the Holy Trinity the following Sunday. "Come over to our church," he said graciously, "and I'll introduce you to Leo."

Through the glass doors, beyond the church atrium, I first saw the white-haired figure of Pericles Lantzounis, handing out candles and religious pamphlets to the faithful. The service had already started when my companion and I entered. Greeting us with a nod, Pericles solemnly escorted us to a pew off the center aisle. "Come down to the basement auditorium for coffee, afterwards," he whispered. "This is the church, you know, where Maria was baptized."

The cathedral was a bit of Greece transplanted to the center of New York City. The long, Byzantine faces of the Virgin and saints with their melancholy eyes observed us from the archways and vaulted ceilings. They were richer replicas of those found throughout Greece in every village church and roadside sanctuary. The chants took me back to the Church of St. Sofia, in Bulgaria's capital, where as a small child clutching my grandfather's hand, I myself had attended the Orthodox services.

We watched the worshipers lined up in the center aisle, their arms folded solemnly in front of them or crossing themselves from right to left, three times. When they reached the priest—or Pop, as he is called—they bent over his hand to kiss his ring before receiving communion in the form of bread and wine.

It was the pageantry of the Greek Orthodox Church, I think, that appealed to Maria. She had a very personal approach to religion. Although a believer, she was not a churchgoer. Her religion was a combination of Greek Orthodox ritual mingled with superstition and Greek mythology. Fate was a thematic element in her spiritual life: she accepted the course of events imposed on her as she accepted the phenomenon of her voice. Throughout her career, she made it a point before a performance to visit the nearest church, to light a candle in front of the Madonna. But Maria did not feel that the ministry of the Church as a communal institution was applicable to her. Hers, I think, was a loner's alliance with the Almighty.

After the service we joined Pericles downstairs for lunch in the auditorium. Seeing new faces, curious parishioners clustered around our table, waiting for Pericles to introduce us.

"This," he said, "is Nadia Stan . . . Stich . . . never mind, and that is her husband," he said, gesturing toward my surprised companion. "They are a Bulgarian couple writing a book about a Greek! How do you like *that!* Nadia is writing about Maria Callas."

Everyone showed great interest. Fragments of stories were told in Greek and English, elaborate repetitions of information they had gathered from books and television and come to believe was personal and fresh. Their main interest, of course, was Onassis' betrayal and Maria's voice loss, for which they held him responsible.

"It is a fact that when Meneghini was her manager, she was extraordinary," I added. "I don't suppose anyone here ever met him."

The mention of Battista Meneghini brought on the embarrassed silence of the forgotten. As far as the eager group gathered around the table was concerned, Onassis had been the *only* man in Callas's life. Then suddenly, Henry Stavrakis, a regular church member, perked up.

"Oh, Meneghini? Sure, that was Callas's *Italian* husband. I remember, when I first came over to this country, I had a job at Western Union and telegrams from overseas passed through my department. I remember Meneghini used to send wires to George Kalogeropoulos—you know, Maria's father— to tell him how great she'd been in the last opera. It was in the fifties, when she was at La Scala. The messages always closed with 'I miss you,' 'I love you' or 'Wish you were with us tonight.' Signed, 'Your loving daughter, Maria.' After her signature, there was always Meneghini's name."

"Leo would have known him," someone added.

"Yes, your cousin, Dr. Lantzounis. Is he here?" I asked Pericles.

"I'm sorry, Nadia, he's too sick; he didn't make it. But don't be disappointed. I talked him into seeing you anyway. He's expecting your call. Just remember, don't tire him out. He's not well."

Leonidas Lantzounis's living room overlooks the East River. He was wearing pale blue pajamas and a brown-checked dressing gown when I was escorted in by the housekeeper.

Lantzounis was Maria's godfather and, by many accounts, the doctor who had brought her into the world. His story was slightly different, though. "I don't know a damn thing about babies," Lantzounis chuckled. "Sure, I was in the delivery room, but I didn't bring her into the world. I'm an orthopedist. Where did you get that idea from?"

"I read it in Maria's mother's book."

"Godfather, yes. That I was. In my country, when you hold a baby at a baptism, it means you are responsible for it for the rest of its life. In our church, babies are usually baptized between six and eight months old, before the baby is old enough to pull the Pop's beard. When Maria was baptized, she was two years old and big enough to cause more damage than tugging at his beard. When Methodios Kourkoulis—he was our priest then—dunked her, she loved it. She splashed around and didn't want to get out. I remember she didn't mind the sacred oil smeared on her head, and she didn't complain when they cut her curls as is customary. You know, in the shape of a cross on her forehead. But she screamed bloody murder when they dressed her in the christening gown. Her father had given her the name of Sophia, but Litza didn't like it, so she was baptized Maria Anna. You see, Litza usually won.

"But one of the few situations she couldn't control was Maria's being born a girl. . . . I know she didn't want another girl," he added.

"Maria said that it was because her little boy, Vasily, had died of typhoid fever that they decided to leave Greece."

"I don't know. I couldn't understand *why* they came over," said the old man. His frail frame slumped back in his easy chair, late afternoon winter light accentuating his pallor and thinning white hair. "They had plenty of money, you know. You come to America when you have a hard time— like I did. You bet your life! I arrived with fifteen dollars. But

to leave Meligala, a drugstore, the best house in town, maids—
for New York! That's crazy!" He shook his head. "If you don't
know the language, you're good for nothing here. You go to
the Greek store and nothing else. . . . Evangelia did not plan
it that way. She didn't use her brains the way they should be
used. She was too ambitious. And George, when he came to
New York, he came like a banker, but he ate up all his money
right away. He came from a small town and acted like a big
shot!"

Like his goddaughter, Dr. Lantzounis didn't mince words.
Perhaps that was one reason she liked him so much, I thought.
Leo and her father were the only people I know of with whom
Maria sustained a lifelong relationship. They were the only
family members Maria ever mentioned to me fondly.

"The big mistake on George's part was that he didn't
figure the amount of time he'd need to learn the language so
he could pass his pharmaceutical exam and set himself up in
business," Leo went on. "He thought he'd do it like me, in
one year, but it took him five. They were used to living well
in Meligala and thought the next dollar would come very easy,
but George didn't have an income here."

Upon arrival the Kalogeropoulos couple and their six-
year-old daughter Yacinthy, nicknamed Jackie, first settled in
Astoria, Queens, in the Greek community still known as Little
Athens, where they were surrounded by foods and customs
similar to those they had left behind. George soon found work
in a pharmacy, which apparently gave a note of premature
encouragement to their new life in America.

"But George had to ask me for a loan so that he could
open his own pharmacy. Can you believe it?" Leo looked at
me incredulously. "In five years they'd eaten it all up. They
had no income, but that didn't stop Litza from taking the

girls to Florida for six months, just to visit her cousins, the Kritikos. Finally, they didn't have anything left, so I loaned them what I had saved out of my yearly salary."

Litza's somewhat vague reference in her book to George's pharmacy prompted me to ask Dr. Lantzounis if it still existed.

"It was torn down. It was somewhere around the Port Authority bus station, but Litza always thought she was fancy, so she wouldn't admit it was in that part of town."

I had to laugh at the mention of this neighborhood. It had come up in a conversation with Maria, and it was a subject that made her blood boil. "Journalists will invent anything!" Maria used to rail. "First it was Brooklyn! Now there's a myth that I was born and raised in Hell's Kitchen! I was raised in Washington Heights," she added firmly.

Nonetheless, George Kalogeropoulos's Splendid Pharmacy was located at 483 Ninth Avenue, at Thirty-seventh Street (the area known as Hell's Kitchen). Like Astoria, the neighborhood was a Greek community in which many émigrés started their new lives before moving on to more prosperous neighborhoods. It was a convenient location for George; most of his customers were Greek and he was spared the daily battle of tackling English. From Astoria the family had moved to a modest apartment on Thirty-fourth Street, off Ninth Avenue, to be nearer George's pharmacy. It is true that Washington Heights, a middle-class residential neighborhood on the northern fringe of Manhattan, is where the family lived longest. Before settling there, however, they moved from one drab walk-up apartment to another, nine times in eight years.

George apparently worked diligently, but the pharmacy enterprise was ill timed. He opened his store four months before the Wall Street crash, and the Depression killed his business.

But Maria's sympathies had always leaned toward her father in spite of his failures. "My mother? Forget about my mother," she had snapped at a reporter who questioned her as we were leaving Rome's Cinecittà after a day on the set. "Why don't you ask me about my father, whom I adored?" she said, slamming the car door.

The question had touched a nerve, and during the drive to the Grand Hotel, Maria turned to me. "Like you and your father, Nadia, my father and I had a good relationship. I remember he loved Greek dance. He'd put on one of his favorite records but it never lasted long; my mother would rush over and change it for an aria, and that was sure to start an argument. I always sided with my father. I was his favorite when I was a child . . . or maybe always," she had added.

"After he lost his pharmacy," Lantzounis resumed, "George went on the road all over the United States. Like a traveling salesman he went, with a bag of cosmetics for beautiful women." Lantzounis arched an eyebrow. "But he was never able to build up his own business again. The only thing George had was good looks and beautiful bearing: tall, straight, distinguished. He wasn't ambitious, not even particularly interested in money, and that made Litza always more annoyed and nervous. He owed me over ten thousand dollars. That was a lot of money in those days—it still is—but he never mentioned his debt or made any attempt to return the money. Only once he said, joking like, 'I'll see you after we die, Lantzounis.' He slapped me on the shoulder and laughed and that was the end of that."

"Was money the cause of friction between Litza and George?" I asked.

"Part of it. . . . Also, George was chasing around. Litza was only a kid when she got married. She was seventeen and

[51]

George was thirty. She was a good-looking blond. She thought everybody who looked at her was in love with her, but they weren't," Lantzounis chuckled. "That's the only difference. And then, after George lost the drugstore, her mind turned. He put her in Bellevue as crazy, and probably she was crazy! She was an ambitious, neurotic woman who never had a friend. She was in Bellevue for a month."

Jackie's report of her mother's unbalanced period is rather different. She told me her mother had swallowed poison that she'd taken from the pharmacy. Her desperate gesture had been brought on by George's precarious financial status and the gloom of the Depression. "This was the reason," as Jackie put it, "which started a not happy situation between our parents and reflected on us, the children. Until then we were a happy family."

"And what memories do you have of Maria as a child, Dr. Lantzounis?" I asked now.

"Oh, I don't remember. I was too busy at that time. I was married to my work. But, later, I saw Maria more frequently. I followed her career at a distance and we corresponded."

"What about the feud between Litza and Maria?"

"When she was a little girl, Maria was very good friends with her mother. People say that her mother didn't like her because she wasn't good-looking—that's another story—but they had good relations. She and Maria were best of friends up to the time Maria went to sing in Mexico and her mother joined her. After that, they started to cool off.

"Litza exploited Maria. She even made Maria Callas dolls. She was a real money digger. I ought to know, I was the one who corresponded back and forth between them. I got Maria to increase everyone's checks. Three checks every month! Maria took care of her sister and mother although Jackie was never poor—she was very well supported. Maria sent money to her father too, but Litza wanted to have more and more."

Lantzounis looked at his watch and reached for the pills on the end table beside him. It was time for me to leave. From the living-room windows I could see the glimmering headlights of homeward-bound traffic.

I left feeling exhilarated. Dr. Lantzounis had given me a fleeting but animated glimpse of the Kalogeropoulos family. I followed it up with a trip to Washington Heights and a stop in at P.S. 189, where Maria received her primary education. The record of that school's most illustrious graduate was meticulously preserved in an acetate folder.

Judging from the school nurse's report, Maria weighed 119 pounds at age eleven, which, for a tall girl (five feet three inches) of big build, is not excessive. She started wearing glasses in the seventh grade, but her severe myopic condition had not yet developed. Written evaluations reported she was a quiet, reserved child with a keen mind, and her grades show she was an above-average student.

The school staff encouraged me to look up Mrs. Georgette Kokenakis while I was in the neighborhood. She was a former schoolmate of Maria's who worked at P.S. 189 and lived nearby. Mrs. Kokenakis suggested I come right over. "If you are walking," she said, "you might like to go by the Kalogeropouloses' house. It's on the way to my place. After you pass George Washington High School, which Jackie attended, make a turn on 192nd Street. Their house was number 569."

A group of Hispanic teenagers sat on the steps of number 569 blocking the entrance of the ill-kept building. Their conversation competed with the music blasting from their radio. Opposite the windows at which, her mother said, passersby once clustered to listen to Maria singing "La Paloma," plastic garbage bags and mangled beer cans surrounded a withering tree hung with orange paper streamers, the remnants of a New Year's party. I tried to imagine what the neighborhood had been like when Maria walked these streets on her way to school or church.

Mrs. Kokenakis's immaculate, two-room apartment was in a Fort Washington high rise that dominated the drab, older buildings once considered fashionable. The affable Georgette, a vivacious and motherly woman in a print blouse and navy skirt, plied me with Greek pastries and coffee, apologizing for the nonexistent disarray, before settling down to give me her account of Maria and her family.

"They were well-mannered, obedient children, overly protected like most Greek girls of our age and background. Their first home was right across the street from the school. Her mother walked Mary Ann or Mary Anna—that's the way we called her then—across in the morning and was always there to pick her up at the end of the day. She was not allowed to linger with the rest of the students after class, unless she was involved in a school play or operetta. None of us ever became friends with Jackie or Maria. They kept to themselves. They were a bit . . . uppity, would you say? George had a pharmacy, which in those days was like being a doctor. The family attended church every Sunday, but they didn't mix.

"Mary Ann was a loner," Georgette recalled, offering me another sweet. "She wasn't invited to many kids' houses and I guess she was not encouraged to have us over. Most of the time she studied and practiced. I can still hear her voice," Mrs. Kokenakis said, closing her eyes. "She sang at my graduation. She was eleven years old, although her voice could have been that of a much older girl. She sang 'Play Gypsies, Dance Gypsies' from *The Countess Maritza*. Usually she was very quiet. She wasn't outgoing, but when she sang, those dark expressive eyes flashed. With her hands on her hips, she twisted to and fro. You could tell that she enjoyed it!"

Mrs. Kokenakis rose, placed her hands on her Rubenesque hips and, with dexterity and grace, swayed to the remembered rhythm of "Play Gypsies, Dance Gypsies." She skirted the marble inlaid coffee table and ice-blue velveteen couch, spun around once more and returned to her seat.

"That's how it was," she said with a nostalgic smile. "Even when the chorus joined in, her voice stood out. We were spellbound by her voice."

On my way home I wondered what Maria's life might have been like if Litza hadn't aimed so high for her. Perhaps, without her mother's delusions of grandeur, Maria would have remembered Hell's Kitchen and the Splendid Pharmacy, and might have become a Washington Heights housewife, caring for her family in a tidy apartment decorated with her children's graduation pictures and mementos of her family's Greek past.

5

The War Years

In 1936, when Maria was thirteen years old and in her last year at P.S. 189, Litza decided to take her daughters back to Greece. She wanted to put some distance between George and herself and was anxious to further the girls' musical careers, convinced that her family in Greece would give her the needed financial and moral support. Although I'm certain that Maria was desolate at leaving her father behind, she must have been excited by the adventure, like any child her age. Nineteen-year-old Jackie was sent ahead to stay with her maternal grandmother in Athens while Litza and Maria packed Litza's beloved Pianola and her maroon silk couch and gold chairs for storage. Two months later the three were reunited when the *Saturnia* docked at the port of Patras and Litza disembarked with Maria, to open a new chapter in their lives.

After a few months with her family, Litza and the girls moved into a spacious apartment at 61 Patission Street, in Athens. There Jackie resumed her piano lessons while Litza set out to find the ideal teacher for Maria. To her chagrin, neither her immediate family nor her numerous "rich" cousins were in a position to help her financially. Had she built up as many illusions around her return to Greece as she had around the departure for America? If so, it appears Litza would not admit defeat, a trait Maria certainly would inherit from her.

Undaunted by Maria's insignificant musical training (which consisted, besides piano lessons, of the music appreciation class in her New York grade school), Litza, it seems, inflicted her daughter's raw vocal talent on anyone who would listen. In her book, Litza tells us she even managed briefly to get the attention of the famous bass Nicola Moscona, who was impressed enough to suggest Maria enroll at the Athens Conservatory. Maria was too young to be admitted, but that apparently didn't faze Litza. Demonstrating her usual flexibility with the facts, she added two years to Maria's age. Maria would be the youngest student the conservatory had ever had.

It was Maria's good fortune to find the necessary musical guidance and enthusiasm in Maria Trivella, her first teacher in Athens, who in 1937 taught her the power and beauty of music. From Litza's account, it seems the young student plunged into her studies with fervor.

After two years with Trivella, Maria entrusted her musical education to Elvira de Hidalgo, a Spanish soprano who had made her Metropolitan Opera debut in 1910 as Rosina in *The Barber of Seville,* and later sang Gilda in *Rigoletto* at Covent Garden, before devoting herself to teaching. "It was examination day, on a humid afternoon at the Athens conservatory, at the end of 1939," Madame de Hidalgo said in an interview given to the Italian magazine *Oggi*. "Maria was sixteen when I first saw her. It was laughable to think this youngster wanted to become an opera singer. She was very tall and fat. . . . She wore glasses, her face was covered with pimples and her dark hair was braided into two unbecoming rolls over her ears, over which she wore a little white cap. She wore a school apron buttoned down the front and sandals that had seen better days." But as Maria started Weber's "Ocean! Thou Mighty Monster" from *Oberon,* Hidalgo said, she closed her eyes and listened. "I heard a violent cascade of sound not yet in control, but dramatic and moving. I had secretly been looking and waiting for that voice for some time. It was as if it were an appointment with destiny."

Elvira de Hidalgo became the young girl's mentor and confidante. They spent hours together discussing voice and theater technique, or sometimes Maria just listened to anecdotes of her teacher's career with Caruso and Chaliapin. Through de Hidalgo, Maria was introduced to the works of Rossini, Bellini, Donizetti and Verdi. It has been reported she memorized entire pages of a score after one hearing, building a very unusual repertoire for a student of her age.

By then, Maria wore thick glasses to correct her increasing myopia, but needless to say, she couldn't wear them in performance. Since Maria couldn't see the conductor's baton onstage, she obstinately memorized every note of the score and thus turned her disability into an asset. This lack of dependence on cuing from the very beginning of her career would allow her great freedom to combine her vocal talent with meaningful physical movement onstage.

The years in Athens offered Maria the first opportunity to test her developing skills in actual performance. In 1940, she took part in a student production of Puccini's *Suor Angelica,* preceded by her role as Santuzza in *Cavalleria Rusticana,* which, at the age of sixteen, singled her out and earned her a first prize. After the lead in the conservatory's production of *Aida* and excerpts sung from *Ballo in Maschera* in November 1940, Maria was chosen as one of the four girls in von Suppé's *Boccaccio*. The part called for singing and dancing in a barrel, but I gather this somewhat limited role left no lasting impression on the spectators. It was only of major importance to Maria because it was the first performance for which she received payment.

Perhaps her debut seemed less than momentous because the world outside the conservatory had just been profoundly shaken. Only a month earlier, on October 28, 1940, war had been declared between Italy and Greece. The Germans would invade Greece the following April. Like all their compatriots, the Kalogeropoulos family found themselves bewildered and unprepared. The bitter winter spread hardship and disease. Every day food and other necessities were harder to come by and the lines in front of half-empty stores became longer. But thanks to Milton Embiricos, a young man Jackie had met in 1938 and became engaged to soon after her arrival in Athens, Litza and her daughters did not endure the privation of the war as grimly as most. It was their good fortune that the handsome Milton belonged to the Embiricos shipping family, one of the wealthiest and most prominent in Greece.

"He was, at the same time, fiancé, brother and father for us," Jackie told me. "He saw my family as his own. He was rich and in spite of difficulties during the German occupation, he carried on with his money to provide us with a big apartment, food, clothes and even a maid. The story that Mary told about how she kept us all on the salary she received at the Athens Lyric Theater is absolutely untrue. Her salary was symbolic, and I would say she spent it all to buy a lipstick, or some pastries. Everything was provided by Milton. He did all this for my sake, because he adored me. We were very happy together from the time I was nineteen until he died in 1962. We never married because his family wanted him to marry his own crowd, his own people, otherwise they were going to disown him. That's the way it is in well-known, rich families in Athens. . . . But I was never obligated to work. My former fiancé would never permit me to work. We were very lucky and Mary was very indebted to me. During those years of the German occupation, Mary was able to devote herself to her art without any care of how to live, to eat, to dress! Without Milton we would have starved. The small amount of money my father sent us from America was blocked by the war, and never arrived."

Even if the Kalogeropoulos family was privileged due to Milton's generous intervention, I know the war left its mark on Maria. Maria and I had often shared the fear and uncertainty the experience had brought to our young lives. I too had lived through the German occupation, in Bulgaria: I remember stern-faced German soldiers with pointed rifles, at every street corner. Enemy trucks, being loaded with goods pillaged from shops, sped away while the long line of people waiting in the bitter cold since dawn for their means of survival watched helplessly. I remember many conversations when Maria recalled the wail of the sirens, walking past the sick and the dying on her way to the conservatory, blackouts, rushed trips to the cellar and the eerie silence that followed the curfews. Even when success ultimately brought luxury to her life, Maria considered it a sacrilege to throw away a piece of bread.

One of Maria's close friends told me that during the famine, Litza sent Maria out with Jackie, warning them not to come back empty-handed. "Unless they brought food," the friend added, "their mother wouldn't permit them to eat. Maria literally ate out of garbage cans during the war."

I found that story disconcerting; Jackie insisted her family had been among the more fortunate, even during the civil war. It made me want even more to speak to someone who knew Maria during those years in Greece. Then, through some Greek friends, I happened on an unexpected discovery: Arda Mandikian, a singer living in Athens who had been a pupil of de Hidalgo's with Maria. Like Callas, she had gained recognition outside of Greece and returned to settle in Athens after a successful career in England and on the Continent.

On a September afternoon, Mrs. Mandikian received me in her penthouse apartment in the center of Athens. She had just returned from a holiday on the island of Poros, and her deep tan accentuated her dark, Armenian good looks. She is a lady with the vitality of a woman younger than her years matched by a sharp wit and beautiful speaking voice. As she excused herself to answer a telephone call, I looked around the L-shaped living room. The decor was elegant yet unpretentious. There were no trophies of her achievements nor the usual autographed pictures of famous people that accompany a successful career.

"One thing which was marvelous about de Hidalgo," Mrs. Mandikian recollected, "is that she left the voice in its natural state. We all sang with our natural voices. She herself had a fantastic voice and was an excellent actress. All the coloratura Maria had in the operas she sang later, she got from de Hidalgo. However, I wouldn't say de Hidalgo was an extraordinary teacher. She was a very good coach, not a technique teacher. What she did for Maria and me, in a way, was wrong because when you are seventeen and eighteen it's not right for the voice to sing heavy roles, duets from *Gioconda*, *Norma* and *Aida*. But we did it. We both shouted and screamed. It was very bad for the voice, but fortunately it didn't harm ours.

[61]

"Maria and I saw a lot of each other then," Arda went on. "You might say we were the two stars of the conservatory and we were always paired off to sing together. We met in class with de Hidalgo, where we listened and watched all the students, learning by their good and bad points, and Maria often came to my house to rehearse. But I can't say we were very close. She wasn't an outgoing, friendly girl. She went her way; besides, we didn't mix socially."

I was a bit surprised. "Oh, I got the impression that you often went to their house."

An odd look came over Mrs. Mandikian's face. Her relaxed posture stiffened and she shook her head back and forth.

"Never," she said firmly. "I never went to their house. I wasn't allowed to."

I pondered over that for a minute. Assessing Litza's description of her own background, it would appear her family was socially established. Her father, she claimed, was a very rich man and came from a "fine family" in Stylis, the little town of Litza's birth. Judging from her pleasant apartment and Mrs. Mandikian's cosmopolitan air, I would venture to suppose that the Mandikian family was recognized in Athens society; but considering the change in Arda's easy grace, I had a hunch there was more to the story than any obvious social discrepancy.

"But I understood you to say earlier that Litza frequently entertained, had open house?"

"Yes, she did," Arda agreed, "to promote her daughters and rise socially. She would have liked to get into Athenian society, but couldn't. She was a pushy woman. Not a likable person."

"I was under the impression Litza came from a very good family."

"If that is the case," Mrs. Mandikian answered, amused, "it didn't show at all. She was a handsome woman, but not at all distinguished."

"Who were their friends, then? Who did they invite?" I asked. "And where did they get the food and drink—this was during the occupation, wasn't it?"

Mrs. Mandikian wavered for a second before she answered.

"Yes, yes it was. They saw artists . . . and . . . some Italians and Germans. As for food, they managed. Those who had money could buy supplies on the black market. They could get anything they wanted."

"But I thought the situation was desperate, that people in Greece were starving."

"Yes," said Mrs. Mandikian pensively, her dark eyes lowered, "our country was the worst hit. Most of us had nothing. Bread? We didn't know what bread was. One could get a bit of lettuce, some beans full of worms and bugs and at times some meat, but you didn't know if you were eating a cat, a dog or a donkey. We were very unhappy in a way, but we kept that strong youthful feeling of looking forward to something better . . . which never really came. In many ways, we lived the normal things of youth. Simple things: singing, swimming, dancing and excursions. Of course, there were curfews, but Athens was never bombed."

It would appear, in fact, that the presence of the enemy Italian troops was actually a boost to Maria's budding career. Her mother also writes that her voice proved to be a rewarding bond of friendship with a group of Italian officers who often visited the Kalogeropoulos house to listen to Maria sing.

With her inborn facility for languages, aided, I have now been told, by the amorous attentions of one of the officers,

Maria learned Italian fluently in a matter of months. The young man's interest in her brought her the self-confidence she so badly needed after years of watching her sister's romantic conquests from the wings. She discovered she loved the language of Rossini and Verdi, and the roles she had memorized suddenly came alive. The fraternization of the Kalogeropoulos household with the occupying forces, however, stirred angry sentiments among some of the Greeks who knew Litza and her daughters.

Even today, the photographs of German officer Oskar Botman and Italian Colonel Mario Bonalti, published in Litza's book, still raise Greek eyebrows. The subject was touched upon during dinner with Jackie, but I was totally unprepared for the long handwritten letter I received from her two weeks later. After answering several questions we hadn't had time to dwell on during our first meeting, Jackie proceeded to explain the matter of the photographs:

> To publish the pictures of German and Italian officers was the strongest proof that there was absolutely not a blameworthy story about these very polite and cultured men. If mother had felt guilty, she would never have published these pictures. These gentlemen were honest friends of our family. They were very fond of opera and adored Maria's voice. In the admiration of Art, we are all human beings connected in brotherhood.

Meanwhile, as the war raged in the streets of Athens, de Hidalgo had managed to place her young pupil as a full-time artist at the opera, a position for which Maria received the modest salary of 1,300 drachmas, or about $65 in today's money, for each role that she performed. The opera house by this time was totally supported by the occupying troops and headed by the German commander, Wilhelm Speidel, whose keen interest in opera would keep its doors open throughout the war.

Maria's talents were quickly recognized. In August 1942, the nineteen-year-old soprano sang her first *Tosca*, a work that Dr. Marchand discovered was intentionally staged for her. Her performance received an ovation and she was unanimously praised for her vocal qualities and acting abilities.

But Dr. Marchand also told me that this breakthrough, added to her rank as first soprano of the Athens conservatory, brought about her first taste of jealousies and backstage rivalry. Still, Maria had worked hard for what she had obtained and seemed determined to let neither these rivalries nor the occupation stop her. "Maria," her mother wrote, "would not let a war interfere with her ambitions."

"I don't recall her colleagues being so awful to her," said Mrs. Mandikian, "but of course she and I worked in perfect harmony. We had absolutely different voices and repertories. We would never have clashed professionally. I think it was her determined attitude which annoyed her colleagues. She knew what she was, she knew her value and she wanted to be recognized. I must say, I admire her more than anyone in the world! There is no one that can touch her, absolutely no one. The amazing phrasing that Maria had, no one had. Maria was Maria. Now everyone takes credit for having *made* Maria. Maria was already made then. You don't acquire that, you either have it or you don't. Maria was Maria."

"Do you think her professional achievements gave her the contentment she needed in those days?" I had to ask.

"No," said Arda Mandikian thoughtfully, "I can't say she was a very happy young girl. She was big and fat. Even her hands, which were amazingly beautiful later, were fat at the time . . . and then, the mother pushed and pushed and pushed.

She made Maria go through all kinds of home beauty treatments to improve her complexion. In a way she was right, since Maria was in the theater, but it seemed never-ending!"

"Could it be that part of Maria's isolation came from her physical insecurities? I mean, besides the flirtation with the Italian, did she have any love affairs?"

"Oh, she did," said Mrs. Mandikian emphatically, "a very well-known love affair with the baritone Evanglios Mangliveras. They sang together in Eugen d'Albert's *Tiefland,* sponsored by the Nazi occupying forces. He was an artist past his prime, but still greatly admired. Perhaps it was just an affair, but on his part it was a love affair. Later, when he was ill— she was famous by then—he asked to see her, but she refused. She behaved very badly toward him . . . she was very strange that way."

Arda said Mangliveras had guided Maria through the *Tiefland* production. Intrigued by her combination of talent and intuition, he fell in love with her and proposed. But Maria refused him. He was too old, she said.

Maria's next accomplishment was Leonore, in Beethoven's *Fidelio,* which she sang in Greek. The Herodes Atticus open-air theater was packed that August 1944 evening with Athenians and occupying soldiers. According to reviews, Maria sang with such emotion that at the end the audience burst into an unrestrained demonstration of joy.

More than twenty years after that event, during a dinner party in Paris, a Greek friend of mine asked Maria, "What is your opinion of the Athens Opera? Did it function when you were there?"

"For heaven's sake don't let on I told you this," Maria whispered, "but the only time the Athens Opera functioned professionally was during the occupation, under the Germans. The rest of the time, it was total chaos, a disaster!"

Two months after *Fidelio,* on October 12, the Germans and Italians evacuated Greece, and Athens was liberated by the Free Greek Army troops. Athens was jubilant, but the euphoria was short-lived. Soon tension came from within. EAM-ELAS, the Communist guerilla group, requested the abdication of King George II and his government. On December 3, 1944, civil war broke out. The chaos and street fighting that ensued proved to be more violent and bloody than the occupation. Even Milton's help was not enough to protect Maria and her family from the hardships of those months. It was also a period of personal struggle for Maria. Though she hated the Germans for the suffering they had imposed on her country, the artist in her had more ambivalent feelings, since their contribution had gained her an artistic acceptance she now relied on heavily.

Finally, on February 12, 1945, thanks in part to British intervention, the civil war was over. But when the Royal Theater reopened in the spring, Maria was not part of its new operatic season. Some of her colleagues who had left the opera during the occupation, in protest of its German management, had now taken the reins.

Dr. Marchand told me: "The last years at the conservatory were very difficult for her. Callas found herself demoted to third soprano. That's why she left. Her jealous colleagues declared war on her and I think she never forgot the way they treated her. She was full of bitterness when she left Athens and she knew there was no future for her here. At the time, I don't think she liked Greece or was happy here."

After seven years of silence a letter finally arrived from George Kalogeropoulos, truly a joyous surprise. It contained a hundred dollars for Maria and a message urging her to return to America so as not to jeopardize her American citizenship. Swayed by the comforting knowledge that her father awaited her, and with New York's Metropolitan Opera as her aim, Maria left Piraeus on one of the first freighters bound for the States. Opinions differed as to Maria's motivation for returning. Jackie said that de Hidalgo did not agree with Maria's decision, that she saw better opportunities for her pupil in Italy, but Maria was steadfast. She was twenty-one and felt she should make her own decisions; follow her destiny. Jackie also voiced doubt that their father had greatly influenced Maria's decision to return. "You see, Nadia," Jackie reminded me that night in Athens, "I chose to stay here in Greece with Milton and my mother. I gave my life to my family. Mary gave her life to her career."

6

To America and Back

"I was so looking forward to seeing my father and returning to America," Maria told Dr. Lantzounis's wife, Sally, shortly after her arrival, "but it isn't at all the way I expected. I've had quite a shock. My father is living with the woman upstairs. I'm certainly not ready to share his affections with that Papajohn woman."

Maria's hurt pride quickly turned her adoration and possessive love for her father into a prudish moral code. Both Lantzounis and Jackie told me that Maria never forgave their old family friend, Alexandra Papajohn, for robbing her, as she saw it, of her father's affection. Maria no doubt felt cheated of her long-awaited reunion with him.

When she first got home, Dr. Lantzounis remembers, "She couldn't get over the opulence of New York. She spent a lot of time looking at the stores and picking out furniture for her room in George's apartment, but eating seemed to be her full-time occupation. She was always hungry. It was as if she had to catch up on all the years of the war." Her over-indulgent diet soon had its effect. Before long she was tipping the scales at 210 pounds.

After the initial taste of American plenty, Maria found it difficult to adjust to the indifference of the average American to what was happening across the Atlantic. She was shocked by the waste in the United States and (she told me years later) memories of the war invaded her dreams. Back in the country of her birth, she was a stranger. As she once said to me, "I am an American with the mentality of an émigrée."

The pleasure of seeing old friends, visiting her godfather, shopping with Sally and pampering her father soon wore off. Maria grew restless. She tried to contact Nicola Moscona, the Greek bass, now at the Met, who had admired her voice years before in Athens and who had assured her of his help should she come to New York. She hoped he would be her intro-duction to the Metropolitan Opera and possibly to the great Arturo Toscanini. But her efforts proved futile, and her calls and messages remained unanswered.

Meanwhile, Maria made the rounds of auditions. Un-known, overweight and disliked for her haughty attitude, she was rejected. Each rejection only made her more aggressive and determined. She now understood de Hidalgo's warning and missed the attention and success she had become used to in Greece.

"Maria was about to take a job at Macy's when soprano Louise Taylor introduced her to my husband," Louise Ca-selotti told me during a telephone conversation in New York. "Eddie Bagarozy, my husband, was a lawyer and impresario and I was a singer coaching on the side. After listening to Marianna—we *all* called her Marianna then—sing 'Casta Diva,' I agreed to coach her. The voice was professional material,

New York, 1935. *Left to right:* Alexandra Papajohn, Evangelia (Litza), George and Maria Kalogeropoulos. *(Courtesy J. Stathopoulos Kalogeropoulos)*

At home in Washington Heights, about 1936. *Left to right:* Evangelia, Alexandra Papajohn and Yacinthy (Jackie). *(Courtesy J. Stathopoulos Kalogeropoulos)*

ABOVE: Maria, Evangelia and Jackie at Xylocastron, near Corinth, Greece, during the spring of 1940. *(Courtesy J. Stathopoulos Kalogeropoulos)*

LEFT: Maria *(in light dress)* and Arda Mandikian singing Pergolesi's *Stabat Mater,* 1943, Athens. *(Courtesy A. Mandikian)*

ABOVE: Bathing beauties during
the summer of 1943, Athens: Arda
Mandikian *(center top)* Maria *(center
bottom)*. *(Courtesy A. Mandikian)*

LEFT: Maria and Gerasimos
Koundouris, accompanist for de
Hidalgo's classes, Athens, 1945.
*(Courtesy Polyvios Marchand Archives,
Athens)*

ABOVE: Leaving New York
for Italy: Louise Caselotti *(left)* and
Maria on board the *Rossia*, June 1947.
(Gina Guandalini collection)

RIGHT: Leaving Hotel Cavalieri,
Milan, 1950. *(Gina
Guandalini collection)*

FAR RIGHT: A "trimmed"
Maria photographed by
Semo, Mexico, 1950. *(Semo)*

ABOVE: Giulietta Simionato, Alejo Villegas Rebelo and a caped Maria dine at the Prince Hotel, Mexico City, 1951. *(Semo)*

LEFT: Maria in her dressing room during *La Traviata*, Parma, Italy, 1951. *(Studio Montacchini)*

LEFT: Evangelia Kalogeropoulos, 1951. *(Courtesy J. Stathopoulos Kalogeropoulos)*

BELOW: Holding hands with her father *(left)* and Meneghini in Mexico City, 1951. *(Courtesy J. Stathopoulos Kalogeropoulos)*

ABOVE: Jackie Kalogeropoulos
(*Courtesy J. Stathopoulos*
Kalogeropoulos)

RIGHT: George Kalogeropoulos,
aged thirty-five. (*Courtesy*
J. Stathopoulos Kalogeropoulos)

FAR RIGHT: Brief cease-fire
between Ghiringhelli and
Maria, after her *Macbeth* at
La Scala, 1952. (*Gina*
Guandalini collection)

ABOVE: Maria at Teatro Verdi, Trieste, 1953. *(de Rota)*

LEFT: Maria in *Madama Butterfly*, Chicago, 1956. *(Luxardo)*

ABOVE LEFT: Vacation time—Maria with Meneghini *(center)* and Giovanna Lomazzi *(right)*, Ischia, 1956. *(Courtesy G. Lomazzi)*

ABOVE RIGHT: A playful Maria with Giovanna Lomazzi in Ischia, about 1957. *(Courtesy G. Lomazzi)*

BELOW: *(Left to right)* Carla Nani Mocenigo, Giovanna Lomazzi, Meneghini, Wally Toscanini and Maria backstage after a performance at La Scala, 1955. *(E. Piccagliani)*

A lesson in glamour with designer Alain Reynaud at Biki's studio.
(Courtesy E. Bouyeure)

ABOVE: Maria and Toy with Valeria Pedemonte after a performance in Milan. *(Courtesy V. Pedemonte)*

RIGHT: At the Paris Opéra, gala evening in honor of General de Gaulle: *(far left)* designer Alain Reynaud; *(far right)* Bruna Lupoli. *(Courtesy E. Bouyeure)*

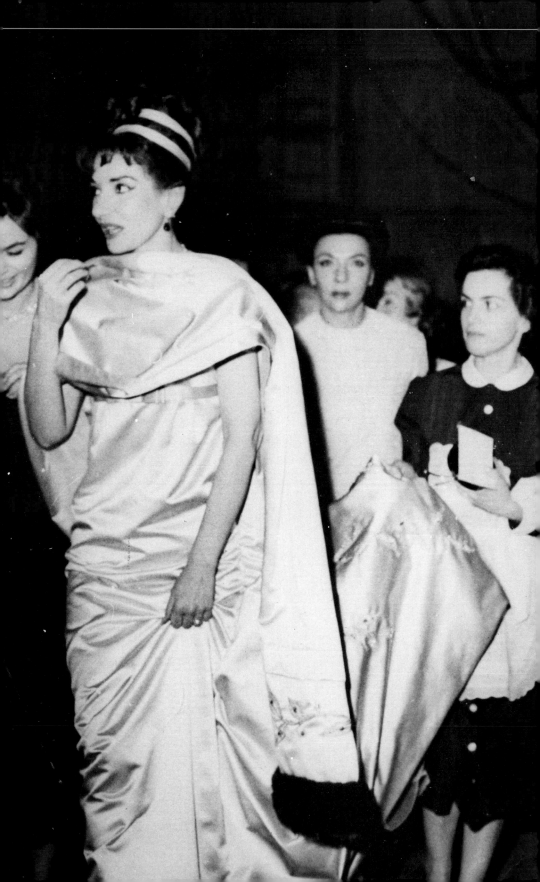

Domestic bliss in Milan, 1958. *(Federico Patellani)*

but the high notes weren't good. They needed work and Marianna was fully aware of that. Our apartment became a second home for Maria. She arrived punctually at eleven in the morning, wearing the same dress day in and day out, and walked the five blocks home at midnight. In a year and a half she missed five days in all. Of course there was no way she could let us know if she was unable to come, as her family didn't have a phone. They had no money, so she never paid for any of the lessons. She sang all day without getting tired and would get furious if she couldn't reach the high notes she aimed for. She would cry, out of rage. But soon there was nothing that girl couldn't do!"

In conversation Louise Caselotti mentioned that Nicola Rossi-Lemeni had, like Maria, been a frequent visitor to their home, where he also studied. Therefore, I was delighted to have a chance to clarify a few points with the Italo-Russian bass during one of his trips to New York. The fair-haired green-eyed Rossi-Lemeni has an easy offstage charm which makes a captivating contrast to the regal characters he portrays onstage. Now a teacher at the Indiana University School of Music, he remembers that he and Maria were "rather lost and penniless at the time . . . the Bagarozys said we could come over for a meal whenever we wanted, so we ate there at least once a day. When I first met Maria in 1947, she was to laugh at; fat and provincial, she weighed 210 pounds. She was conscious of this and, to defend herself, she was aggressive. I used to call her Roly-Poly."

Contrary to the Bagarozys' counsel, Louise Taylor persuaded Maria to audition at the Metropolitan Opera. Maria claimed that her singing was well received, but when I asked John Ardoin what he knew about Maria's Met audition, he gave a different version of the story than the one Maria had always told. "That audition has never been dealt with properly because we all accepted the party line that Maria put out," he claimed. "In 1945, she went to the Met and auditioned. She said, and maintained to the end, that they offered her *Fidelio* in English. She also said they had offered her *Butterfly* and she said she was too fat. There is no truth in that. I now understand totally. Edward Johnson, who was general manager in those days, told her that if she could straighten out her upper and lower registers and lose some weight, he would consider her for the Met. But, there was *no offer, no contract*. Reflect a moment on Maria's psychology at the time. She's come from Athens, where she was the most beloved singer in Greece. She was it! She returns to her father in New York to tell him she was the big star of Greek opera. She has an audition at the Met, and is turned down. What is she going to do? Go back to her family and tell them the Met is not interested in her? That she wasn't offered a contract? It was a question of saving face. That was very important to her. So, she lied. And that was one of the reasons she was so anti-Met. Of course, after a while, she talked herself into believing she'd had the offer."

In fact, in 1971, when I made arrangements for my friend Naomi Barry to interview Maria for the *International Herald-Tribune,* Maria insisted again on her version of the much discussed event at the Met. "In 1946," she told Barry, "Edward Johnson wanted me to make my debut at the Met in *Fidelio,* in English, and *Madama Butterfly* in Italian. I don't believe in opera in translation and I didn't consider Butterfly my best role. For a debut, you must make sure you are a success. So, I refused and had to wait for years." She didn't add, as has been reported, that she tried her ace in the hole, offering to sing *Tosca* and *Aida* gratis—but the answer was again, "Thank you, but no thank you." She was rebuffed, her pride wounded.

"I'll be back," she said. "You'll beg me on your knees to come and sing here."

The audition for the San Francisco Opera followed the same pattern. Impresario Gaetano Merola suggested Maria make her name in Italy and then return to him. Meanwhile, Eddie Bagarozy, whose dream was to manage his own opera company, had teamed with Italian impresario Ottavio Scotto to form the new United States Opera Company. Bagarozy's idea was to gather top European artists who were eager to work in the thriving postwar United States for reasonable fees. A large number of stars were Italians who had had difficult careers because of the war. Among them was Nicola Rossi-Lemeni.

A born optimist, Bagarozy was confident of success. The company planned to open with *Turandot* in Chicago and the lead was to be sung by "Marie Calas," a Greek soprano whose name, at that period, seems to have been as variable and uncertain as her career.

The Chicago press followed the progress of the new opera company with interest and gave it ample coverage. The opening date was scheduled for January 6, but financial and union problems intervened, postponing the performance. At length, Bagarozy and Scotto were obliged to declare bankruptcy, leaving a penniless "Calas" stranded in Chicago.

For Maria, the United States was turning into an artistic nightmare; she seemed to be getting nowhere. Litza's arrival did not improve the situation, although it had been Maria's idea to send for her mother. Perhaps to discourage her father's relationship with Alexandra Papajohn, she had borrowed seven hundred dollars from her godfather to pay for the passage. Her father's cramped quarters on West 157th Street further strained family life. Litza regularly nagged Maria for refusing

"that *Butterfly* offered by the Metropolitan Opera," and reminded her of the sacrifices she had made to promote her
career.

When the legendary tenor Giovanni Zenatello (acclaimed for his portrayal of Otello, and at that time the artistic
director of the Verona Festival) arrived in New York looking
for new voices, Nicola Rossi-Lemeni used his Veronese con-
nections to arrange auditions for himself and Maria. Although
Zenatello had come with the idea of contracting Herva Nelli,
a young singer from Philadelphia, for the role of Gioconda,
he agreed to hear Maria at Rossi-Lemeni's request. The Metropolitan's eager young Richard Tucker, already cast as Enzo,
was asked to sing the duet with Maria, but when the seventy-
five-year-old Zenatello heard Maria, he was so struck by her
voice that he insisted on singing it with her himself. Maria
was offered six performances of *Gioconda* in Verona at sixty
dollars each.

Still disbelieving and frightened that Zenatello might
have a change of heart, she asked Bagarozy to act as her agent.
He drew up a contract that was signed on June 13, 1947, "as
we went out the door, on our way to the ship," says Louise
Caselotti. Maria's signature guaranteed that she would turn
over 10 percent of her gross earnings to Bagarozy, her "sole
and exclusive agent for a period of ten years" in exchange for
managerial and promotional services involving her career, which
included opera, radio, concerts and television. A similar contract was signed by Rossi-Lemeni.

Once her role was assured, the problem of Maria's passage to Europe remained to be solved. George's fifty-dollar
contribution could not get her very far, so, once again, Lantzounis came to the rescue, advancing the necessary funds. He
added a little extra, he told me, to allow his goddaughter to
buy herself an evening gown for the Italian premiere.

"I remember the crossing on the *Rossia* well," Rossi-Lemeni told me. "I was already on board when Maria arrived. She turned up in a black limousine, hired by her parents as a going-away present, like a diva leaving the Metropolitan on her way to sing at La Scala. She was wearing an enormous red hat. I couldn't believe my eyes!"

"Of the three of us," Louise Caselotti recalled, "Maria had probably experienced the most hardship in her lifetime, yet her complaints on board the *Rossia* became a litany. What did she expect? It was a cargo, not a luxury liner. Anyway, it really wasn't that bad," she said, laughing at the memory. "We were young, everything seemed fun then!"

"I was happy to be going back to Verona, which was my home," Rossi-Lemeni added, "and the *Rossia* was an economical way of getting there. But the accommodations were terrible. There was no service to speak of, and we were constantly scolded if we arrived a minute late for a meal. At the end of the journey, the Russians asked everyone to sign a document saying what a wonderful crossing we'd had. Maria was very upset. It was the first time I became aware of that side of her character. She exploded! 'It's a filthy ship and we've been treated like soldiers. The whole thing was horrible and I refuse to sign this document,' she said, throwing it aside."

Perhaps this was a preview of her later behavior, which did little to endear her to her colleagues. But I don't think so. It seems to me just Maria's blunt integrity surfacing, a trait she rarely managed to repress. As she once remarked, "They say I'm stubborn. No, I'm not stubborn; I'm right." Who can fight that?

7

Meneghini

May 2, 1949
I don't have anything else to tell you, dear, except
that I adore you, I honor you and respect you, and
that I am so proud of my Battista! No woman is
as happy as I am. Even though I am well known
for my singing, most of all I have the man of my
dreams! I challenge any woman to say that she has
as much as I do.

The feelings expressed by the enamored bride to her
"Titta" or "Santo Benedetto," as she lovingly nicknamed him,
had been totally erased by the time I met Maria. By then the
memory of their ten-year marriage had faded and she only
chose to speak of Meneghini as the greedy impresario, thirty
years her senior, who catnapped through rehearsals and opening nights. But Rossi-Lemeni assured me that in June 1947,

when he introduced them in Verona, Maria's feelings for Meneghini were very different.

The stocky, gray-haired Meneghini, with his double chin and aquiline profile, was a familiar figure in Verona's industrial and musical circles. A simple man from a reliable bourgeois background, he had a solid place in the business community. When he was not attending to his family's construction business, he spent his leisure time with the musicians and organizers of Verona's famed Arena listening to singers, attending rehearsals and otherwise nourishing his passion for opera.

"You know, Maria Callas is not the only singer he helped," Rossi-Lemeni told me. "Before her, there was Fusinato, another soprano. She was a monster. Big like Maria, but with a head like a pyramid and a huge fantastic voice. He tried to help this girl because he was in love with her voice, but she was so stupid and antimusical that she was very easily replaced by Maria.

"After a *Gioconda* rehearsal, Meneghini came up to me and said, 'Who is this Maria Callas and what is she going to do after she finishes here? Will she leave Italy?' There was a lot of talk about Callas. There were those who said she had talent, an interesting voice. Others said no, the voice is ugly and she's fat. I told Meneghini this was her only engagement and if nothing came up after *Gioconda* she'd be going back to the United States.' "

" 'That's impossible,' Meneghini said to me. 'I must meet her and at least invite her to see Venice before she goes!' "

"Maria's first reaction was typically hers: insecurity mixed with pride. 'No, I don't want to meet him. I don't need anybody's help. I don't want him to get the idea that he can take advantage of me because of his money.' I assured her Meneghini was a gentleman."

MARIA

In his biography, *My Wife Maria Callas,* Meneghini's eulogy of love to Maria, he assures us that by the time they got back to Verona, it was 2:00 A.M. and Maria was delighted with the outing and touched by his tender good-night kiss.

Apparently the enchantment of Venice worked its magic, as tête-à-tête luncheons and dinners followed. With each meeting Maria became less withdrawn, until she let down her defenses and poured out her heart to Meneghini. He says she told him of her parents' unhappy marriage, the painful separation from her father, her artistic success at the conservatory followed by the letdown and humiliations she had endured in New York. Verona was her last chance, she had said bitterly. If it didn't prove successful, she was ready to give up her career.

Meneghini listened attentively, offered to help and says he saw a helpless, childlike honesty in this physically commanding woman. On her side, I think, the beleaguered Maria was beguiled by her suitor's chivalry and kindness and, though he might not have been a romantic ideal, she was overwhelmed by his attentions. At any rate, all seemed to agree, during the next months Maria and Giovanni Battista fell in love.

At last, on August 2, 1947, the opening night of Verona's first postwar operatic season took place in the city's ancient Roman amphitheater. *La Gioconda* was conducted by Tullio Serafin, the well-loved maestro who had conducted the Arena's inaugural performance twenty-five years earlier. The production was lauded, but Maria herself received only lukewarm reviews. She pretended to dismiss them as unimportant but she was terribly upset.

Meneghini saw her pain and tried to console her. "Don't pay attention to what they write," he told her. "They don't understand a thing. You just keep on singing."

But no engagements materialized from Maria's *Gioconda* performance. Everything in her future had rested on this success, and failure meant leaving to face further uncertainties in New York.

Meneghini did everything he could to keep Maria in Italy. He put her in contact with Milan's theatrical agencies and arranged for an audition with La Scala's artistic director, Mario Labroca. Maria chose to sing "Casta Diva" from *Norma* and "O Patria Mia" from *Aida*. Labroca, however, was unimpressed and suggested she go back to America.

As the moment of her departure approached, Maria's mood darkened. I can imagine how she must have felt. She had found, in performing, the personal approval and security she craved, yet now the opportunity was denied her again and again. It seems as though she had confidence only in her singing—if that failed, all was lost. I think perhaps this is why she had such difficulty in accepting criticism. "The only person who has the right to criticize Callas is Callas," she was to say later. When, after *Gioconda*, Louise Caselotti tried to point out the technical errors that caused her voice to tire (a fact that critics had noted), Maria snapped back, "I'll do what I want! What matters is *that* you sing, not how you sing. Battista says he can get me to sing in all the theaters in the world."

With Meneghini's faith as her only shield, she launched into a heated argument that was to bring her long friendship with Louise to an abrupt close. "Maria would no longer listen to *me*," Caselotti says today, with a note of sadness, "so I suggested she study with Gina Cigna, an extraordinary singer. Do you know what her answer was? 'What is Cigna going to teach me?' "

But Rossi-Lemeni maintains Maria knew she had more to learn. "At the beginning no one wanted her," he remembers. "The books written about her give the impression that her career just took off. That's not so. Even in *Gioconda* she didn't have success, and afterwards she worked very hard to rid herself of the ugly sounds in her voice which sometimes seemed to come through a thick fog. These ugly sounds were due to a particular defect which we call 'the potato in the mouth'—that is to say, some sounds go back by themselves even if you try to support them. It depends on the conformation of the resonator. Maria worked to make her voice more pleasant. She worked with my mother, who was a singer and a coach. Maria was the hardest worker I've ever met."

At the last minute, Maria's perseverance paid off. Tullio Serafin, who had made his reputation discovering and forming voices, wanted to stage *Tristan und Isolde* to restore the prewar tradition of singing Wagner's opera in Italian.

"The problem was the singer," Rossi-Lemeni recalled. "Who was there in Italy, at that time, who could sing Isolde? Serafin decided that if Maria studied with him and his wife every day for the next six months, he was sure she could do it. But Maria was scheduled to leave and had no money to finance the rigorous training period in Italy. At this point, 'Santo Benedetto,' her guardian angel, spoke up. He offered Maria a six-month arrangement whereby she could concentrate on her singing while he took care of practical matters, lifting the financial burden from her shoulders."

Maria happily placed herself in Meneghini's and Serafin's hands. Time and again, she would surrender herself to others—particularly men—during her career. Although, given her options and the opportunity, one could hardly call this a surrender. Spurred by Meneghini's offer and Serafin's faith in her, Maria moved to the Quirinale Hotel in Rome to be coached by the "vocal magician."

"It was when she took up her studies with Serafin that her voice really started to improve," Rossi-Lemeni continued. "Serafin had a big musical influence on Callas and he was very smart with the way he coached her. He would say, 'Well, this note is not good, so try to do it in some other way' or 'You must cover this note, Maria,' but he wouldn't tell her how to cover it."

When Maria accepted the role of Isolde, she was unfamiliar with the opera, but her six months of relentless work would be rewarded when she and the little-known cast conquered a critical audience in Venice's La Fenice Theater. Sharing her success were two other singers who would go on to achieve fame: Boris Christoff and Fedora Barbieri.

"Her presence was imposing," Rossi-Lemeni told me, "even if the interpretation was a little banal. Her voice was so strong, so beautiful. She was immediately a box-office draw."

After her success in *Tristan und Isolde* with Serafin, Maria went on to sing *La Forza del Destino, Turandot, Aida* and *Norma*. With Serafin's help, she was on her way to conquering the Italian opera world. Later she would often remind people that after her teacher de Hidalgo, Serafin had been the most important person in molding her musical future: "He made me," Maria used to say.

Only a year after her success in *Tristan und Isolde,* Maria returned to La Fenice Theater as Brünnhilde in *Die Walküre,* again under the direction of Serafin.

My friend, the composer-conductor Franco Manino, who had been Serafin's assistant during the *Walküre* production, was in Rome between conducting tours when I spoke to him. "At that time," said Manino, "she was unsightly, unimaginable! She was immense, with huge sagging arms, but her attitude to her art never wavered. From the start she was intransigent, precise and strove for perfection, qualities difficult to retain once a singer becomes great. To my mind, the tantrums and scenes of hysteria that numerous publications linked to her artistic work were unfounded. She was a complete professional. I believe that her exceptional training and her willpower are what sustained the enormous demands she made on her voice and body during *Die Walküre* and *I Puritani*."

Rossi-Lemeni agrees it was an unprecedented tour de force. "It was crazy! Margherita Carosio, who was supposed to sing the lead in Bellini's *I Puritani,* got sick a week before the opening and they didn't have a replacement for her." So Serafin said, 'The only one who can learn to sing *I Puritani* in time is Maria Callas.' Can you imagine! A singer who sings *Die Walküre* cannot sing *Puritani!* But with seven days' preparation with Serafin, she did it . . . and she sang her last three *Die Walküre* performances while working on *I Puritani.*

"Perhaps," Rossi-Lemeni continued, "her theory of supporting the voice by eating well was not to be dismissed! As a rule, performing artists do not eat for at least three hours before they go onstage. Maria was an exception. Before a performance of *Puritani,* Maria would tuck away a huge steak and a plate full of vegetables. Her colleagues could not understand how she could move, much less sing, with all the food she had eaten an hour earlier, but it didn't seem to bother her at all. Once onstage she was like an island of intensity. Her voice in the second act overpowered everyone else's and her energy was boundless."

The thing I found fascinating as I pored over reviews and accounts of this period is that until Maria lost weight, it didn't seem to occur to many people that she was too fat or wrong for a part. Apparently she was never clumsy; her graceful gestures were in harmony with the character and the opera. The illusion she created was complete.

In 1948, shortly after her *Tristan* in Venice, Meneghini and Maria began to make serious plans for their future together. By this time, Maria could hardly believe her good fortune. Through this difficult turning point in her career, Meneghini had become her axis. Friends tell me she hung on every word he uttered and was totally subjugated by her mentor. The minute she stepped offstage, she found her "Titta" waiting in the wings to reassure and praise her. "You were great!" he'd cry out. "Fantastic! Go out there again and give them all you've got. Brava!"

To most people's surprise, the unlikely couple proved well suited. Maria adapted remarkably to her benefactor's environment and language, picking up the soft cadence of the Veronese dialect and its accompanying mannerisms. Friends and colleagues dispel any suggestion that she might have married him only out of self-interest. Maria's longtime friend, translator and music critic William Weaver (with whom I've kept in touch since our collaboration at the Spoleto Festival in the early sixties), remembers that Maria was drawn to Battista's cushiony figure as to a magnet. "Really, Nadia—she constantly embraced and hugged him and just couldn't keep her hands off him. She was enormously proud of 'my husband the industrialist,' as she liked to call him."

Fedora Barbieri also remembers them. Barbieri sang Brangäne in the Venice *Tristan und Isolde* and would often share the applause with Maria thereafter. Like Maria, she is straightforward and professional but blessed with a wonderful sense of humor, which—I must admit—Maria lacked. When we met in Florence, I knew instantly that we were going to hit it off. She started our interview by crying out, *"Basta con*

Maria Callas! Basta! Books, articles, endless TV coverage—one would think she was the *only* voice in opera. There were, and are, others, you know. For instance, what about Fedora Barbieri!"

Barbieri agreed that Maria and Battista were obsessed with each other. "It was as if he had made a bet with himself: he was going to make her into the greatest diva ever. He did everything for that woman. He really did it out of love, because Maria had little or nothing to offer: She was poor and ugly. She was so fat, at the time, that she couldn't find shoes to fit her and came to rehearsal in her bedroom slippers. There was nothing physically appealing to fall in love with, yet he really loved her and lived for her."

". . . I'm lonely without you," Maria wrote Meneghini. "I don't have or want friendships. You know that I am a misanthrope, and I'm right in being that way. I live only for you and for my mother: I'm shared by both of you!"

Having such tangible proof of Maria's love, Meneghini in turn proved his own. When his brothers protested his relationship with Maria, he gave up his share of the family's flourishing construction business for love of the plain penniless foreigner, gambling his own financial future on the unpredictable frailty of a voice. He was known for his parsimonious ways and friends were amazed at the money he spent on Maria with no assurance of an immediate return. Barbieri remembers that "if Meneghini offered someone a cup of coffee it became the talk of the town. In later years, when he realized the importance of cultivating press and social contacts, he spent more readily, but everyone remembers him as tight, and so was she."

Finally, the twenty-five-year-old Maria refused to leave for her Buenos Aires singing engagement without a gold band on her finger. She later admitted to a friend that her obstinacy was strengthened by fear that something might happen to Battista during her long absence. "His brothers were just awful to me. They thought I loved Battista for his money. They went as far as to say they'd murder him so as to keep him from becoming my husband."

Maria was married on April 21, 1949, the day of her departure for Argentina, in the somewhat disorderly sacristy of Verona's Filippini Church. The sacristy, generally used as a storage place, was littered with broken statues, dusty incense burners and other church paraphernalia, none of which was noticed by the shortsighted bride, who further dimmed her vision by bursting into tears of happiness. While the priest, assisted by a scruffy old sexton, pronounced them man and wife, Maria repeatedly thanked the Madonna for blessing her with so much love.

Eight hours later, the new bride sailed off alone for a three-month tour in Argentina. The company, headed by Tullio Serafin, was made up of old friends: Nicola Rossi-Lemeni, Fedora Barbieri and Mario del Monaco, who were to sing in *Norma, Turandot* and *Aida*. For Maria, the tour meant another giant step in the struggle to establish herself as a major performer. But while she was thrilled by the attention and accolades, her daily letters to Titta were homesick and lovesick.

It struck me that Maria's letters from Argentina, between the lines of love promises and plans for their reunion, seem to show her loneliness and deep insecurity mixed with a strong consciousness of her talent. She writes of "hostile winds," of "her enemies," and gives frequent if unsolicited demonstrations of her superiority. When the voice of her colleague, soprano Delia Rigal, cracked as she was ending the *"O Patria Mia"* aria in *Aida* (a role Maria was to take over shortly), Maria, in a letter to Titta, attributed the mishap to "God's justice."

MARIA

It seems that ever since Athens, Maria had begun to feel that while God in his fairness had protected her, many people remained against her. This paranoia seems to have only grown with her fame. When I met Maria, these fears were still a recurring theme. Although she desperately wanted to trust people, she was constantly on guard.

When Maria finally returned to Verona from South America, she and Meneghini moved out of the Accademia Hotel into their own apartment. Maria was beside herself with joy. It was the first time she had a home of her own that she could arrange as she wished, after years spent in impersonal hotel rooms and close quarters shared with her family. Domesticity, with its tangible comforts, was of utmost importance to Maria. She became a zealous housewife, taking pride in the inedible meals she prepared for Battista, endlessly moving furniture around or hanging the paintings her husband collected.

"The house looked like a stage set," recalls Rossi-Lemeni. "It was almost empty and there were no books in the library. She didn't have the taste of being cultivated in anything other than singing."

When the Meneghinis moved into their Milanese house a few years later, mutual friends told me that the bareness Rossi-Lemeni describes was suddenly replaced by antique furniture, and valuable objects of various periods and styles placed next to overstuffed fringed sofas scattered with lacy pillows all trimmed with a profusion of bows.

Even when I met her, twenty years later, Maria's domestic side was frequently evident. It surfaced in odd and sometimes charming ways. On my first visit to her Avenue Georges Mandel apartment in Paris, I found her busily moving the living-room furniture around.

She loved "staying in" and fussing around the house. Her favorite rooms were the kitchen and bathroom. The latter had the function of a private study, in which she spent a good part of her time calling friends, doing her makeup, soaking in the tub or studying scores.

I remember her bathroom in Paris was spacious enough to be a reception room. Creams, brushes, perfumes and magazines were lined up in regimental order, while the cupboards were carefully replenished with supplies by Bruna. Always neat and precise, Maria claimed she could not function in messy, confused surroundings.

One of her relaxations and favorite pastimes was fiddling in the kitchen. It was part of what I call her dollhouse syndrome. To Maria, cooking symbolized the height of domestic creativity. She loved the pouring, stirring and chopping that complicated recipes involved. Judging from the effort put into these sessions, one would have expected succulent results, but a gourmet does not necessarily make a gourmet cook and Maria's cooking was a disaster.

I once sampled her talents when I had the flu. Maria was alone at the Grand Hotel in Rome and wanted company. I had a high fever and felt wretched, but neither my protests nor a deluge sweeping over the city was enough to dissuade her.

"If you are so sick," she said on the phone, "I'd better come right over. You need someone to care for you and cook you a good hot meal."

A few minutes later, a drenched and breathless Maria appeared at the door of my fifth-floor walk-up, laden with a pile of wet magazines. She ordered me to bed and headed straight for the kitchen. Colorful exclamations in Veronese dialect accompanied the clatter of pots and pans. The first course was packaged alphabet soup to soothe my feverish state. I silently blessed Maria's visit, when a shriek came from the kitchen. "Help! I can't turn the gas off!" I leapt out of bed to find a volcanic eruption of mashed potatoes spattering all over the kitchen. What was left in the pan took its place next to a shriveled chicken breast, which by now was cold. No sooner had I eaten this repast when the doorbell rang.

"Don't move, I'll get it!" Maria called out as she rushed to open the door, the apron still tied around her waist.

"Hello, I'm Doctor Stella. I've come to see Nadia. How is she?"

"She feels a bit better now that she's eaten," Maria answered. "I'm Assunta, the maid. Please let me hang up your wet coat."

From her vocal inflections I could imagine the expression on her face. Maria accompanied the doctor to my bedroom, then cleared the luncheon dishes and disappeared into the kitchen.

After he had finished examining me, Maria offered the doctor an espresso. He took a sip, winced, and added more sugar as he pensively studied the maid. It was evident that Maria was enjoying herself enormously.

When Dr. Stella prepared to leave, he whispered, "Your maid. . . . You know . . . she reminds me a lot of someone. . . ."

Rossi-Lemeni told me that he too had the privilege of sampling some of Maria's home cooking. "When Maria invited me to their apartment in Milan, she had set a beautiful table with her finest silver, china and candlesticks. After drinks, Meneghini suggested we go to the table. Suddenly, Maria looked distressed. She had forgotten to prepare dinner. 'Well,' she said, 'maybe I can make a risotto with the rice left over from last night.' " An unpardonable offense to the North Italian risotto lover. " 'I'll sauté it.' She sautéed it so much that it was completely burnt and we didn't get any dinner." Rossi-Lemeni smiled. "She was very simple that way. She didn't create a problem for herself about things like that. It was the same with her singing. You'd ask her, 'Maria, will you sing something for us?' And she'd say 'yes' right away, not like my voice students, who always find some feeble excuse. She was ready to sing anywhere, anytime, even if she was doing the dishes. No warm-up, no nothing; she'd go right into 'Casta Diva,' nothing less."

In some respects, I think now that the years of her first successes in Italy were very happy ones for Maria. She seems to have accepted the heavy artistic commitments Meneghini arranged for her with enthusiasm. As long as he was there, she could do anything. She felt safe. In fact, during the 1948–49 season, Callas sang eleven highly demanding roles, some with totally different vocal *tessituras*. She was always either preparing a new role, performing or traveling. In those two years she covered all of Italy with Florence as her testing ground. There, at the Teatro Communale, the artistic director, Francesco Siciliani, recognized Maria's unusual vocal versatility and gave her the opportunity to sing roles modeled on the repertoire of Giuditta Pasta and Maria Malibran. She sang *Armida, Norma, Lucia di Lammermoor, Medea* and *Traviata*.

Opera expert Sergio Segalini explained to me, as one of opera's less initiated, that Maria was the first singer in a century to regenerate the *soprano dramatico di agilità*—"until she came along," he said, "a lot of operas had been abandoned because of the impossibility of finding proficient singers for those roles. Maria could, for instance, sing both *Norma* and *Sonnambula*, parts usually performed by a dramatic soprano and a light soprano, respectively. Callas sang both, as did the prima donnas in Bellini's time."

By the beginning of the fifties, Maria Callas Meneghini was making an important impression on the Italian critics. They compared her Norma to that of Giuditta Pasta, who had created the role: now she too was hailed as *"la divina."* Her Violetta was full of "poetry and ardor"; her Elena in *Vespri Siciliani,* "phosphorescent in beauty and agility." Unanimously, they lauded her inexhaustible technical abilities, her superior intelligence, her voice, her presence, her acting.

These hard-earned achievements were important to Maria, but, from everyone I spoke to, I got the impression that her relationship with her husband came first at that time in her life. Loving and being loved was her raison d'être. She could finally assert her identity as a woman in a situation of acceptance and security. In fact, she felt so secure that she invited her mother and sister to visit her in Verona in 1949. At first Maria had been somewhat hesitant, remembering the discord that arose after brief periods with her family, but eventually she gave in to her mother's pleas. I think, in fact, Maria was anxious to impress her with her new respectability. The visit was a success, Jackie told me. She and her mother found Meneghini "likable and a very good influence on my sister." Maria flaunted her success and Litza still insisted on taking the credit; nonetheless, the stay ended in perfect harmony. Litza returned to New York delighted that her difficult daughter had found a man.

The only element missing to complete Maria's happiness was a child. Both she and Meneghini wanted children, but their long separations and Maria's growing professional commitments kept postponing that dream.

Frequent engagements in Mexico often separated the couple. In the early fifties, Maria spent a lot of time working at the Palacio de Bellas Artes in Mexico City, where she maintained a very full schedule in spite of the respiratory problems and insomnia caused by Mexico City's altitude. It was during one of those stays that she met opera lover Alejo Villegas Rebelo, the manager of the Prince Hotel. He knew Callas and saw her daily. My sister who lives in Mexico City had invited the slight, perfectly groomed Villegas Rebelo to meet me.

"I was a great admirer of Maria's," he told me, "and my ambition was to lure her from the Hotel del Prado, where she was staying, to the Prince. After a performance I went backstage and invited her to lunch at the Prince the following day. She accepted, and since I knew she liked meat, I gave her a huge, tender steak. She loved it! She moved in the same day. On the first visit she stayed a couple of weeks and then returned again in 1951 and 1952. That way I had the pleasure of seeing quite a bit of her on- and offstage."

"I see, Mr. Villegas," I joked. "You really got her by the stomach!"

The shy Mr. Villegas gave an embarrassed laugh. He was totally absorbed in his memories of Callas.

"Her Tosca was my favorite. She was so powerful, so dramatic that she hardly needed to sing. I totally forgot her shape. Everyone felt that way, because the whole theater stood up at the end of the performance and she got many curtain calls."

"Yes, I've seen photographs of Maria taken during that period. But she was so large!"

"At that time she was a huge, amiable giant. When Maria came through a doorway, her frame would block off all the light. I will show you some photographs, taken by my good friend Semo, but they flatter her. I introduced her to Semo, who was a very good photographer, and what he did was to take her picture, and then, with a pair of nail scissors, he'd cut what would amount to three to five inches off her figure. After that was done, he rephotographed the slim, cutout Maria on a black background. Of course, she was delighted with his work and kept going back to Semo for more pictures. She was very conscious of her shape. She must have suffered a lot from it, because she always wore a big black cape down to the ground to cover her body."

The black cape only confirmed what Maria's colleague mezzo-soprano Giulietta Simionato had told me regarding Maria's frustrating weight problems. While they were singing in Mexico together, Maria desperately tried to find a solution to her appearance, which she had grown to hate.

She asked Simionato to accompany her to a plastic surgeon to see if an operation could improve her heavy legs. The answer was negative. So she subjected herself to endless tortures: electric massage, hot-wax treatments and frequent Turkish baths.

"I went with her," Simionato told me, "because I was worried that with her weight and poor circulation she might have unpleasant side effects. I was like an older sister to Maria. We often worked together and she always respected me and listened to my advice. From me, she even accepted criticism. While we were in Mexico City we had adjoining rooms, so I kept an eye on her and calmed her until another letter from Meneghini arrived. She was desperate when she was without him. At night, after Maria went to bed, I took care of the flowers she had been given that evening at the theater."

Simionato says at that time Maria was "beautiful from the waist up. She was fat, but well proportioned and had healthy skin. From the waist down, she was deformed." Simionato leaned forward and whispered confidentially, "What's more, her large legs were covered with long, thick, black hair. It reminded me of an animal. When I told her to do something about it, she just laughed. But I assure you, the director of Las Bellas Artes was not laughing when he saw her step off the plane. He was appalled. He thought the Americans had played a joke on him. He couldn't believe the fat woman in the long green skirt, black shirt and the green flowered hat decorated with a rhinestone brooch and a veil draped over her thick glasses could be the Maria Callas they had chosen as the star of their lyric season."

For Maria, the months in Mexico were long and lonely. In her solitude, her dream of having a child became an obsession. She missed Titta and worried about her parents' health. Her father was hospitalized in New York with diabetes and heart trouble; her mother had a serious eye infection. But what worried Maria most was her mother's untimely request for a divorce from her sick and aging father. She couldn't understand it.

Perhaps she sent her mother a round-trip ticket to Mexico in the hope of acting as mediator between her parents; obviously, she wanted to speed her mother's convalescence. Whatever Maria's hopes were, Mrs. Kalogeropoulos's visit in 1951 is vividly remembered by Alejo Villegas Rebelo, since she stayed at the Prince Hotel.

"She was a very attractive woman but she complained constantly," Alejo said. "She told me all the time how rude and selfish Maria was and that she had such terrible financial worries because her daughter wouldn't take care of her. Maria would come to me afterwards and say, 'Alejo, don't pay any attention to her. She's always nagging and complaining about me because she wants more money, that's all. But you see, I cannot do more than I am already doing; I must also think of myself. I want to take time off and have a child. Maybe even buy a house and retire.' "

At this revelation I put a few other pieces together and wondered if Maria's fight with her mother might have had its start because Litza thought Maria was pregnant. The reason for my speculation has to do with a remark Jackie made to me in Athens. Jackie said that, unlike herself, her sister had always wanted children and that when their mother visited Maria in Mexico, Maria had said, "Mother, all I want is to have twins and then I can die!" Did her mother panic with fear that the rising star would abandon her career and end her financial support, just as Litza's divorce was coming through? Whatever the ultimate cause, the emotional rift that started in Mexico was crowned by Litza's accusations when she got back to America. She told friends and family that her rich daughter was allowing her to die in economic distress. Somehow Litza disregarded the sacrifices Maria had made for her: the Mexican trip, a mink coat, a present of $1,500 and Maria's complete payment of Litza's pending medical bills.

Maria was hurt by her mother's unfair accusations but remained silent until Litza asked for more money a month later; then Maria exploded. Her disgust at her mother's persistent greed and lack of loyalty to her father overruled the responsibility she had once felt toward her. Their relationship deteriorated to such an extent at this time that Leonidas Lantzounis was called upon to act as mediator.

When I asked him about the growing resentment between mother and daughter, Lantzounis replied, "Her mother did some nasty things. She humiliated Maria by telling everyone that her daughter left her without money. That's not true. I know because I took care of the monthly check Maria sent to her mother and sister."

Since Leo, Litza and Maria are gone now, I must go to Jackie for the last word. She wrote me: "When my mother divorced my father in 1951, she asked Mary to help her economically with the sum of a hundred dollars each month. Mary refused to help her, although she was indebted to her mother. Mary was a rich woman from her art and from her husband. She refused to help Mother. Instead she wrote, 'Go back to your husband!' Mother was very much insulted and sent an accusing letter to Mary for her wrong behavior. Mary became very angry and that was the end. They never spoke or saw each other again."

8

La Scala

With Meneghini's tireless promotion, Maria's career rapidly gained momentum. He pushed, argued and won increasing fees while she put all her energy into her craft. The "brick salesman with a sprinkle of music" (as a girlfriend of Maria's once referred to him) was determined to make his wife the most famous opera singer in the world, by applying the down-to-earth rules that had brought him success in commercial dealings. Together they patiently paved Maria's way to La Scala, but that conquest was still as laborious as everything else she had achieved professionally.

The opportunity first presented itself in April 1950, when Callas was asked to replace a suddenly ailing Renata Tebaldi in La Scalas production of *Aida*. Callas wasn't well known in Milan, but Meneghini was convinced that once the Milanese heard her sing, his wife would have an excellent chance for acceptance. The audience at the gala performance, however, gave Callas a cool reception. After the performance, Antonio Ghiringhelli, the director of La Scala, congratulated all the artists with the exception of Maria. Much to her dismay, no Scala offer followed this guest appearance.

Aside from working at La Scala, Maria's other great aspiration at this time was to perform under Arturo Toscanini's baton. "I arranged for her to audition for my father, here, in this very room," Wally Toscanini said to me over tea in her Milan apartment. "I'd heard her sing and loved her voice. I felt it was timely for them to meet, and as I expected, my father was fascinated by her voice. He had no doubt he'd found the perfect Lady Macbeth. Maria had a special, wicked quality in her voice which my father had been looking for. Unfortunately the project never materialized because of delays, and the usual complications and jealousies at La Scala. You know how it is.

"Maria was a strange person, Nadia. When my father died, his body lay in state at the Casa Verdi, near Maria's house. She had just come back to Milano from New York and she found a big crowd gathered in the street. Someone suggested to her that it might be fitting that she render homage to the Maestro whom she had so admired. 'Toscanini is dead,' she said. 'I'm alive and very tired,' and with that she closed the door on the crowd and went inside the house.

"When the news got around that Maria had auditioned for Toscanini and that he'd liked her, everyone perked up and paid attention to the Callas voice; even Ghiringhelli listened. He went to Florence to hear her in *I Vespri Siciliani* and offered her a contract for the 1951 La Scala season, which was to include *Norma, Don Carlo, The Abduction from the Seraglio* and *I Vespri Siciliani* as the inaugural performance. Maria was twenty-eight years old."

From the beginning, Ghiringhelli didn't know how to cope with Callas. Though he had ruled La Scala with an iron hand and calculating ambition, he was used to the gentle character of Renata Tebaldi, the reigning queen of La Scala. The vague promises that were part of his style got him nowhere with Maria and her unyielding attitude did nothing to endear her to Ghiringhelli. The growing Callas-Tebaldi rivalry only added to the progressively strained relationship.

"Maria was still fat when their feud started," says Fedora Barbieri, who toured Latin America with them at that time. "She and Tebaldi sang on alternate nights. The public in Brazil was divided, but personally, I think the prize went to Callas. I will never hear anything to equal it. It remains something sublime. It's with those performances and the gimmick created by the press that the Callas-Tebaldi rivalry started. Of the two, it is Tebaldi who benefited. At one time, the press tried to create the same kind of antagonism between Simionato and myself."

Comprehending that it was unrealistic to hope for Ghiringhelli's assistance, since his sympathies and those of the critics lay with Tebaldi, who had well-established roots at La Scala, Maria turned to the audience for support. The only way she could surely gain recognition was by establishing her artistic supremacy onstage. She went about preparing her part with meticulous precision. First she memorized the score, then planned every move and counted every step she was to make onstage. "You must remember," Segalini reminded me, "Maria couldn't see the conductor nor his baton so *she* gave the go-ahead. [Victor] de Sabata always marveled at her uncanny timing and precision. He used to say, 'Maria, you are a monster; you are not an artist nor a woman nor a human being, but a monster.' Her shortcoming gave her greater concentration, but the fabulous entrances she made, ending up in the correct stage position at the exact moment required by the music and action, were by no means chance happenings. She knew everyone else's movements as well as her own and was as familiar with every inch of the stage as she was with her home. Like the ancient Greeks, Callas saw things as part of the whole; she was interested in everyone's part. After a while the role became like a second skin. Her interpretation gradually took hold of her and became totally instinctive."

The Maria I knew was extremely intelligent but by no means cerebral. For ages she fooled the critics into analyzing her intellectual, historical and mythological character portrayals. But Maria actually knew little about the background of her characters and cared less. As John Ardoin puts it, "All that was useful to her was the kernel. For her, Medea was an awesome priestess-witch, Carmen a gypsy, Anna Bolena a queen, Violetta a courtesan. That's all she needed to know. She watered the seed and let it grow. Out of that little nothing came the incredible multifaceted, amazing, transfigured creation."

I only saw Maria onstage in concert at the end of her career, but having watched her work in the *Medea* film, I have to agree that her art was totally instinctive. That is why those who saw and heard her in her opera roles report that her performances were never the same twice. The critic Jacques Bourgeois summed it up for me: "By following the instinctive truth she was endowed with, she never made a mistake in her art. As soon as she reasoned, she made mistakes."

In fact, if one asked her why she did certain things onstage or what a certain action meant, Maria was usually at a loss for words. For instance, she was seized with panic when she was invited to appear on a talk show to discuss the Medea she was then portraying nightly at La Scala. She frantically called Rossi-Lemeni, who was to be on the same show to talk about his role in *Don Carlos*.

" 'Nicola,' she said to me, 'since we are on the same broadcast, could we go together? Could you pick me up, please?' That was her way of economizing," Rossi-Lemeni added with amusement. " 'I have to ask you about Medea, Nicola. I know nothing about her.' So I had to give her a crash course about Medea in the cab on the way to the radio station."

At the beginning of her fame at La Scala, interviews were torture for Maria. Giulietta Simionato said Maria would often ask her to go in her place. " 'I just can't do it, Giulia,' Maria would say to me—she would work herself up into a state. 'I don't know what to tell them. I get so tongue-tied that I even have difficulty talking about music. Please, go for me!' "

Listening to Simionato, one wonders how a woman with such lack of confidence could have had such a powerful impact on her audience. Perhaps in Maria's case, part of her power was that sheer act of will. She *became* her characters. Jacques Bourgeois, who saw her in all her famous roles at La Scala, swore to me she never faltered. "She managed to persuade us [the audience] that truth and reality could derive from the illusionary yet conventional art form of opera. What we witnessed onstage was *reality,* and *we* were the unreal element. Her words and actions made it seemingly *normal* that one should sing one's feelings instead of speaking them, which placed the audience in an absurd state of unreality."

Valeria Pedemonte often experienced that "absurd state of unreality." She was fortunate to have been present at most of Callas's Scala performances. Then in her teens, Valeria made friends with the rehearsal directors, who allowed her to slip, unnoticed, into empty boxes from which she could watch and listen to the famous directors and singers of that golden period while doing her homework. Although few knew her name, Valeria was familiar to the Scala staff, and to Maria. At the end of each performance, the young student came down from the gallery and waited backstage to offer Callas a bunch of violets with her congratulations.

"I was no more than a kid, but I had a tremendous admiration for Callas. Nothing fanatic, mind you; she hated fanatics," Valeria told me solemnly one afternoon in her tiny Milan apartment. "The sacrifices I made to buy her the violets were really worthwhile. I watched her leave the theater followed by doting admirers laden with the huge bouquets she had received, but my violets were the only flowers she carried. So . . . I became known as Violetta."

It can't be said she ever considered Valeria a friend, but Maria faithfully answered her telephone calls and fan letters, while Valeria spent her allowance on tokens for the young diva.

"She loved animals and little things. I used to arrive at Via Buonarotti with a flower, an ice cream, a turtle or a couple of goldfish. I remember these silly things thrilled Maria." Valeria continued: "They meant much more to her than objects of great value. She adored animals of all kinds, but was partial to small ones. I can still see her squeezing her toy poodles, Thea and Toy, to the point of excess. The day I brought her the goldfish, she was overjoyed. She rushed over to the pond and put them in with the other fish, saying, 'There, now they won't be alone.' " Occasionally, Maria would give Valeria a ticket to one of her performances, as she did with other young admirers whom she had taken under her wing.

I owe my friendship with Valeria to an article in *Connoisseur* magazine about an intriguing association called the

Amici del Loggione, the Friends of the Gallery. Valeria had been a member of the group, created to protect the singers from the gallery members' boos, bravos and whistles during performance and to prevent rowdy fights between rival clans. Valeria is as passionate about music as she is about her native Milan, and through her eyes, I tried to get a picture of that city as it was almost forty years ago.

"The postwar Scala, when Maria started singing here, was very different from what it is today! It was a period of renewal and we needed frivolity to help us bury our memories of the war. Those were years of such panache—crowded restaurants and custom-made clothes! La Scala was the pivot of Milanese life. It staged twenty-four operas per season, compared to the nine that are put on today, even with the help of all our modern technology.

"Of course, we went to hear the music, but most of all we went to listen to the divas. The folly that they inspired in those years was unparalleled. Opening night was a great celebration. People arrived early so that they could see and be seen. The lobby was full of beautiful people, and the women were blazing with precious jewels, not like today, when everybody comes in blue jeans. On those opening nights, Meneghini always cruised around La Scala's lobby greeting people and promoting his wife's performance."

Valeria graciously offered to take me on a "Callas tour." It was a hot summer weekend and Milan was virtually empty. She picked me up in her Fiat and we drove toward the center of town.

"This is the route Maria usually took to get to La Scala," Valeria explained. "Usually some young fan would pick her up at her home, at Via Buonarotti, and drive her to the theater. You see that house?" Valeria said, pointing to a handsome stone house surrounded by a large garden. "That used to be Ghiringhelli's house. Maria always made it a point to drive past it. Perhaps just to check up on her enemy, who knows. . . ! And from here, she usually asked to be driven through the winding streets we'll soon get to, which are full of little stores and wonderful houses that make up the heart of the old city. She loved that part of town."

We parked at Piazza del Duomo, near Milan's famous cathedral. We walked to the side entrance of La Scala, which is adjacent to the café-restaurant Biffi Scala. "You see, Nadia," Valeria was saying, "this is where Callas entered the theater, but when she became very famous, her car had to be driven inside the courtyard; otherwise the fans would have torn her to shreds. They would try to get a hairpin, a piece of her dress, a strand of her hair. Really crazy. That is Biffi's, the famous café where all the socialites and artists meet. Maria loved their blend of coffee, and when she moved to Paris, she had Biffi's barman send her a monthly supply. Do you know it?"

In fact, I had lunched in Biffi Scala the previous day with one of Maria's former colleagues, a member of what Valeria would call the anti-Callas group. At first she had been reluctant to talk about Maria, although I knew she had agreed to meet me so as to tell me how much she disliked her.

Italians have a strange fear of speaking negatively of the dead. Before embarking on a conversation regarding Callas, a number of people crossed themselves; others muttered "May she rest in peace" or made the "horns" gesture to ward off evil, as an extra precaution. Maybe they were afraid that Callas the *strega*—the witch, as she called herself—Callas the demigoddess might strike back!

Anyway, this lady insisted that Maria's ascent at La Scala was helped by a claque subsidized by Meneghini and that the cartloads of flowers were distributed by Meneghini to the gallery audience and friends, to be showered on Callas at the end of each act or curtain call. I've heard enough about Meneghini's frugality, though, to suspect it would have pained him too much to put such an extravagant plan into action.

Maria's first two seasons at La Scala were artistically full and intense. The *La Gioconda* production followed soon after *Macbeth,* then she went on to Venice and Rome for *La Traviata, Lucia* in Florence and back to La Scala to sing *Il Trovatore.* Recognition satisfied Callas's ambitions, but offstage, Maria was by no means a jolly fat girl. Physically, she was still the self-doubting "Roly-Poly" with swollen ankles and boils on her neck and back that Rossi-Lemeni had known in New York five years earlier.

On the subject of weight, Maria had grown desperate. The sacrifices she made to lose a few pounds went unnoticed, as she usually gained them back quicker than she'd lost them. With the growing attention she was receiving as a singer, it was imperative she find a solution to her problem. She gratefully accepted Luis de Hidalgo's invitation to visit Biki's high-fashion boutique, one of Milan's most prestigious.

"Luis de Hidalgo, the great soprano's brother, was the director of my boutique at the time," designer Biki Bouyeure, told me when I visited her in her penthouse, which overlooks a glorious hidden garden in the heart of Milan. "He was thrilled at the prospect of remodeling Maria's ungainly look." The "grande dame" of Milanese fashion sat in a dark green velvet chair. Her distinctive features, powdered in porcelain white, were framed by a green-and-white turban. Around the room every available space was filled with objects she had collected during her world travels.

"Getting her to the boutique was comparatively easy," Biki recalls, "but Luis was supposed to convince her that she had to be totally refurbished. That was another story. His courage failed him so he came to me in the back of the shop looking for moral support. When he pointed out his prospective customer to me, I sized her up in a glance. Mrs. Meneghini Callas was wearing a shapeless suit, flat shoes and plastic earrings. 'Don't waste your time,' I told de Hidalgo. 'No one as plain as that can wear our clothes. Our styles and prices are not for everyone. Besides, you know how stingy they say she is. Forget it! She'll never be a client of ours.' "

Biki observed Maria as she inspected the models on the rack, pushing each garment aside after a myopic scrutiny of the price tag.

" 'A peasant on her Sunday outing,' I told de Hidalgo. She kept up a running commentary in Venetian dialect with Meneghini, who looked on. Meneghini, on the other hand, had pretty good taste, though his frugality got the better of him. 'Maria,' he said in dialect, 'we'd better go, this is not for us. There's nothing here that's our style.' As he encouraged Maria to leave, she turned to thank Luis. 'I'll be back,' she said, but neither of us believed it."

9

Diva

She was still the fat prima donna loved for her voice and not for herself. No one noticed or seemed to mind Maria's girth when she impersonated a character in an opera, but time brought fame, and fame brought attention from the media. The attention the press now gave to Maria's weight problem humiliated and enraged her. Women's magazines and gossip sheets were full of diets and cures Callas was supposed to have followed without success.

I know she experimented with a number of crash diets and diuretics, but she told me she always went back to her basic meat diet, which she followed most of her life: rare beef or (raw) steak tartare, sometimes accompanied by a salad or vegetable. I get quite nauseated at the thought of all the raw meat I watched Maria eat during our meals together in Rome and Paris.

Then, at the end of 1953, the incredible Callas meta-morphosis began. She gradually lost 65 pounds over the next couple of years. She went from 210 to 144 pounds. The press, of course, reveled in her transformation, exploiting the before-and-after pictures. Her fan mail, she once mentioned to me, became a sort of Dear Abby for fat people. Nonetheless, in a matter of months the unpleasant publicity proved to be in Maria's favor: it doubled her popularity and made her a house-hold name throughout Europe.

According to Maria, there was no secret diet or potion; the answer was a taenia, or tapeworm, which is sometimes acquired from raw or rare meat. Maria told me she had one twice, which made me wince in disgust.

"You don't have to make such a face," I remember her saying. "It's a perfectly harmless, clean animal. In my case, instead of making me lose weight, it made me gain. As soon as I got rid of it, I started to lose weight. What hap-pened to my body after that was nothing short of a miracle, Nadia."

Maria's medical theories sounded a bit original to me, so I asked some specialists for their opinion. As far as medical science is aware, they told me, it is impossible to gain weight when one has a tapeworm. Illogical? Yes. But then, that was Maria's thinking. As in other matters, she was often an ex-ception.

Who would have believed that the obese "peasant" who visited Biki's fashionable dress shop a year earlier would return as the svelte young Callas, La Scala's chief attraction.

"It was uncanny, Nadia," Biki said, clasping her hands. "The caterpillar had turned into the multicolored butterfly. She was unrecognizable. And I don't only mean the loss of weight, but her expression, her state of mind had changed!

She had the radiance that comes from the knowledge of beauty, from within. The revelation of her beauty as a woman was as important if not more so than her artistic success.

"When she came back to us, I handed her over to my late son-in-law, Alain Reynaud. He is responsible for doing away with her terrible clothes and making her into a trend setter. Alain made her into a high-fashion model."

The dapper Alain, who had trained with Jacques Fath in Paris, had a ready smile and an appealing aura of mystery. He viewed the world, and women in particular, from behind the dark glasses he was rarely without. When Biki entrusted Maria to him, Alain's intelligence and sensitivity told him he'd have to be patient and win Maria's confidence gently before he could rid her of years of ingrained bad taste.

Biki believes "their relationship was one of instinctive understanding and total trust. It was friendship at its best— no romance, no complications. Maria learned everything about clothes from Alain, starting with the basic rules of color. He had endless patience. He taught her how to drape a shawl, assemble an outfit and walk in high heels . . . everything. But do you know why it worked, Nadia? Because Maria was intelligent and humble. She listened. She listened carefully and applied what she learned to her life, or her art, as the case may be. When she left for America, Alain made lists telling her which hat she should wear with which dress, which gloves, purse, shoes and so on, down to the last detail. Of course, she had that natural carriage and peasant dignity, and when she was all dressed up, she looked as if she were of noble birth. The only territory she wouldn't allow Alain to interfere in was her makeup. She insisted on doing her version of the *Medea* stage makeup: a thick, black line that swept up beyond the natural contour of her eye. When Alain remarked that it gave her a hard look she said, 'Listen, you worry about your clothes and I'll worry about my makeup. I'm an actress. I know how to make up!' "

Maria came to rely on Alain more and more. The minute she had doubts about her clothes or her personal matters, she called him. The call for advice and reassurance became a daily occurrence whether she was in Milan or on tour at the other end of the world. For Maria the telephone was a major necessity that kept her in communication with those she loved. It is one thing she never skimped on—I can vouch for that, as I think of the hour-long conversations we had between Paris, New York and Rome. Her bills must have been horrendous, but she didn't seem to mind. She talked on and on, and asked endless questions.

"She wasn't satisfied with a yes-or-no answer," Biki remembered. "Maria loved detail. For instance, on a transatlantic call she'd ask Alain, 'How is Roberta?' That's my daughter. 'Did she go to so-and-so's wedding? What did she wear? Who was there? What about the reception? Food good? Was the bride pretty? Did Francesca'—my grandaughter—'pass her exams? What about Jacques'—my grandson—'has he lost weight?' It went on and on. I don't know how Alain put up with it. After she was through with the family, she wanted to know all the Milanese gossip and then she'd go on to her wardrobe, her performances, successes, admirers. . . . You couldn't get her off the phone and we couldn't get our work done. It drove me up the wall.

"As time went on, we no longer considered Maria a client; she became part of our lives. And for her, my couture house was her second home. Alain's collections were often designed around her, and when she was away on tour, Alain's office paid her staff and took care of her household bills. Later, when she no longer had her home in Milan, she knew she could always count on a room at our house."

To the end, Alain Reynaud remained Maria's designer. She refused the offers from Dior, St. Laurent and Balenciaga.

"She'd made a commitment to a friend and was unbending," said Biki, smiling. "However, she strayed once. Since you knew Maria well, you'll appreciate this. She strayed because the dress was free!" Biki laughed. "A Greek designer had given her a dress and she didn't want to offend her compatriot, or at least that's what she told us. She wore it once but felt so guilty that she called Alain the minute she got home. . . . Before you leave, Nadia, I want to show you something." Biki went to a glass case full of little treasures and picked out a malachite cigarette box, a lighter and an ashtray. "You won't believe it," said Biki, handing me the objects, "but I swear to you Maria gave us these. The day she brought them, my son-in-law and I laughed so much after she left! I remember Alain saying, 'Please put these under glass, Biki. They are prized possessions.' Neither of us could get over these presents, the first and last, mind you, in all the years we knew Maria."

It was about this time that Ghiringhelli made his about-face with Callas. It coincided with Maria's weight loss, which was rapidly changing the opera connoisseurs' Callas into the Great Callas. John Ardoin told me: "She was given rehearsal time that would be unthinkable today and Ghiringhelli satisfied all her other professional demands. Ghiringhelli's shrewd and ambitious nature slowly shifted his support from Tebaldi to Callas. Tebaldi's voice was glorious, but it caused no inner turmoil and Ghiringhelli could no longer close his ears to the public's declaration of love for 'La Callas' nor jeopardize his empire by ignoring it."

In 1953–54 the Callas-Tebaldi competition was at its peak. When one diva got the better of the other, terrible fights ensued between the opposing fan clubs. On several occasions, the gallery seats nearest the proscenium had to be put off limits for the safety of the singers.

"They went completely wild," Valeria told me. "They threw shoes, heavy objects, eggs, whatever they could get hold of. Both singers showed exceptional courage and iron nerves just to step out onstage, let alone sing. Those were the days when the atmosphere of division was so pronounced that the tension in the theater could be physically felt. One could detect who was breathing with or against Callas. Ultimately, an esprit de corps developed in Callas's favor. The declaration of love had been long in coming, but then it became idolatry."

Maria undeniably enjoyed her role as the imperious Diva Callas. "After her stage performance," Valeria recalls, "she gave a second performance in her dressing room. She received her fans reclining on the sofa. Being idolized became a habit, though she did hate the morbid devotion of some of her fanatic fans. There was a group that trailed her everywhere. To keep them at arm's length, she assigned them chores that made them feel privileged, but when they became too possessive, she used cool indifference to ease them out of the picture. Callas was very good at that!

"Oh yes, another thing I must tell you about, Nadia, which belonged to that Callas era and would be unthinkable today," Valeria added, "is the 'promenade with the Diva.' At the end of a performance, *loggionisti,* in their Sunday best, gathered under the portico and waited for her to come out. A radiant, chatty Callas would appear, usually attended by a few friends. Titta would be seen a few paces behind trying to balance Callas's beauty case and some of the flowers she had been given. He waddled along collecting the names and addresses of fans who wanted Callas's autographed picture." These, Maria confessed to me, were signed by Meneghini most of the time. He had become an expert at simulating her signature. "Being around the Scala so much, I got to know Titta quite well, and after Maria died, I went to visit him on Lake Garda. I felt sorry for the old man.

"What was amazing," Valeria went on, "was that the 'Divina' didn't seem tired. She seemed to draw the sap of life from the performance itself and the audience's reception. Callas would slowly cross Piazza della Scala and make her way to the famous Galleria. In winter the Milanese fog adds a particular aura of mystery to the nearly deserted arcade. Callas's followers would walk alongside of her, without crowding, their eyes glued to the woman they truly regarded as a kind of divinity. When she reached Savini's restaurant, she would turn, smile and call out, *'Grazie! Buona notte!,'* and her fans cheered and clapped until their goddess was out of sight."

Later during her Scala reign, Callas and her court moved from Savini's to Biffi Scala. A permanently reserved table, slightly to the left facing the entrance, allowed Callas to scrutinize the coming and going of Biffi's patrons without being in full view herself. It relaxed her to watch the parade, while she devoured her steak tartare, fruit and glass of Lambrusco, her favorite red wine. After finishing her meal, she would rise, bid friends and colleagues good-night and head for home accompanied by Battista. "It's so tiring to be with people," she once said to John Ardoin, "because they all see me as a goddess, so I have to be a goddess for them."

While Alain Reynaud was the Professor Higgins of Maria's offstage image, the man who played a significant role in perfecting the persona and making a "lady" out of her was Count Luchino Visconti. A theoretical Communist who liked to put on a tough-guy act, Visconti belonged to one of northern Italy's oldest and most distinguished aristocratic families. He transferred the refinement of his heritage to the stage and screen and, through his superb taste and realistic staging, taught

Maria the ways of upper-class life and of royalty—he polished the rough diamond.

"It was actually her name that first intrigued Visconti," William Weaver told me. "He'd seen it on a poster in the streets of Rome announcing the 1949 opera season at the Baths of Caracalla. The following winter he heard her Kundry in *Parsifal* and was fascinated by her voice even though her headdress kept falling on her nose and her abundant figure was sparsely draped in bits of gauze. The actress in her attracted him. So after the performance, he called and suggested a meeting. 'Sorry,' she answered, 'I'm leaving for Argentina tomorrow and I'll be gone four months.' "

When Callas got back to Italy, huge bouquets announced Visconti's presence whenever and wherever she sang. Visconti sat in the front row, following her every move through his opera glasses.

"You can imagine," said Franco Manino. "Maria thought he was a madman, but Visconti wouldn't give up, he was dying to work with her. He pestered me for months so that I'd introduce them. Finally, I got them together at Serafin's house in Rome. Franco Zeffirelli, who was then Visconti's assistant, was there too. 'I have a surprise for you,' Serafin announced. 'Look who's here to sing for you, Luchino.' Serafin went to the piano and played the *recitativo* 'E strano, è strano' from *Traviata*. As Maria reached the high C's of the cabalettas, the crystal chandelier started swaying as if there was an earthquake. We were all flabbergasted by the sound and its effect," Manino remembered.

Their collaboration at La Scala began in December 1954 with Spontini's *Vestale*. It was followed by four other productions that are now part of operatic history: *La Sonnambula, La Traviata, Anna Bolena* and *Iphigénie en Tauride*. The Callas-Visconti relationship was a strange and intense one. True to her nature, once Maria decided to trust Visconti she broke down all barriers as she allowed herself to fall completely under his authoritative spell. But unlike the fatherly Serafin, her infatuation for Visconti bordered on love. She was enthralled with his genius and totally subjugated by it. Though she knew he was homosexual, like many women she found his virile charm irresistible. And when it came to work she was ready to obey him like a slave.

"Visconti enjoyed the hypnotic effect he had on her," William Weaver assured me when I told him how mystified I was by their friendship. "He had a cold, sometimes sadistic side to his nature and often made Maria do things she really didn't want to do just to see how far he could push her. He took pleasure in the power he had over her. He could tell her to enter on all fours, and she'd do it! She called him Luca, an intimacy reserved to his closest friends and family. She disapproved and was jealous of the time he spent with his male friends and unsavory acquaintances. She was shocked by his abruptness and use of four-letter words, yet she put up with his idiosyncrasies because she had found her artistic equal in him."

Valeria Pedemonte, spying on those rehearsals from her orchestra box, agreed. "Visconti guided her through every gesture and detail. 'Maria,' Visconti would instruct, 'get up, walk three paces to the right and open your umbrella. . . . No, more slowly.' Or 'Walk like a ballerina. Pretend you are walking on a moonbeam.' "

When Visconti staged *Traviata,* he broke with tradition by moving Verdi's usual 1840 setting forward to 1880. His idea was to bring the veracity of the middle-class drama closer to the audience by stripping it of its grand-opera trappings. But the changes for the sake of realism were not well received by the critics. A number of unconventional bits of business stirred endless discussion at the time.

William Weaver, who saw the Scala production several times, remembers, "Maria loved the production. She agreed to most of Visconti's direction, but the details she didn't agree with she slowly discarded. She pretended she'd forgotten or that circumstances had not permitted them to happen. At the end of the first act, amidst the disordered remnants of the party, as she launched into her *'Sempre Libera'* aria, Visconti had her kick off her shoes and sink into an armchair. Maria went along with that. It's what an exhausted hostess would do at the end of a party after all the guests had left; but when he insisted that Violetta die with her hat on, Callas wouldn't have it. She cheated her way out of it. Visconti wanted Callas to get up, as Violetta believes she's getting better, stagger on *'Non posso . . . non posso,'* collapse and die.

" 'It doesn't make sense,' Maria told me. 'Luca knows *nothing* about women . . . the last thing a woman puts on is her hat! First she puts on her shoes, then her cloak, and the hat would be positively the last thing she'd put on. What he wants is ridiculous, but what can I do?'

"What she did," Weaver explained to me, "was wait until the fourth performance, when Visconti had returned to Rome. She wore the hat, but when she sat back in the chair, she did it in such a way that it managed to fall off. It always fell off as if by accident, and she sang the last part of the scene with her long hair flowing. It was much more effective, and the detail of the falling hat added to the poignancy of the action."

Maria couldn't always get away with her changes and little inventions, as she knew that Visconti was watching her from the prompter's box, stage center. She couldn't see him, but she *felt* his presence. At times, when she was within touching distance, he would whisper directions, to which she would reply with an amiable 'shut up,' knowing full well that, on-stage, *she* was in command."

Artistic differences between two such opposite person-alities were bound to arise, but they were not the cause of their gradual separation. It was their offstage life that created the break. Maria became disenchanted by his "unpleasant and vulgar ways," and without further explanation started her re-treat, avoiding Visconti and his entourage and disregarding his frequent letters.

The aura she had created around Luca began to dissolve for her. Instead of blaming herself for idolizing him, she turned away and diminished her loss by rearranging the past to suit herself. Visconti had refined her art and it was time for her to move on.

As her infatuation lost its fervor, she became interested in the young Florentine costume designer Franco Zeffirelli, who had been schooled by Visconti and whose talents had gradually branched out to directing.

The first opera he staged with Callas at La Scala was *Il Turco in Italia*. In Zeffirelli's production, Maria was enchanted by the costumes and the director. She particularly appreciated the gentle, sensitive young man with good manners and a quieter approach to his work, after her disillusionment with Visconti. But her *entente* with Zeffirelli didn't go down well with Visconti. He was not used to being avoided and he was extremely annoyed that his ex-assistant and friend, whose ini-tial success he was largely responsible for, was now competing with him. Meneghini claims that Visconti got a group of his devotees to spread slander about Zeffirelli around Milan and attribute the malicious gossip to Callas.

After confronting Callas and realizing that she had noth-ing to do with the nasty gossip, the young Tuscan director challenged Visconti. They had a serious fight, which, it is said, ended in physical blows but ultimately a renewed and even closer friendship ensued. She who had been the cause of their quarrel now became their link. In the end, they both saw Callas as La Traviata and dreamed of doing a filmed version of the opera with her in the title role so as to have a perfect documentation of one of the greatest interpretations of that work.

In those Scala years, as Maria's popularity soared to unbelievable heights, millions of people lived through Callas's fame. The public thirst for possession of the singer was insatiable. No sooner had she won over the public than it began to devour her. It was no longer satisfied with her art; it now claimed a piece of the artist. Her fans knew nothing of the physical and emotional strain she had to cope with; they could not have imagined her anxieties, her insecurities, her undeniable need to be led by someone she believed in or, more important, who believed in her.

Like Callas, Giuseppe di Stefano, who had frequently been her leading man, was also at the pinnacle of his career. Maria had always been physically attracted to him; in fact, she had been in love with him (or maybe she had been in love with the idea of being in love with him) since their Latin American tour. Now that she was slim, she hoped that he might cast an interested glance in her direction. It would have been an infinitely important conquest for Maria as a woman, a confirmation of her newly acquired beauty. But to her chagrin, he took no notice of her. Wrapped in his success and surrounded by adoring women, di Stefano had no time for her. In fact, he went so far as to tell her that she didn't appeal to him, that her new gauntness repelled him.

A still insecure Maria may have played out her romantic fantasies during rehearsals and backstage, but as the curtain rose on a performance, the uncertain beauty, the putty in Visconti's hands, became the hypnotic Callas that immobilized audiences.

"They stood," Valeria Pedemonte remembers, "crying out her name with repetitive cadence—'Cal-las, Cal-las, Cal-las'—until the last syllable melted into the first, making them interchangeable: 'Sca-la, Sca-la.' When you came right down to it," says Valeria, "in those years La Callas was La Scala and La Scala was Callas."

But even at the height of her glory she was rarely satisfied with her work. She needed direction and reassurance. Rossi-Lemeni remembers that when they sang *Norma* together, after she'd finished *"Casta Diva,"* she'd pass in front of him making an awful grimace and whisper, "I didn't sing well. Right?"

"She did this every performance. I told her, 'Are you crazy, Maria! You sang beautifully.' You have no idea how dramatic and tragic the second and third acts were. Later the insecurity got worse. In *Anna Bolena,* when her voice started not to be so sure, she was very nervous onstage. Besides, the claque against her didn't help."

I imagine it was on one such occasion that she was over-heard to say, "I'll show the audience tonight. I'm going to ring its neck like a chicken." She showed her belligerence toward the audience on a number of occasions, but I firmly believe Maria's relationship with the audience was one she might have had with a demanding lover. She wanted to give, to meet her lover's expectations of her, however grueling, so as to remain the one and only.

At thirty, Callas was one of the most famous and sought-after women in the world. She once said to me, "God was good to me, Nadia. I'm not saying all the credit is his. No, I earned my place at the top the hard way, but he did give me success beyond my expectations."

With all her money and glory, Callas still retained peculiar vestiges of her simple tastes and frugal upbringing. Giovanna Lomazzi, a very attractive young girl who loved music and was a close friend of Maria's during her years at La Scala, told me that Maria hardly ever carried any cash with her. She was so conditioned by Meneghini, who managed all her financial affairs, that it never entered her head to ask for money that, after all, was hers. Giovanna recalls that Maria's wallet was a most unusual sight. "It was a beautiful leather wallet in which I would have expected to find wads of bills. Well, there wasn't a penny in it! It was stuffed with visiting cards, addresses of stores, telephone numbers or notes from friends. She rarely carried money with her, and when she did, she misused it, causing delight or embarrassment. She once tipped a waiter the same amount as the entire cost of a three-course luncheon, and another time she gave a seamstress who had worked over-time on her costumes and had personally assisted her for weeks, five hundred Italian lire, the equivalent of fifty cents! Some-times when Maria and I went to the hairdresser, she had to borrow from me to pay for her shampoo and set. On the other hand, she showered presents on those she cared for. She gave me fabulous clothes she'd only worn once, if at all." Clothes had become very important to her and she spent lavishly on them. After she had acquired her slim figure in the fifties, they were the tangible proof of victory over her physique. She prized her world recognition as a beautiful woman.

She also loved jewelry and was thrilled by Meneghini's opening-night tokens. She would have loved to buy some for herself but didn't dare. When she got her first checkbook, Carla Nani Mocenigo, a Venetian friend from *Tristan* days, suggested Maria celebrate by buying herself a piece of jewelry she had coveted for some time. "She couldn't bring herself to do it," Carla told me. "She'd earned that money, God knows, but she was afraid Battista would think her frivolous. For that matter, she wouldn't even buy herself a nightgown without checking with Battista first. After all the time we'd spent drooling over the jewelry in Bulgari's window, you know where we ended up? In a Lucite shop! She had an obsession about that place. She'd rush there whenever she was in town and buy loads of useless objects that would find their way to a cupboard shelf."

Carla's story reminded me of the reaction I had when I first saw Maria pack a suitcase. Every bit of clothing was swathed in plastic. Her suitcase was reminiscent of the mystery in Christo's "wrapped art." Maria encouraged me to do the same, insisting her method kept clothes from wrinkling.

In the 1950s, Maria's moments of leisure became more and more infrequent. Now an international personality, she belonged everywhere and nowhere. She had a great gift for languages, but the muddle of tongues sometimes created an obstacle in expressing what she intended to say. Her French, English and Italian were charmingly peculiar in their originality. It must be remembered that she grew up speaking Greek at home, English at school, Italian and French onstage and Veronese dialect in the kitchen. When it came to prayers or counting, she reverted to English, the language in which she had learned them. She misused expressions and words because she translated them from one language to another. "All her languages were somehow a kind of translation from something else; it was like Houston, a city that is all suburbs with no downtown," said William Weaver. "Her English was very strange, full of misused words and foreign expressions. For instance, she always used *possibly,* even when she meant 'if possible.' " Similarly, she misused Italian words, because she translated English directly into Italian.

Whenever Maria and Battista did get away, it was usually to their favorite beaches: Venice and Ischia. There Maria could forget about her image and be herself. These were escapades she fully enjoyed. Hidden under a floppy hat, her long hair flowing down her back, Maria would hire a fisherman's boat and row out far enough from shore to secure privacy. When Battista was busy, she would go with a friend—often Giovanna Lomazzi. After a swim, she would burst into song and encourage Giovanna to join her. Maria usually chose a *Norma* or *Sonnambula* duet. She got a big kick out of her private concert, even though Giovanna didn't know most of the words and admits that her voice was not particularly harmonious.

Those were joyous moments. Maria bubbled with laughter and silly stories. She'd go on about the merits of home life and her love for Battista, the perfect husband. " 'With all my heart, Giovanna,' she'd say, 'I hope you find his equal,' " Giovanna laughingly told me. "Maria was touching, she really meant it, but I was only twenty then and Meneghini certainly didn't correspond to my dream of the ideal husband."

One day when Maria, Carla Mocenigo and Battista were on the Lido Beach in Venice, a young man that Carla knew approached them, inviting them to a party the following evening. Maria introduced herself, giving only her first name. At the time her hair had been tinted blond for a role and that day by the sea she had braided it, which made her seem much younger than her age. The unsuspecting and somewhat flirtatious young man asked her to join the party. She was very flattered by his attention and eagerly accepted. "I'd love to come . . . but . . . I don't know if my father will allow it. I'll have to ask him." And as she said that, she glanced in the direction where a plump Battista slept soundly in a deck chair. "OK," said the young man, "check with your father. The party will take place in a very respectable house. If he gives you any trouble, I'll come and pick you up and I will escort you home." As soon as the young man was out of sight, she turned to Carla and said, "You see, he invited me because I'm attractive, not because I'm Callas."

As a rule, the admiration that was lavished on Callas the artist was rarely bestowed on Maria the woman. Those who only knew her slightly found her rather banal, while others saw her as tough or boring. Most were disappointed that her artistic genius did not carry over to the everyday woman. "I don't understand," Wally Toscanini said to me during our meeting in Milan, "how an artist of such sensitivity and talent onstage could be so devoid of personality in real life. She was a very dull woman."

Though they didn't all see her as a goddess, most people conjured a fictitious Callas, only to be disillusioned by the real one whose changing moods and complicated life-style frequently colored her behavior—even her beauty, for at times, she appeared heavy-featured and plain. But no matter how people saw her, music critic Fedele d'Amico's words struck me as most insightful: "The importance of Callas is that this woman didn't have any models from whom she copied. She was created out of her own intuition."

IO

The Met

Now that Callas's international fame had reached boundless proportions the Metropolitan Opera finally took an interest in her. As in the case of La Scala, the Met's approach had initially been hesitant and financially unsatisfactory to the increasingly brazen Meneghini.

While the Metropolitan Opera was endlessly studying and negotiating, Lawrence Kelly, the energetic founder of Chicago's Lyric Opera and Dallas's Civic Opera, wooed Callas and won the great soprano's first U.S. appearance. Perhaps she would never have agreed to giving the Met that honor, just on principle, but John Ardoin believes Kelly still deserves a lot of the credit. "It was Lawrence Kelly who gave Callas her American debut in 1954 and who, through his musical and human affinities, became like a brother to Callas," Ardoin wrote me, and included an unpublished interview he'd done with the late Kelly recalling Callas's Chicago opening.

In 1954, she was a 138-pound, stark-white-blonde who had come to sing *Norma, Traviata,* and *Lucia di Lammermoor.* In *Norma* the wobble [in her voice] existed at the first performance . . . she was nervous, it was her American debut. The wobble existed most of all at the *"Son io"* in act four, because her crown became entangled in her dyed blond hair. So she did an A-flat or an A, I've forgotten which—*"Son io-o-o-o"*—and she kept holding it, and there was the poor conductor Rescigno holding his arms out— they grew longer—and then began *o-o-o-o,* you could have thrown grapefruits through the "vee-bratto," as she called it, because it lasted five minutes, and she wouldn't let go. Then she got rid of the crown and the wobble ended. Her Norma was terrific enough to put her on the map on this continent.

By the time *Lucia* was staged, she had the Chicago audience in the palm of her hand, they gave her a forty minute ovation. However, *Butterfly* and her last *Trovatore* were the most memorable things I've ever heard in my life."

Remarkable they must have been. In fact, only a month before receiving Kelly's interview, Vera Zorina, Balanchine's beautiful wife and prima ballerina, also told me at great length of the intensity of Callas's acting in that 1955 Chicago *Butterfly.* Callas sang the role only three times, all with Giuseppe di Stefano as Pinkerton. She was hesitant about doing it because, as she told Lawrence Kelly, her opinion of the role had not changed since 1945—"it is destructive vocally."

"Conductor Rescigno had recommended Hizi Koyke as the director," said Vera Zorina, competing with the noisy luncheon guests in the St. Regis dining room. "Koyke was a Japanese lady who had sung *Butterfly* and, knowing the traditions of her country, could give authenticity to Puccini's opera. Maria had said to Koyke, 'I'm tall and thin, I'm not a Japanese doll. Now let's make me into one.' She must have worked and worked because she mastered the delicate mannerisms, the sliding walk of the sixteen-year-old girl who matures into womanhood and faces despair within the span of one act."

Zorina, who during her career was a marvelous interpreter in her own right, had seen Callas in *Il Trovatore* and could not get over her transformation in *Butterfly* in 1955. "Maria's five-foot-ten figure had shrunk. It was unbelievable; she was small onstage." In the scene in which Cio-Cio-San commits hara-kiri, she went upstage to the shrine and, with her back to the audience, prepared to die. "In those days, Maria had her own hair down to her waist, which the Japanese director had taught her to arrange with one pin. When she jabbed the dagger in, her head snapped back and her hair flew out like a flag! . . . She then conveyed incredible pain, managed to get up, stagger to a chest from which a bit of georgette hung out of the drawer. In agony, she grabbed the piece of georgette and it came and came and came as Callas moved towards the center of the stage. When she finally collapsed, she pushed it into her wound. Unbelievable! I have never seen such acting!"

Maria's third and last *Butterfly* performance was most memorable for a backstage incident after the curtain fell. With Maria's consent, the performance of November 17 had been added to satisfy a large number of Chicago fans. Like the preceding two performances, it was a triumph. After endless curtain calls, a moved and exhausted Callas, making her way to her dressing room, was accosted by a group of process servers who had come with a breach-of-contract suit brought against her by Edward Bagarozy. Their intrusion and lack of sensitivity totally astonished Callas. Once she had recovered her speech, she burst into a rather remarkable tirade.

"Get your hands off me! Don't touch me. I will not be served. I have the voice of an angel! No man can serve me." The "tigress" raged on while the postperformance press and photographers eagerly recorded the incident. It made news around the globe.

It seems that after eight years, the last-minute representation agreement signed by Callas and Rossi-Lemeni as they boarded the *Rossia,* bound for Italy, had turned up with a vengeance. Bagarozy had come to collect what he considered his due as sole agent to the now famous diva. Maria vehemently claimed that no contractual arrangements had been made between them. But to her embarrassment, she was faced with the evidence in black and white.

Rossi-Lemeni admits that their nonchalant attitude in signing was the cause of their later problems. "Bagarozy warned us. He said, 'You aren't even reading the contract!' But we were excited about going to Italy, so we answered, 'We trust you.' But what I never understood is why Bagarozy took so long to surface and collect. Through my lawyer, I settled for five thousand dollars and the contract was annulled." But with Maria the lawsuit dragged on for three years.

Callas flew to Milan the following day to rehearse *Norma,* the production that was to inaugurate La Scala's 1956 season. Upon arrival she confided to Simionato (who would sing Adalgisa in the production) that she was overjoyed to be home, back in the theater where she was loved, singing her favorite role, away from "those Zulus," as she called the American process servers. Norma had then become an essential part of Callas. The role was her specialty, her trademark, so to speak, and she would tell critic Jacques Bourgeois with great seriousness, "Bellini wrote *Norma* for me."

By 1955, when the Metropolitan Opera finally offered Callas a contract, she had achieved world renown and could choose any conductor or theater she fancied. Perhaps she agreed to sing at the Metropolitan to fulfill her long-standing challenge. The prestigious opera house was finally "on their knees" (more or less), as she had aggressively predicted ten years earlier, and now "they would pay."

The price the dogmatic Rudolf Bing paid was high. Callas made her entrance at the Metropolitan on a carpet of U.S. dollars paid in advance, in cash. She was also given confirmation that all legal claims on her work presented by her former agent, Bagarozy, would be settled by the Metropolitan Opera.

On opening night of the Metropolitan's *Norma,* which Bing had revived especially at Callas's request, a cool public listened to a nervous Callas, whose vocal efforts in the first act were evident. "A puzzling voice"—wrote *The New York Times*. "Occasionally it gives the impression of having been formed out of sheer willpower rather than natural endowments." Yet, soon the New York public loved her, though Maria was never overly enthusiastic about a career in New York. She always maintained that the major period of her career belonged to La Scala and that her operatic experience at the Metropolitan was really not significant if considered in the totality of her work.

She told me that with the exception of *Pirata,* which she sang at Carnegie Hall, she was never in form when singing in New York. She felt that the climate wasn't good for the voice. I wonder whether it was the New York air or the fact that she was burning the candle at both ends. At this time it seems amazing she wasn't devoured by her very existence.

"She had discovered the pleasure of being slim and elegant," says Giovanna Lomazzi. "So she ate little and hardly drank anything except coffee. After a late night and with an upcoming performance, she'd manage to make her way through most of Fifth Avenue's major department stores and at the end of the day she would go straight to the Met, laden with shopping bags full of clothes and useless objects she'd bought. She didn't even stop off at the hotel! I don't know how she did it. I'd curl up in a chair, exhausted—I was in my early twenties at the time—and watch her put on her makeup knowing she had to go out there, onstage, and sing a full-length opera. Maria claimed her voice didn't need much rest. 'I keep it exercised by keeping active,' she'd say. 'If I sit and do nothing, my voice gets that thick, foggy sound!'

"When we were in New York, Maria's father came to see her frequently," Giovanna told me. "He'd come to have dinner with Maria and Battista at her hotel suite. His visits enchanted her. He always arrived with sweets and little presents for her. It was amusing to watch the relationship between father and son-in-law. They were contemporaries, you see. But the father spoke Anglo-Greek, while the son-in-law spoke neither English nor Greek. Their dialogue consisted of bear hugs, smiles and friendly slaps on the back. It was a happy moment in Maria's life, though. She was surrounded by success and the men she loved."

The year 1958 brought with it two major crises that significantly altered Callas's career. The most notorious took place at the Rome Opera during that performance of *Norma* attended by Italy's president. Everyone in Rome knew of this scandal. For years I'd heard the scandal discussed and argued at dinner parties and felt its palpable presence in the air that night when Rossellini and our film crew valiantly "re-pre-sented" Callas to the Roman press. Well, I've looked into it now, and I really *don't* think this one was Maria's fault. Though the occasion meant a lot to her, Maria was not well. After finishing the first act with difficulty, she knew she couldn't continue. Her throat was inflamed and she had a high fever. As usual, there was no understudy for Callas. After an inter-minable hour the management announced that the perfor-mance would not continue. The enraged crowd stormed the box office for refunds, shouting, "Callas get out of Rome." Callas personally apologized to President Gronchi and in a press conference the following day asked "everyone to un-derstand and forgive her"; instead, the press asked for proof of Dr. de Martini's diagnosis of an inflammation of the trachea and bronchitis and made the incident a diplomatic and na-tional scandal. They tried to bribe their way into Callas's room. They offered Dr. de Martini and Meneghini, whom they mis-took for hotel employees, large sums so as to be allowed to photograph her in bed. Rebuffed, they attacked with greater tenacity.

That evening left a deep wound in Maria's life to which she frequently referred. "The public can be so cruel," she often told me. "They only accept you when you are great. They have no mercy if you are not well and will neither forgive nor forget your failures."

The public had helped fill her emotions and ego as a lover would, but now that lover had rejected her. For the first time Callas realized she could not count on her audience. I think it was a tremendously painful revelation. Perhaps she received her first inkling of the fact that the great devotion she had given music would be ultimately unrequited. Perhaps it dawned on her that evening that there was something be-yond music, something she was missing.

The litigation that ensued from the Rome Opera scandal lasted thirteen years. In 1971, she called to tell me that the Supreme Court of Appeals had pronounced the conclusion in her favor; but to her distress, only a couple of papers acknowledged her victory.

"It's not fair," Maria said plaintively. "Life really isn't fair. Now that I've won, I'm tucked away on a back page where no one will see it, but when I was sick, I was on the front page because I'd cancelled. I've *never* cancelled unless it was completely necessary. The press ruined my Italian career that night in Rome. They have no one to blame but themselves."

I gather the fabled "tigress" had been built up to such tremendous proportions that the public could no longer discern the truth. This, in addition to the antagonism that was mounting at La Scala, would ultimately lead her to leave Italy and resettle in France.

At the Metropolitan Opera in New York that same year, Callas continually sang to packed houses. But Bing's and Meneghini's contrasting temperaments and the latter's unreasonable financial demands were pushing Bing's patience to its limit. Maria's refusal to sing alternate performances of *Macbeth* and *Traviata* and her final no to Bing's efforts to accommodate her by offering *Lucia* instead of *Traviata* caused the rift between the Met and Callas that eventually led to her dismissal.

On November 6, 1958, while Callas was engaged at the Dallas Civic Opera, she was informed that Rudolf Bing had announced to the press that "Maria Callas was fired from the Metropolitan Opera." Meneghini's purposely engineered scheme to get Maria away from the Met and have Bing break her contract, had been successful. After an electrifying performance of *Medea*, Maria arrived at her friend Mary Mead Carter's house, where she was to be feted. She found the major television networks and endless press camping out on Mrs. Carter's front lawn. Much to Bing's irritation, Maria seemed quite undisturbed by the dismissal.

"She wasn't really upset. She had a wonderful time that evening. She danced and partied until dawn," Mrs. Carter told me. Maybe she was just sick of it. That night her whole career seemed less important than simply being with friends.

I had found Mary Mead Carter on my own, through a mutual friend. How strange Maria was, I thought, as I listened to Mrs. Carter's soft Southern accent. Here is a person who had been a really close friend of Maria's, someone who had spent a lot of time with her during her career in the United States, yet Maria had never mentioned her to me. I wondered about Lawrence Kelly, and John Ardoin in Texas, Maggie van Zuylen in Paris, Giovanna Lomazzi in Rome, Carla Nani Mocenigo in Venice . . . and so many others scattered all over the globe, who were her good friends, who loved her but didn't know of each other's existence. I asked Mary Mead Carter what she thought of this odd state of affairs.

"Maria was possessive about her friends in a pragmatic sort of way. She was self-centered and unimaginative and it never occurred to her that a friend in Paris or Milan could be interested in one of her friends in New York, let alone that they might meet. She assumed everyone else thought the same way. It was friendship on a one-to-one basis."

Perhaps it was also her superstition and mistrust that kept us apart, for I recall she had said to David Frost in an interview for the *New York Post*, "Celebrities don't know who are their real friends."

"Maria to me, as a friend," said Mrs. Carter, "was like an old shoe, a comfortable old shoe. I always found her co-operative, understanding, concerned and very caring. Just the opposite of what you read. We were together off and on for years, we traveled together a great deal and I never found her difficult."

Maria had an immediate gut reaction to people and situations and followed it consistently, though this could sometimes mean she played roles to suit people around her. She was Callas the legend, when she felt that was expected of her; then abruptly she'd shift to Maria the woman for those she cared for and was comfortable with. But I think this duality sometimes caused alarming problems for her.

"The role she assumed depended on how you first presented yourself to her," John Ardoin agreed when we discussed Maria's personality. "She immediately decided whether you were going to be on her side or 'the other side.' She pigeonholed you. If you were on her side, if she liked you, she would go out of her way to help and back you with her strong sense of friendship and loyalty. She tested people's reaction to her outspokenness, launching into the subject closest to them, which at times made people extremely uncomfortable. She sensed people's feelings and moods to a frightening degree. When she was in Dallas, recovering after cracking her ribs, she spent a lot of time with Larry Kelly and me. One day I was driving her to the doctor when she said, 'John, you're not quite yourself today, you seem ill at ease.' I answered half jokingly, 'Oh, I suppose I am, I just have to get used to the idea of running around with you all the time.' 'I see', she said, 'your problem is that you're still thinking too much about Callas and you really don't know Maria. Well, don't worry dear, we'll take the time to get to know Maria.'

"She was also paranoid about people making money at her expense. 'He did that book to make money on me,' she said about the Callas book I did with Gerald Fitzgerald, although she knew full well it was not the case. Her kindness evaporated the minute she felt she was being used or betrayed and then there was no way the friendship could be patched up again. As she said, 'If I'm a friend, I give. If I'm not, I am indifferent but I believe in love and lots of loving.' "

Friendship, for Maria, was measured by her unique personal standards, a yardstick that often led to disillusion. As time went on, she lived in terror that friendships and relationships she had commenced would not last. Aware of the changing sentiments of the human heart, she often predicted their end before they had time to mature, preparing herself for the eventual letdown. Her godfather, Leo Lantzounis, is the only person I know of whose friendship covered her entire life-span.

As a friend, Maria was thoughtful and liked to find "the right present, a present that had meaning." She once gave Giovanna Lomazzi a charm for her bracelet, a little gold dog, saying, "You're such a faithful friend, I want to give you this as a symbol of your fidelity."

"That was her way," John Ardoin agrees. "When she was happy and comfortable in a friendship she was generous. She'd find something to her liking that amused her and she'd want to give it to you. She was an impulsive giver. 'Do you like this?' she'd ask. 'Do you like that? Pick out something for yourself, pick out something you want.' At Neiman Marcus in Dallas, she bought a dozen three-dimensional tic-tac-toe games to give to her friends. She loved the transparency of the purple and white glass balls and she actually kept one for herself, which lived in a corner of her living room at Avenue Georges Mandel. Do you remember it, Nadia? On the same shopping trip she bought a four-hundred-dollar gold swizzle stick encircled with diamonds. It was for Mary Mead Carter, who always swizzles her champagne. This was after the O-nassis breakup, when she had started attending to her own business affairs. Her wallet was crammed full of bills. I couldn't believe the number of one-hundred-dollar bills that were appearing! I ventured to say, 'Maria, that is the biggest waste of money I've ever seen. You know Mary is going to use it to ruin good champagne!' "

The manifestations of her affection were often delightfully unexpected. On one occasion she arrived at the Savoy Hotel in London after Tito Gobbi's performance in *Figaro*. She rushed into the Savoy dining room during a dinner party in Tito's honor, fell into his arms and said, "It's your birthday, isn't it? Well, I just flew in from Paris to wish you a happy birthday!" Her surprise appearance with Onassis at her side added a special touch of merriment to the celebration, which went on late into the night. Tito was happy and extremely moved by her gesture. The following morning he rose at dawn to send Maria a bunch of flowers. Much to his astonishment, the concierge informed him that "Madame has already left. She and Mr. Onassis have returned to Paris on his private plane."

It was in 1959, while singing *Lucia* in Dallas, that Maria first became aware of impairment to her voice. She had a few faltering moments with some difficult high notes, but thanks to her uncanny ability she managed to solve the problem without revealing it to the audience. Nevertheless, she was distraught. When she got back to her dressing room, drenched in perspiration, she told Giovanna Lomazzi, with evident fear, "I gambled my career tonight, my career ends here." But according to Meneghini, her vocal problems started earlier. In an unpublished interview with my friend filmmaker Fiorella Mariani, he said that the "deteriorations" coincided with Maria's exposure to the gilded life-style when she set aside her total commitment to music: "Although she went on singing,

Maria, surrounded by fans, after a performance in Milan, 1958.
(Courtesy V. Pedemonte)

ABOVE: Maria faces a crowd of reporters after her Teatro del Opera walkout, Rome, 1958. (Messaggero, *Rome*)

OPPOSITE: Maria and fans after the last performance of *Pirata* at La Scala, Milan, 1958. *(Winfried Stiffel)*

BELOW: Maria with Luchino Visconti in *Anna Bolena* at La Scala, Milan, 1958. *(Federico Patellani)*

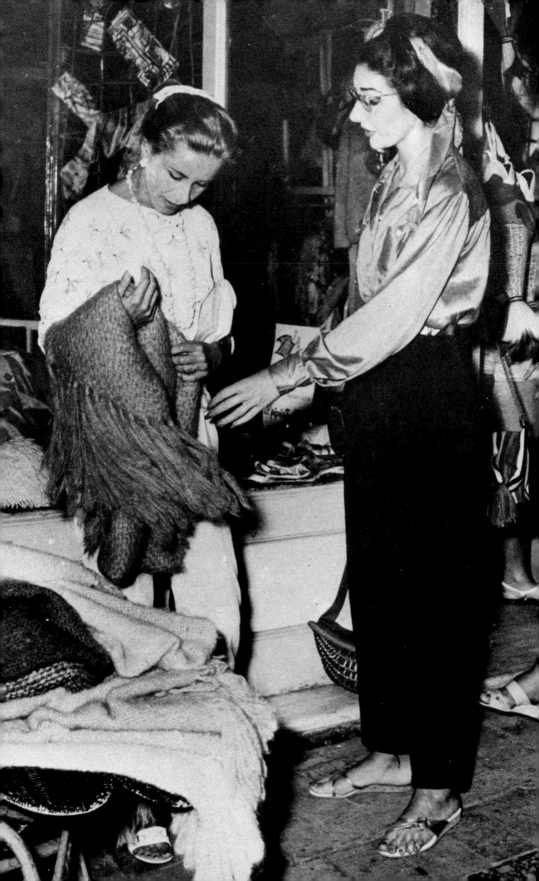

LEFT: Shopping with Tina
Onassis in Capri, 1959. *(Gina
Guandalini collection)*

BELOW: Maria with
Winston Churchill, on
board the *Christina,* 1959.
(Gina Guandalini collection)

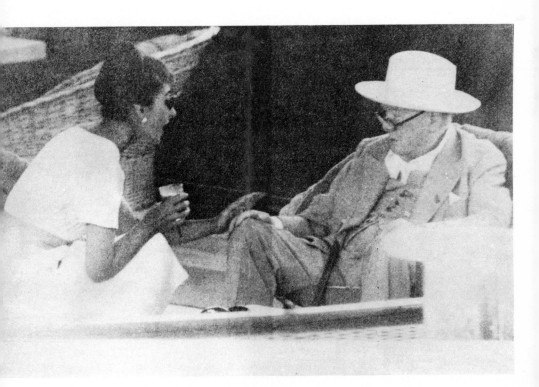

ABOVE: Marie-Luise von Criegern and Aristotle Onassis during the christening of *Olympic Challenger* in Kiel, Germany. *(Courtesy M. L. von Criegern)*

BELOW: Another christening! Maria with Marie-Luise von Criegern. *(Courtesy M. L. von Criegern)*

Maria with Rudolf Bing, backstage at the Met. *(Metropolitan Opera Archives)*

ABOVE: Departing with Aristo. *(Gina Guandalini collection)*

BELOW: Maria applying makeup to Callas mannequin at Angel Records. *(Metropolitan Opera Archives)*

ABOVE: *Left to right:* Cesare Siepi, Fedora Barbieri, Maria, Fausto Cleva and Mario del Monaco, after a performance of *Norma* at the Met, 1956. *(Metropolitan Opera Archives)*

BELOW: Christening Medea. *Left to right:* Pier Paolo Pasolini, Franco Rossellini, Maria. *(Mario Tursi)*

LEFT: With Pier Paolo Pasolini on location in Turkey. *(Mario Tursi)*

BELOW: The two Medeas, Maria and I, with an unpaid extra. *(Mario Tursi)*

ABOVE: A day off from the set, Rome. *(Mario Tursi)*

BELOW: Protected from the intense heat, Maria is borne to location, as Rossellini heads the procession. *(Mario Tursi)*

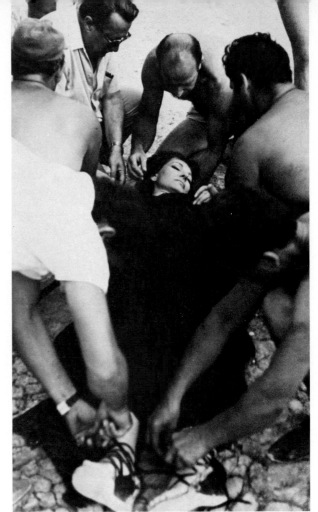

RIGHT: Maria faints from exhaustion on location in Grado. *(Mario Tursi)*

BELOW: Cooling off between takes. *(Mario Tursi)*

"Do you think I'm a tigress?" *(Mario Tursi)*

ABOVE LEFT: Picnic at the beach in Greece, 1970. *(Courtesy George Embiricos)*

ABOVE RIGHT: Maria getting away from "Callas." *(Courtesy George Embiricos)*

BELOW: At La Scala, after the opening of *Vespri Siciliani*, 1971. *Left to right:* Maria, Ghiringhelli and myself. *(Courtesy estate of Maria Callas)*

ABOVE: Maria with Raina Kabaivanska *(right)* at the rehearsal of *Vespri Siciliani*, Turin, 1973. *(Pier Giorgio Naretto)*

BELOW: During a recording session. Surrounding Maria are *(clockwise from upper left)* Eric Smith from Philips records, Antonio de Almeida, di Stefano and Harold Lawrence. *(Mary M. Lawrence)*

A relaxed moment. *(Mario Tursi)*

her voice, the Callas voice, ended in 1958, with *Pirata,* at La Scala."

But even before her voice suffered, I think a change had taken place in Maria. She was torn between the simple needs of her true nature and the overpowering invasion of fame. She wanted more freedom. Now that she was rich and beautiful, she sought the recognition of the *'bel mondo.'* Secretly I think she envied some of her new friends, and wished for a title herself. Although she didn't feel totally at ease in her new surroundings, society life represented everything her work had denied her.

"She started to lose her voice when she lost confidence in herself as a performer and lost it altogether when she decided to fulfill her ambition to be the First Lady of European society. That really ruined her," Rossi-Lemeni told me.

But Maria wanted to live. She'd had enough of Callas.

By September 1957, when Callas and Onassis first met in Venice, at the ball Elsa Maxwell gave in her honor, Maria's vision of life was already undergoing this drastic change. Elsa Maxwell was partially responsible for it. She had chased after Callas, doing her utmost to project her into the realm of social celebrity. For a while Maria resisted—but soon succumbed. The most famous singer in the world was now tempted to become the most famous woman in the world. And inevitably, the sparkle of this new world showed up the tarnish that was beginning to collect on the old. With new eyes Maria also began to notice her husband's shortcomings. The limitations of his father-husband role became much more evident to her. Psychologically, I think she had lost the need for a parent figure and was now craving a sexually fulfilling husband-lover, a role Titta could no longer fill.

Her devotion was slow to fade, but she was increasingly

irritated by Titta's professional possessiveness and by his obsession with the Callas career as a money machine. Maria had become a commodity that he juggled as he saw fit. Although friends had tried to make her understand that Meneghini was using her in that regard, she had never questioned or interfered in his business dealings, trusting his honesty and capabilities as an administrator, and dismissing the idea of any impropriety. But when she finally understood, she burst open like a steam valve. When she learned that he had kept huge percentages on her record rights, made investments in his name alone and stashed away tidy sums for his own dealings, her pain flared into angry reproach and then shifted to contempt and indifference.

What she now saw was her "Santo Benedetto" without the halo she had created for him: a potbellied, unsophisticated little gargoyle. He was and always had been simply out of his depth. He was handicapped by age and couldn't learn a foreign language. His provincialism left him unprepared for meetings with royalty and heads of state. He struggled to cope with the journalists, the impresarios, the crowds, the social events but made one gaffe after the other. His tactics with Rudolf Bing had proved disastrous, as he had no idea how to confront the measured coolness of the Germanic temperament. After one difficult meeting with Bing, Maria was overheard snapping at Battista, "If you are not capable of being my secretary, don't do it." At cocktail parties Meneghini was bored and usually napped in a corner. A friend remembers him dozing off at a dinner party given in Maria's honor by Lord Harewood, at which the Queen Mother was present.

But now, Meneghini's days of contentment at Via Buonarotti were numbered.

II

Onassis

"When I met Onassis, I was so taken by his magnetic charm that I forgot how ugly he was," I admitted to Marie-Luise von Criegern at an embassy party in Rome. "From the pictures I'd always seen of him with his baggy suits, dark glasses and plastered-down hair, he looked to me like a Chicago mobster boss out of a forties movie."

Marie-Luise, the lovely wife of Cristoph von Criegern, then the German naval attaché in Rome, knew Onassis for over twenty years. She laughed. "I've never thought of him that way! I've known him too long. I met him and Tina when I was a young bride. My first husband, Adolf Westphal, was twenty years older than I. Adolf and Aristo's friendship dated back to Onassis' whaling-fleet days. All of Onassis' ships, from tankers to the *Christina,* were built at Kieler Howaldswerke then, under my husband's direction. Aristo and Adolf did most of their business from tables in nightclubs, bargaining and making arrangements and then sending telegrams all over the world. My God, when I think of the endless nights I sat listening to those two talking business, it makes me dizzy! You have no idea how boring it all was, but Adolf refused to go anywhere without me. I don't know that Aristo was ever *attractive*, but there was something about him, a kind of sexual-animal strength, I remember noticing even then. I think that is what overwhelmed Maria when they met at that Opéra do in Paris."

The Paris Opéra Gala in December 1958, where the paths of Onassis and Callas crossed for the second time, was a benefit concert for the Legion of Honor and Callas's Parisian debut. Politicians, intellectuals, movie stars, *"le tout Paris"* filled the orchestra and boxes to listen to the Diva and watch France's president, René Coty, present her with the Legion of Honor.

Maria swept majestically onstage in Alain Reynaud's latest creation, a champagne satin gown with a square train trimmed in sable.

"She looked glorious!" Biki told me. "Later Maria ruined the gown. She couldn't resist picking off the sable trim. 'It's wasted on the train,' she said. 'I'll do something with it.' Of course it ended up forgotten in a closet. But we all agreed, she looked glorious!"

She must have because Onassis was immediately drawn to her. That evening, he decided he wanted to possess the unattainable Callas and went about planning his conquest. The perfect occasion presented itself a few months later at a ball in Venice, given by Countess Castelbarco in Maria's honor. There Aristotle Onassis and his wife Tina invited the Meneghinis for a cruise along the Turkish and Greek coasts on the *Christina.*

Although Meneghini had enthusiastically welcomed the Greek couple's invitation, Maria was strangely reluctant. She made elaborate wardrobe preparations, all the while insisting she didn't want to go, predicting that the trip was going to be a "crashing bore."

The voyage turned out to be one of happiness for some and tears for others.

"Meneghini stood out like a sore thumb on the *Christina*," said Biki. "When Maria compared him to Winston Churchill, Gianni Agnelli and Lord Moran, she realized he was part of her past."

Life on board the *Christina,* swimming, sight-seeing or making occasional visits to dignitaries in ports of call, appeared idyllic on the surface. But as the journey progressed, the casual conversation and card games stretched into dawn, with asides and whispers about Maria and Aristo. Meanwhile, Tina sobbed in humiliation and the baffled Battista awakened to the disquieting smoothness of his wife's unslept-in bed.

In his memoir, Battista says Maria was cool with him, but she would neither discuss nor make excuses for her behavior during the voyage. The only mention of change was professional. She wanted to retire, she said. She had spent the better part of her life working; now she wanted to enjoy the fruit of her earnings. "You can't retire," Battista replied, "because you can't afford to." As the discussion unfolded, Maria discovered that Battista had not only generously helped himself to the communal funds but had blocked most of her money in long-term investments. Needless to say, this did not help his case.

Meneghini says it was during a visit to Mount Athos on August 6, 1959, that he understood his marriage was doomed as he watched the revered patriarch Athenagoras join Maria's and Aristotle's hands in his own, blessing them as if in matrimony. Maria was deeply moved and saw it as an omen. She confided to a friend that it was on the evening following the blessing that their union was consummated.

The Meneghinis' return to Milan did not restore their marital tranquillity. Maria was irritable and moody. She found excuses to spend time alone, which was most unlike her. Battista's troubled state of mind was aggravated by his mother's ill health, which required his attention. By the time he returned from visiting her in Zevio, the bubble was ready to burst. Maria, weighed down with guilt and unable to make subtle shifts, had to clear her conscience instantly. She told Meneghini that Aristo was in Milan and wanted to speak with him. They needed Meneghini's help, she said. He must free her from their marital commitment, but avoid scandal. She wanted a separation, immediately. She said she felt jailed. She accused him of being a "country bumpkin who fulfilled his ambitions through her glory." She had given him ten years; now it was over. She was caught in a "twist of fate" that bound her to Onassis.

To clarify the situation, a meeting was arranged at Meneghini's villa in Sirmione, on Lake Garda. Onassis apparently had too much to drink, insulted Battista, and in the same breath asked for his handshake of approval. Then Meneghini turned on Onassis, cursing him. "May you never find peace for the rest of your days," he cried out.

Painfully aware of the storm she had unleashed, Maria wept. She left abruptly for Milan with Toy and Thea, her miniature poodles, forgetting her green jacket hanging in the entrance.

"It was still there when I went to visit Meneghini three years later," Valeria Pedemonte told me. "It was like a symbol of hope which he thought might bring her back. But she never came."

Onassis and Callas managed to meet secretly between her professional engagements and keep in touch through Bruna. But when Maria was in London in September, the press got wind of her relationship with Onassis. The hunt was on. Neither could make a move without being trailed.

Meanwhile, Meneghini gave reporters his version of events. "He was unfair and vindictive," Biki insists. "He behaved stupidly and provoked Maria. Of course, she overreacted and they had a terrible fight about money. Maria asked for the house in Milan, her bank account and her jewels. It was all very ugly, and that was the last time they spoke to each other. After that they communicated through their respective lawyers."

"Even though they never spoke to each other again," says Carla Nani Mocenigo, "his presence obviously still affected her. I remember when I accompanied her to Brescia for the separation hearing, she was very nervous. She needed a distraction. As we drove into town, Maria said, 'Carla, I'd like to buy a nail file.' We chose a shop in a side street so as to avoid the mob of photographers waiting in front of the courthouse. When the salesgirl saw Callas walk into her shop, she nearly fainted. 'I'd like to buy a nail file, please,' Maria said. The request was so anticlimactic that the salesgirl insisted Maria choose a present. Perhaps a bottle of perfume? What scent did she prefer?

"If you want to give her something she'd go wild over," Carla suggested, "give her some perfume samples." Maria was so happy with them that she forgot her anxiety. As she entered the courthouse, she was still avidly examining the miniature bottles. 'Maria,' I said to her, 'put those away. You can't have everyone see you playing with perfume samples on such a serious occasion.' Maria put the samples in her purse and took off her glasses. 'Now I'm fine,' she said. 'Meneghini will be nothing but a blur.' "

"Maria had totally fallen in love for the first time. Onassis swept her off her feet. All that mattered to her was love," their longtime friend Hélène Rochas assured me when we saw each other in Paris. "He offered her fireworks, which compensated for the problems with her career. But Maria was not a modern woman; she had a nineteenth-century sense of respectability. She suffered from a 'back-street complex'—of being the mistress. She needed the conventional status symbol of being a wife. Another thing that bothered her was social acceptance. She would like to have been, how shall I say, better born. She was uneasy in some social situations and, being anxious, her behavior was often impulsive, awkward. They were the reactions of a proud peasant."

Despite the strict moral views she had professed when any of her friends were going through a divorce or being unfaithful to their partners, Maria considered her adulterous relationship with Onassis irreproachable. "I was not a home breaker, nor was he," she told a friend. "Tina was going to leave anyway. It was something that had to happen. I had to follow my destiny."

"It is that sense of destiny, that Greekness that she and Onassis had in common," explained Prince Michael of Greece, who saw a lot of Maria when he and his wife, Marina, lived in Paris. Come to think of it, we owe our friendship to Maria. She took me to their house for dinner one evening in a rare exception to that exclusivity with friends that Mary Mead Carter and I had discussed.

"She was *profoundly* Greek," Prince Michael said. "Her language was Greek and she spoke it well. When she spoke French or other foreign languages, she put on an air of sophistication, but in Greek, she was herself, totally natural. She wasn't at all divalike, as it doesn't suit the language or the national character. Actually, there was a sort of duality in her language, as in her nature, depending on whether she spoke about professional matters or just trivia. When the conversation was on her art, she was the epitome of the self-assured professional. When it was general, she turned into a hesitant, middle-class Greek discussing curtains, carpeting and little dogs like all those Athenian ladies . . . like the Greek shipping magnates' wives with their tiny poodles who all have ridiculous names. There was, however, a side of Maria which was not at all Greek. She was always a bit reserved and distant. Perhaps it was a defense."

Although Maria had evolved beyond her middle-class education to become an international figure, mentally she had remained very much part of the traditional Greek family structure. She longed for a child—preferably a boy—who would give her the status of a mother, the dominant figure in the Greek household.

"When Greek men are home, they expect their wives to be waiting, their soup to be hot and their guest welcomed in style," says Prince Michael. "It's all very important to them, but they don't stay put for long. Cheating on your wife is a must in Greece. Adultery is a national sport! For the most part, men dislike the confinement of their homes. They enjoy trailing from one café to the other most of the night. It's a very Greek trait, very much part of Onassis. He hated being at home. He loathed the houses he owned and avoided living in them as much as possible. He'd always find a friend who would join him at the café for a drink, and from there they'd move on to another bar or café and pick up other friends, and so on. Onassis was a poor sleeper. His nightly ritual usually dragged out till the wee hours whether in Athens, Paris, London or New York."

I believe that, in a strange sort of way, Maria was actually attracted by Aristo's evasive, domineering traits. It made her feel feminine. She once asked John Ardoin if he'd ever been to Greece. "I have," John answered.

"Don't ever believe what you see there," she said. "It looks European, but believe me, it is totally Eastern. The man is the pasha."

Painter-sculptress Marina Karella, who married Prince Michael of Greece, remembers when Maria Callas returned to Greece in 1960, to sing *Norma* at Epidaurus. "I was seventeen. Right out of school. And I was lucky enough to be one of the assistants to *Norma*'s stage designer, Yannis Tsarouchis. The night of the dress rehearsal, the bay was filled with masses and masses of boats of all sizes. Among the 'floating audience' was Onassis with his son, Alexander. Alexander had brought along the latest gadgets and recording equipment. Then came the opening night—Serafin was conducting. . . . It was very moving. There was an immense crowd. People shouted and cried with enthusiasm. Callas was sublime! But there was no Onassis. He didn't like music and he'd had enough with the dress rehearsal.

"After the performance, I'd been invited to dinner on board the *Christina* by a friend of Maria's. Can you imagine the joy, at seventeen, to be invited on the *Christina*? To see Callas, my idol. I was absolutely thrilled. I'll never forget getting to that dinner. I lost both my shoes as I scurried through the crowd.

"You know what surprised me most when we got on board? It was the undemonstrative reception Callas got from Onassis. He greeted her as an ordinary guest. How could he after such an extraordinary feat? It was a terrible anticlimax, and do you know, the opera was never mentioned during the course of the evening! Onassis seemed much more concerned with his important guests and the buffet than Maria's artistic success. For the most part, their conversation was limited to domestic details. 'Is your steak OK? Is it overdone?' 'Are the shrimps fresh?' 'See to it that Mr. X gets more champagne.' "

Under the grandiose surface, the couple's *petit bourgeois* interests prevailed. Aside from their physical attraction for each other, it seems clear to me their middle-class Greekness was their strongest bond.

For Onassis, business was number one in his life. It came before his family or his pleasure. Actually it *was* his pleasure, a fascinating game that was on his mind at all times. He'd invite businessmen and their wives for an evening on the town or on his yacht with the sole purpose of monopolizing the men in business talk. Perhaps that was the reason one of his favorite couples was the Westphals.

In the summer of 1960, he invited Adolf and Marie-Luise on board the *Christina*. As they drove to Karmena Vourla, where they were to meet, the always outspoken Adolf remarked, "I hope Ari isn't going to bring that singing bitch along now that he's left Tina. That bitch better not ruin our friendship."

"You must understand, Nadia, Aristo's friends and the press blamed Callas for the breakup in the Onassis marriage," Marie-Luise reminded me. "When we got to the house where we were to meet, I saw, among the small group of friends, a very slim lady dressed in a black sweater and pants. She wore no makeup and her large dark glasses hid her face. Her hands were long and beautiful, her nails unpolished. The only jewelry she had on was a tiny, tiny watch. Adolf went to sit beside her and started a conversation. I got very nervous. I had recognized Callas but was aware my husband hadn't. I was terrified that he'd turn to Aristo and say, 'I'm so glad you didn't bring the bitch Maria'! After dinner, before boarding the *Christina*, Aristo suggested we go on a fishing trip—which lasted till two in the morning. As we stepped into that launch, I managed to whisper in my husband's ear, 'Darling, that was Maria Callas you were sitting next to.'

" 'That is Maria Callas!' he said. 'Oh, no, come on! She's much too nice, I'm sure it isn't Maria Callas.'

"Personally, I was glad to meet her. She was a godsend! She and I could chat about feminine things while the men went on with their business talks. We were bored out of our minds until we decided that the lesser of two evils was to learn something about business. With time, we managed to follow. Aristo liked that about us. If we didn't understand, we sat quietly and listened to them talking about ships, ships and more ships. They wrote out deals on cocktail napkins and cigarette boxes. Aristo would empty the Greek No. 1 cigarettes, his favorite brand, on the table, unfold the red-and-white box and jot down his ideas. That's usually how their contracts started, then the office would confirm them later in the day."

Onassis sometimes handsomely rewarded Marie-Luise's patience. In 1960, he asked her to christen his ship *Olympic Challenger*. He gave the "godmother" a glorious diamond and ruby bracelet (ninety rubies) to match the necklace he'd given her as a wedding present. Marie-Luise told me he gave a similar one—diamonds and sapphires—to Princess Grace of Monaco for christening another one of his ships.

I can only remember Maria mentioning two gifts she had received from Onassis: a pair of earrings and the Mercedes-Benz she still drove around in when I met her. Biki also told me that Maria had appropriated a coral, turquoise and rhinestone pin and earrings from her boutique, which she liked so much that she asked Onassis to have Van Cleef and Arpels copy it for her in precious stones. Maybe he gave her other presents I am not aware of. But Maria was not one to brag about such things, nor did she talk much about the grand lifestyle she shared with one of the richest men in the world.

When I discovered Marie-Luise had often cruised on the *Christina,* I was delighted that she could provide some information regarding life on board the ship. "It was casual," said Marie-Luise. "The surroundings were luxurious but the lifestyle was simple. We all did what we wanted in the morning. We could order breakfast in our cabin or have it upstairs. We sat in the sun, swam, read. In the middle of the day we went ashore to have lunch in modest fishing villages. Aristo loved small places and simple food. He ate little. He usually ordered a steak, a salad or a Greek specialty. That was also true of Monte Carlo or Paris. He offered his guests the most extravagant meals, but he kept to plain foods and small quantities.

"A number of times in island villages I saw the Greek peasants kneel and kiss Maria's feet. She was embarrassed, but she liked it all the same. They kissed Ari's hands and Maria's feet while they mumbled prayers of thanks for the honor these two famous Greeks had bestowed on them by visiting their island.

"The days on board the *Christina* were very quiet; it was at sunset that the bustle started. Caviar was served with cocktails—a sort of snack—in a four-pound tin, which everybody dug into with a spoon. We went out every single night. Sometimes we went from harbor to harbor, from one café or night spot to another. Onassis never tired, he never wanted to go to bed. In that way he and Maria were totally compatible. He expected his guests to keep up with him. That was his nature. That was one of the problems he ran into with Tina. She married him when she was seventeen. She followed him for as long as she could, but finally she'd had enough and gave up. It was too much for Tina, but Maria kept up. She did everything Ari wanted, but in return he was often rude to her and showed her little affection. When people were around, there was never any intimacy between them. He never took her in his arms, caressed her or gave her a kiss. The most he ever did was touch her hand. Maybe she didn't like it, I don't know. I have the impression she was a little prudish, but then he'd never been affectionate with Tina either."

What struck Marie-Luise was how little of the *Christina* was actually used. The spacious drawing room, with its fireplace, grand piano and photographs of Tina with the children (which were never removed: *she* was the Greek Mother!) and its delicate white silk chairs, was rarely occupied. "In all the years I went on cruises, I can only recall one occasion when the pale green and white dining room was used for a seated dinner party. It was a beautiful ship, but it just wasn't lived in. The cabins were very large and beautifully decorated with lovely materials and carpets. The handles and faucets in the marble bathrooms were dolphin-shaped, made of gold. Maria's cabin was enormous, with an adjoining boudoir and endless closet space for all her clothes. She loved buying beautiful new dresses!"

Hélène Rochas, another frequent guest on board the yacht, told me the same: "Like the drawing room, her cabin was rarely used. She spent most of her time in Aristo's quarters on the floor above, but when she did sleep in her cabin, it was a sure sign that they had had a falling-out. When peace had been restored, her suite once again became her poodles' playground, and they relieved themselves in the bathtub. Aristo and Maria's quarrels were those of any passionate, noisy Mediterranean couple. In addition, there was the conflict of their celebrity, a rivalry that sprang from the same source, which made their fights all the more violent.

"Like many Mediterranean men, Onassis was difficult and cruel," Hélène went on. "He used language that even made the sailors blush. He attacked Maria's insecurity as a woman, and mocked her art. She fought back in her frightened voice of attack. An unpleasantly shrill voice that Onassis hated. He would say, 'This woman's voice, which can be so beautiful when she sings, can be so ugly, at times, when she speaks.'

"During the years they were together, they spent a lot of time on board ship. Onassis adored the sea. He was a true sailor and had found his equal in Maria," Hélène Rochas remembered. "Whenever time permitted, they went off alone (with a crew of sixty) on the high seas."

Vera Zorina, another sea worshiper, who spent a brief holiday on the *Christina* after Onassis married Jackie Kennedy, liked his toughness and sporty no-nonsense attitude. "He was a real sailor," she said. "He loved being on that boat. He was sloppy, walking around half naked with baggy pants, but he was in command of his ship, you definitely felt that. This was no matinee idol strolling around with brass buttons on his jacket. He talked like a tough sailor."

"His conversation was full of four-letter words," Josephine Chaplin remembers. A young admirer of Callas, she had been invited on board the *Christina* in the summer of 1963. The atmosphere was relaxed and convivial. "Whenever Maria heard him swear, she would say, 'Don't listen, don't listen, Josephine, stop up your ears, don't listen.' I was very shy then. I'd get very tongue-tied and Maria would kid me about it. 'I don't understand you, Josephine,' she'd say. 'You've written me piles of letters, and now that I'm in front of you, you don't say a word!' When I told her it was because she was my idol (she'd always been my idol), she answered jokingly, 'Everybody should have an idol. You are lucky to have me; at least you can be with me, not only admire me but have fun with me too. Look,' she'd say as she slid down a chute into the sea. 'Look at the prima donna now!' "

There was a lighter side to Onassis that Marie-Luise referred to as his "boyish ways." "In the bar, on board the *Christina,* he had a computer-controlled tabletop on which he liked to maneuver a miniature replica of his ships—his fleet of tankers. It was his private game of nautical Monopoly. He also had a street organ on which he liked to grind out his favorite tunes. He loved Greek music, but that was it. He hated Maria to practice within earshot and wouldn't allow her to sing for friends. He loved Callas, the Diva, but wanted her to be Callas without singing," Marie-Luise observed.

In spite of Callas's now infrequent appearances and the critics' opinion that her voice was weaker, her fame continued to grow. So did the challenge. Every time she sang, she had to live up to the Callas past. She was terrified, and there was no Titta waiting in the wings.

The minute she stepped offstage, she was a tracked animal compelled to a life on the run in a world seen through hotel-suite windows. She was met by mobs everywhere. When she was in Hamburg for a concert engagement, she called Marie-Luise to cancel a luncheon date. "I can't leave the hotel, Marie-Luise. There are hundreds of people waiting for me to come out. I can see them from my window. It makes me very nervous. I can't even go out to buy the stockings I need for tonight's performance. I'll have to send the hairdresser." The police had to protect her entrances and exits no matter where she went.

Everyone wanted a piece of Callas—and everyone had an opinion about the radical change in her life.

Madam,

You've never seen me, but I know you well. I am the florist of La Scala of many many years ago: come to think of it, I offered Maestro Verdi a bouquet the very last time he came to this theater. Of course, you came later, when I was no longer there. Nonetheless, you can't imagine how often I cried tears of joy when I listened to you sing.

I thought to myself: finally Ghiringhelli has brought a lady to the Scala like those of the nineteenth century whose hands were kissed by the tsar of Russia: tall, dignified, aloof. A lady who forgets that she is a woman, who lives for Art, disdains money, is capricious, makes demands. Big ones, like Beethoven, who performed his concerts till five in the morning.

I liked the way you slimmed down to a model's figure out of sheer willpower, and the way you married that nice gentleman from Verona. . . .

Even when you were absent, you were always *the* Lady of the Scala. When another singer sang in our theater, everyone compared her to you, to your greatness, because you were the giant of lyric art, you were *unique* in the world. Incomparable, inimitable, unmatched even in your defects.

What have you gone and done now? You've run off with that Greek compatriot of yours, married, with children. Why? Don't tell me for love?

Come on, you are not one of those "chanteuses" who lose their heads over some Don Juan. Matters of the heart for one like you are not an excuse, they are a weakness. Your heart is your voice: It is with your voice that you make us weep, not with your romantic escapades. Your lover is the public, and no one else.

Look here: "Casta Diva" wrenched my soul, even when you were off-key, because you were really Norma from head to foot, before and after singing. Now you can sing "Casta Diva" any way you care to but I won't cry anymore. Onstage you are involved with Romans, but in reality, you are thinking about the Greek. Did she do it for money, as some suggest? I say that's impossible. Not an artist of her caliber. . . .

I cannot absolve your action, because you are guilty of an assassination: You killed the last *lady* of the Scala. It is a crime that others might pardon you, but your ex-admirer will never pardon you.

Elvira (The florist of the Scala)

12

Betrayal

On December 7, 1960, when La Scala opened its season with *Poliuto,* the theater was bursting at the seams. Callas had returned after a break with Ghiringhelli, but everyone knew that it was only a brief truce. They were fully aware that this was to be one of Callas's last opera performances at La Scala.

The turmoil in the gallery increased the tension. The faithful music lovers were understandably upset. Ghiringhelli had refused to decorate the theater with the white carnations that had been flown in from the Riviera for the occasion. Meanwhile, in the orchestra, Onassis was surrounded by his special guests the Begum Aga Khan, Grace of Monaco, Gina Lollobrigida, Elisabeth Schwarzkopf and her husband Walter Legge.

In her dressing room, that night, Maria knew she lacked the stamina to get through the performance. Still dieting constantly, she was a shadow of her former self. Simionato re-members that as the nurse gave her a vitamin shot to sustain her, Maria murmured, "If I don't do a good job tonight, I'll kill myself!" "I was surprised by the change in Maria," says Simionato. "She said it with the usual Callas pride, but behind the words there was a certain humility that was unlike her. She was very frightened. It was as if her wings had been cut off. She knew that she no longer had control over her voice."

"What happened," Larry Kelly told John Ardoin in his interview, "had nothing to do with weight, and there's where I disagree with other people. Callas had different objectives and began to perform accordingly. To be the greatest soprano in the world, that she had achieved. To go further, she wanted to be wealthy, secure, accepted. She disregarded the rules, and that voice which took thirty years to manufacture naturally shattered slightly when she stopped the regime, the discipline of making it work."

The voice did waver. There was tension. But that December evening was to be the final victory for Callas at La Scala. The audience came prepared to preserve the myth intact for as long as possible. They clapped and shouted, seemingly dismissing her vocal weaknesses.

Up in the gallery, her most ardent fans waved handker-chiefs after the performance and implored her not to leave La Scala. *Her* Scala! The following morning the front page of Milan's most important newspaper announced that "thirty years from now, we'll be able to say, 'I was there that night.'"

A year later, when she returned to La Scala for her fare-well performance in *Medea*, fewer bravos came from the star-studded orchestra. Those who had heard the Great Callas could not pretend. This time, the "audience of truth" in the gallery shouted insults and whistled. Valeria Pedemonte re-members looking up through her tears and thinking, "What more do you want? In one evening, you are hearing the great singer and the end of the great singer."

Friends that night had difficulty going backstage to congratulate her. Yet her adoring court was there.

"My dear, you were fabulous . . . you've never been so marvelous," said a fan, hugging her.

"Yes," Callas answered. "I thought I was in marvelous voice tonight."

William Weaver, who witnessed the scene, told me he couldn't bear the charade. He knew that she knew. He turned and left.

Maria's insecurity about her performance came out during dinner, when she joined Onassis, the Westphals, Elisabeth Schwarzopf, Walter Legge and conductor Thomas Schippers. Marie-Luise recalls her questions started with the roast beef at 2:00 A.M., and ended over coffee and vodka at 4:00 A.M. "What did you think of such and such a passage in the second act? Did I hold that note long enough? Why did they start to whistle?" Everyone assured her that she was wonderful and that the whistling came from the Tebaldi claque.

Alexander and Christina, jealous of their father's relationship with Maria, did everything in their power to reunite their parents (although Tina had no desire to return to Onassis, with whom, Marie-Luise felt, she'd never been happy). Meanwhile, Maria's efforts to win over the children's affections, an effort she hoped would help to legitimize her position, were disastrous, in particular with regard to Christina.

As a matter of fact, when Christina once came up in conversation, Maria mumbled to me, "Not a nice girl. Hard. She treated me as if I were the mistress!" As she spoke, I wondered if Maria hadn't put on her coy, charming act to win her over. She did this when she was insecure, not realizing how it played against her. It wasn't natural; in fact, at times it was quite insipid.

In the summer of 1961, the Westphals rented a house in the Spanish hills near Marbella. They were having a drink at the Marbella Club with Prince Alfonso Hohenlohe when Aristo and Maria dropped in. "After a Spanish-scheduled four o'clock lunch, Aristo wanted to move on. 'Why don't you three come back to the *Christina* with us?' he said. 'Come as you are, we have everything on board. We can go to a night-club and then you can spend the night.' I suggested I run up the hill to pick up an appropriate dress," said Marie-Luise, "but Ari couldn't wait. 'Don't bother. Maria will lend you a dress. Won't you, Maria?' Maria nodded but without enthusiasm. When we got on board it was the cocktail hour, so we went on eating, caviar this time, while the *Christina* sailed toward Tangiers. At 11:30, Aristo got up suddenly. 'Let's go ashore!' he said. 'Both of you, slip into a dress and let's go. Come on. Hurry, hurry!'

"Maria and I were the same height, but Maria's waist was smaller. There was not time for alterations. So with safety pins we adjusted the skirt to my size. A few minutes later we rushed back to show Aristo, who was getting very impatient. 'Oh, Marie-Luise,' he exclaimed. 'You look beautiful in that dress! Don't you think it's nice on her, Maria? Look at her bust. Look how beautifully her bust fills out that dress of yours!' I was embarrassed. He put her down and humiliated her in front of people at times to the point of being brutal. She, of course, never got used to it."

Hélène Rochas agrees. She is convinced Maria suffered terribly. "He admired her at first and then degraded her. Emotionally Maria was a child-woman. Her dynamic personality allowed her to cope with everything except the men she loved."

"The men all had quite a bit to drink before leaving the ship," Marie-Luise continued, "and as the night advanced, they left a trail of empty bottles in the most fashionable nightclubs of Tangiers. The party got out of hand. In one of the clubs the men joined the belly dancer onstage, giving a rather rowdy exhibition of themselves. We were upset, but to our relief, no one recognized us. Then Aristo asked me to dance—he danced only when he was drunk. He was very puritanical. He said one shouldn't dance cheek to cheek or body to body. 'The proximity brings on the condition a man finds himself in when he wants to make love,' he used to say. I suppose one could call him a hot puritan? His personality was unexpectedly diverse. For instance, he rarely joined in the general conversation but when he did, his contribution was usually geared toward philosophy and the meaning of life. He liked to quote the Greek philosophers, whom he read in his spare time. He rarely read novels; his thrillers were the great philosophers.

"From the belly dancers we moved on to a club where there was a Spanish singer, and Onassis asked her to sing his favorite Argentine songs. I guess the mixture of the music and liquor took him back to his youth in Argentina. The girl had a pleasant but untrained voice. When she had finished, Aristo looked at her with admiration and said, 'Maria, don't you think she has a beautiful voice?' 'Yes, darling,' Maria replied dryly, 'she really has a beautiful voice for a nightclub singer.' "

I don't speak Greek, so the conversation with mezzo-soprano Kiki Morfoniou turned into a mixture of sign language and Italo-Anglo-French; but actually, we managed quite well. We met in Athens, but the August heat was so unbearable in the city that she drove me out to her pine-shaded villa in the country. There she told me all about the *Norma* [1960] and *Medea* [1961] she'd sung at Epidaurus with Maria.

"Meeting and singing with Callas was like a miracle. When I auditioned for her, she instantly sensed I was terrified, and was very gentle with me. 'Kiki, why are you so nervous? Relax. We'll sing the duet from *Norma* together; that will calm you down and I'll be able to hear your real voice.' When we were through, she said she liked my voice and we'd make a good team. You can't imagine how thrilled I was! You see, I was just at the beginning of my career in 1960. I asked Callas to help me and she did. She was like an older sister to me. She guided me, suggesting ways to tackle the role. Please, you must say that my success was greatly due to Maria. It really was. The following year, when we did *Medea* together, and went out for curtain calls, Maria pushed me forward so that I would take a bow alone. I stepped back to take her hand, but she nudged me. 'Go on, Kiki, go along. I want you to go out alone.' I found this gesture incredible.

"I also remember that during the dress rehearsal of *Medea*, in the scene in which Medea watches Jason betray her by taking Glauce as his bride, Maria started to cry. It was just a rehearsal, but there she was shedding real tears; that's how much she was in the part. To me it was a revelation. When I asked her how she managed to cry onstage with such facility, she answered: 'Kiki, you are too young to cry. That comes with the experience of life, which you then transfer to the stage. Anyway,' she added, 'try not to cry when you are onstage, it doesn't do much for the voice.' That rehearsal will stay in my memory as long as I live. She gave everything each time; she didn't hold back and save her voice for opening night as most singers do."

Friends had flown in from all over Europe for the opening performance, including Wally Toscanini, even though she was not on speaking terms with Maria. Wally confided to her friend Gian Carlo Menotti that her falling-out with Maria had started when she had tried to check Maria's tirade against a Scala colleague. "Wally tried to reason with her," Gian Carlo explained. "She begged her, 'Maria, please listen to me. I'm telling you this out of affection, like a mother.' And Maria turned on her and said, 'Like a mother? You could be my grandmother!'

"Wally was stunned," said Gian Carlo. "You know, she's only about fifteen years older than Callas. After that Wally stopped seeing Callas. She saw no reason to expose herself further to Callas's nastiness. But at Epidaurus, watching Callas's heartrending performance of Medea, Wally told me afterwards, 'Gian Carlo, I began to cry. I had to forgive her because I knew what she was going through. She was losing her voice . . . and . . . *he* was there, in the audience. You could almost see the blood coming out of her vocal cords. She gave an incandescent performance, out of despair. All she wanted was to be loved.' Wally went backstage, and as soon as Maria saw her, she fell in her arms and burst into tears. 'Only you know what I'm going through tonight!' she sobbed." (Menotti says that Wally had been through a number of unhappy love affairs herself.)

There was another person in the audience with whom Maria had broken off relations: her sister Jackie. After nine years of estrangement, George Kalogeropoulos brought Jackie to hear her sister in *Medea* with the hope of a reconciliation and perhaps to discourage the attacks and gossip the Greek press had built around Callas's return.

Polyvios Marchand still can't get over the way Callas was received in Greece. "She returned to her Greece and was greeted with a cold shower. The press criticized her fee, which they found extravagant; they picked on her relationship with her mother, her cousins . . . they were shameless."

Jackie acknowledges that her father's effort to bring the sisters together was not really successful.

"Mary and I did meet a few times during our stay, Nadia, but she never introduced me to any of her friends. The one time I met Onassis—he was very charming with me—Mary interrupted the conversation every few minutes. She kept saying, 'Do you have the time, Aristo? We don't want to be late. What time is it?' On another occasion we went to visit Onassis' sister and brother-in-law on the island of Skiathos. The brother-in-law, who was a doctor, mentioned that he'd heard my recital in Athens and that I had a lovely voice! Mary looked at me with great superiority and said, 'What? You, a voice! *I'm* the one with the voice. You have the hee-haw of a donkey. Ah, well! The innocents live in hope, don't they.' You can't imagine how I felt in front of all those people, Nadia. And when I gave my concert, she was furious. She locked herself up in her house in Milan for three days. She said that if I dared use the name Callas to build a career, she would do everything in her power to stop me."

Maria's professional engagements, acting as hostess on the *Christina* and party hopping all over Europe left her little time with Aristo. It was common knowledge that he had flings on the side, but she closed an eye, knowing there was no relationship unless it was on his terms. Fearful of antagonizing him, she turned into a meek and obedient lamb. Once in a while, when they were at sea or on Skorpios, he spoke of marriage, but he was always vague. To herself, she blamed his indecision on the fact that Meneghini's continual changes and demands delayed her divorce. That divorce was infinitely important to Maria, as it meant legalizing her situation and having a child by Aristo. But when she got pregnant by chance, in 1966, she wasn't prepared for his reaction: abortion. It was an order.

"At first I couldn't believe he was serious," she said on our way from Athens to Tragonissi in the summer of 1970. "He said, 'I don't want a baby by you! What would I do with another child? I already have two.' The decision was torture. As you know, Nadia, I don't believe in abortion. It took me four months to make up my mind. Think how fulfilled my life would be if I'd stood up to him and kept the baby." I remember Maria wistfully looking at the parched Greek landscape.

"Why didn't you?" I had asked.

"*Dio mio,* I had to make a choice. . . . I was afraid of losing Aristo. I guess God wanted it that way."

Mary Mead Carter is convinced Onassis would not have left her. "He would have married her, but she couldn't take the risk of losing him. Besides, Maria was too honest; she never would have blackmailed Onassis into marrying her."

Giving up the child was the crowning disappointment of a difficult three-year period: the move from Milan to Paris, a messy divorce, a hernia operation and a serious vocal crisis that destroyed her confidence. She told musicologist Sergio Segalini, "I know the music world has already dug my grave and I foresee the moment when I'll have to throw myself into it."

In the summer of 1963, Lee Radziwill was on board the *Christina* with Onassis and Maria when she was summoned to her sister's bedside in Washington. Jackie Kennedy, the First Lady, had given birth to Patrick Bouvier Kennedy, who only lived one day.

To Maria's surprise, Lee returned to Greece almost immediately. "I was astonished she hadn't stayed with her sister," Maria said to me. "She repeatedly told us how undone Jackie was by the death of her baby. Both Aristo and I felt badly about it, so he extended an open invitation to the president and Mrs. Kennedy to join us on a cruise."

The historic cruise took place in the autumn of 1963, but two important guests were missing. The president of the United States and Maria.

"I was in Paris," Maria told me. "Aristo had kicked me out! He told me he couldn't have his "concubine" on board with the president and First Lady of the United States. That was just an added insult to the fight we'd had a month before when I discovered an empty Cartier box with a love note from Aristo to Lee. A couple of nights later, I saw the bracelet it had contained, on her wrist."

"How could they! How did they dare have an affair right under my nose. I still can't get over their nerve," Maria repeated, her hands joined in a typical Italian gesture, as if beseeching enlightenment from above. "I have the proof," she said in a fiercely triumphant tone. "I've hidden the note and box. But tell me, how could she accept those dirty diamonds?"

While the international press rushed to Athens to cover the departure of the *Christina,* a proud Maria stayed in Paris. During the next few years she was repeatedly forced to try to come to terms with the fact that she was no longer totally in control of her life or her art.

Maria had gone to live in Paris to be near Onassis and because she believed she might make the Paris Opéra another La Scala, but this was not to be. Callas made sporadic appearances at the Opéra and a return to the Met in March 1965, but there were no great triumphs. Finally, on May 29, 1965, Callas retired from opera. As Sergio Segalini remembers with melancholy, "After the first act of *Norma* at the Paris Opéra, when I went into her dressing room, she seemed almost dead. That night she understood that she could not sing Norma again. When Callas understood that, she ceased being Callas."

And when Onassis understood this, his investment in Callas ended. Their stormy affair continued, but she had to put up with his gallantries to other women and his increasing roughness with her.

On an evening when Maestro Nicola Rescigno was to dine with her in Paris, she called him two or three times to change the restaurant and finally asked him to come to her apartment at Avenue Georges Mandel. When he got there, she wasn't ready; she kept changing her clothes, and he realized that it was because Onassis was going to join them. The outfit she eventually decided on was to be worn with a small headdress made of veils and ribbons created by Biki. During dinner, she tried to attract Aristo's attention; she had primped all evening, but couldn't get a complimentary glance out of him. She finally couldn't stand it any longer. "Aristo," she said, "how do you like Biki's latest creation?" He stared at her briefly and replied, "Either you cut your nose off to match the hat, or you get a bigger hat to match your nose."

"On another evening," John Ardoin told me, "the couple dined out with my dear friend Larry Kelly. Larry's hair loss had started very young, and, being vain, he had submitted to horribly painful and costly transplants. As soon as they settled in the restaurant, Maria propped one of her legs up on a vacant chair. She did this whenever she could to relieve her poor circulation. During dinner it became evident that Onassis was stroking her leg under the tablecloth. He turned to Larry and said, "Poor Larry, you paid so much money to put hair on your head and Maria pays so much money to take it off her legs. Right now, she feels like a plucked chicken."

Notwithstanding his insults, and even after their break-up, Maria was proud of Onassis and of his capacity to have achieved fame and fortune entirely by his wits. To impress me with Aristo's genius in financial deals, she once told me that, on a couple of occasions, he had signed contracts in vanishing ink. Contracts of no interest to him, but essential to the re-alization of his future deals. "He would sign, and lo and behold, the signature had vanished the next day. Clever, no?" I tactfully (for once) withheld my comment.

In 1966, Maria renounced her American citizenship in favor of a Greek passport which she hoped would help in-validate her Italian marriage, but legal bureaucracy kept the situation in limbo for another two years. She and Onassis still spoke of getting married in the autumn of 1968 when the big explosion occurred.

During that summer, relations between the couple were visibly strained. To Lawrence Kelly, who was on the *Christina* with them on their last cruise, it was obvious that Onassis wanted to get rid of Maria. Kelly saw it was time for her to leave, but she couldn't or wouldn't do it on her own. Once again, he proved to be the shoulder she could lean on.

"Pack up and be ready to go next week," Larry said after they returned to Paris. "You are going to come back to the United States with me. I'm not leaving you here in this mess. You need to be with your buddies at such a time."

But a week later Kelly found Maria at the American Hospital in Paris. Her photograph was on the front page of every French paper. The report was that she had attempted suicide, and Larry was convinced she had tried.

Maria's departure brought Onassis the sense of relief he had been looking for and gave him the opportunity to accel-erate his romance with Jacqueline Kennedy. Their marriage plans had matured during their Caribbean cruise in May 1968, but she had decided not to put them into effect until she had Robert Kennedy's approval.

Her brother-in-law asked her to postpone the wedding until the end of his presidential campaign. Jackie agreed to wait. But Robert's death on June 6, only a few weeks after her romantic voyage on board the *Christina,* drastically altered her future. There was no reason further to delay her union with Onassis.

Mary Mead Carter, who saw Maria upon her return to the States, confided to me that she found her destroyed and without purpose. "She was so agitated, she couldn't sleep without pills. I was very worried about her that summer," Mrs. Carter told me, "but Maria was a survivor, and little by little she adjusted to the reality of her situation. She would never have done anything to herself. If she had, it would have been that summer."

Maria had once mentioned to me, in passing, the so-called suicide incident. "Do you remember what a fuss they made when I was put in the American Hospital because of my anemia? The press cooked up a dramatic story about my having attempted suicide. What nonsense all that was! I really was sick; but they didn't want the truth, they wanted melodrama. I admit I was depressed, but you know as well as I do, I would never have done anything stupid like that. No man is worth *that* much. Besides, I love life! It's so unexpected."

Larry Kelly, Mary Carter and John Ardoin, who spent a lot of time with Maria during that restless period in Santa Fe and Dallas, felt that despite her distress she would come out on top. "She never lost her sense of direction and truth," says John. "Onassis crushed her emotionally, but his pasha ways didn't shake the basic Callas integrity. In fact, in a way, she clung to that.

"For example, one evening Larry and I were having drinks in the hotel lounge, when Maria appeared. 'Can I join you? I'm bored, I want to do something. Do you know any card games?' she asked. I'd had about three stingers and was not feeling totally lucid," says John. "I don't know to this day what made me do it. 'Well,' I said, 'I know a silly children's game, called I Doubt It.

"We were having fun. We played several rounds and had gotten down to the fives. Maria, who wasn't quite getting it, said, 'I have no fives.'

" 'No, Maria, that's not how you play the game.' I explained. 'Put down the cards and say they *are* fives. If we catch you lying, you have to pick up all the cards on the table.'

"She stood up, threw her cards on the table and said, 'How can you ask me to do that? How can you ask me to lie? I thought you were my friend. I thought you understood me.' She left the room without another word. Larry and I sat there dumbfounded. After all, it was just a card game."

After a week they moved on to Las Vegas, San Francisco and Cuernavaca, where Maria slipped and cracked three ribs. Larry and Mary flew her back to Dallas, and while Larry returned to his business obligations, Mary cared for Maria, took her shopping, entertained her, shared her daily steak tartare and drove her to the doctor. She came out giggling from her first doctor's appointment. "What's wrong?" John asked.

"Larry would pick the one doctor in town who loves opera! He has all my records. When I took my blouse off, his hands started to shake so badly, he couldn't strap my ribs. He could barely touch me!" she said.

Shortly after Maria returned to Paris, she received a phone call from Onassis' butler, whom she knew well from his years of service on the *Christina*. He was hesitant and more formal than usual.

"Madame," he said, "I'm calling you to tell you . . . to give you . . . I feel it is my duty to inform you of what is about to happen before you read it in tomorrow's paper. I'm distressed to have to give you the news. Mr. Onassis is going to marry Madame Jacqueline Kennedy."

The message was a knockout blow.

"He lied. Do you understand? He duped me," Maria repeated over and over during the years I knew her (usually sitting on my bed at 3:00 A.M.). "What I'll never forgive him for is that he denied everything two days before! How could she marry a man who had had an affair with her sister? Can you understand it, Nadia?"

"Who better than the wife of a president!" Prince Michael of Greece remarked. He wanted a 'lady,' and publicity, which to him was like a drug. He probably regarded the union as another one of his business deals."

The "contract" was signed on October 20, 1968, on the island of Skorpios in Greece. "Mark my words, the gods will get even. There is justice," Maria intoned like a Greek chorus. It was not too many years before her predictions would come true.

The world gasped in disbelief at the news of the Kennedy-Onassis marriage. The American public was dismayed. To them, a national landmark, an institution, was exchanging widowhood for frivolity and financial power, which aroused disapproval rather than compassion.

As for the Greeks, they were outraged. The union was not only the betrayal of a Greek woman, but of Maria Callas, their modern goddess, and an affront to the entire nation. Onassis had apostatized the national honor. "He behaved in a disgusting fashion," an Athenian friend of his told me. "He should never have done that to Maria. Being used to buying everything he wanted, he decided he wanted the sister-in-law of the future president of the United States. That didn't work out, so he bought the widow of a president instead. Poor Maria, she went through hell because of those two. Serves them right that it didn't work."

While Jackie and Aristo exchanged vows, Maria feigned indifference. Beautifully dressed, breathtakingly grandiose in her dignity and courage, she was driven by her chauffeur, Ferruccio, in the Mercedes Aristo had given her, to the film premiere of Feydeau's *A Flea in Her Ear,* then on to a reception celebrating the seventy-fifth anniversary of Aristo's habitual trattoria, Maxim's. She was dying of pain, but refused to indulge in self-pity. When asked what she thought of Jacqueline Kennedy, her answer was, "I cannot tell you, I cannot give you an opinion as I have never met her." Her anger and hurt were directed to Onassis. "He's just a collector of famous women," she said. "The only way he could collect her was to marry her."

It is rumored that during the first year of their marriage Jackie spent $1.5 million on clothes, antiques and decorating. But perhaps the underlying cause of Onassis and Jackie's rapid estrangement was not money; those who knew them feel it was simply social incompatibility. Starting only a few weeks after his marriage to Jackie, Aristo put into action a perverse game to regain Maria's love.

"He's mad. The man is sick," Maria cried out indignantly during a telephone conversation with Joëlle de Gravelaine. "Why does he go on sending me flowers? I wish he'd leave me alone! Drop dead! I have other things to think about. I don't need him!"

13

Back to Turkey

"When the news broke, pouf! like this!" said Franco Rossellini, throwing his arms in the air, "that Jackie and Onassis had married, I called Maria the same day. She was in a rage and very depressed," Franco recalled during our lunch in Rome. "I told her, 'Maria, I'm coming to see you in Paris, tomorrow. I have a lot to talk to you about. So when I arrived, I said at once that I wanted to do the *Medea* film and that it was about time she worked on something she liked. Her conversation was vague. She pretended she didn't care about Aristo, but the incentive of doing a film just to show him was in her. The next problem was the director. She hated the idea of Pasolini. Particularly after seeing his *Teorema*. You know, she walked out in the middle of the screening!"

In fact, I'd heard about her reaction from Jacques Bourgeois.

"Maria called me at three A.M., and without prologue or apology launched into her version of *Teorema*.

" 'Jacques,' she said, 'I have just seen something absolutely disgusting! Pasolini's latest film, *Teorema*. The man is mad!'

" 'Maria, what are you talking about?' I asked drowsily.

" '*Eh bien, Jacques, voilà*. . . . A young man goes to spend the weekend with a family in the country. He makes love to the mother, then he makes love to the daughter, and then he makes love to the *son!*' "

Although Bourgeois had not seen the film, his sleepy subconscious remembered having read an article on the subject.

" 'Oh, yes, of course, that's God,' I told her.

" 'What, Jacques? What do you mean, God?'

" 'Maria, the young man in the story represents God. It is to be taken symbolically.'

A long silence followed.

" '*God?* But that is blasphemous!' Maria gasped."

"It took a long time to convince her to make the film," Franco went on. "She made my life miserable. She kept saying, 'You are going to exploit me like that crook Zeffirelli.' This response reflected back to the film version of *Tosca* that Zeffirelli had wanted to do with Maria two years earlier. She was still with Onassis then, and although she didn't believe opera should be filmed, she wanted to work, to be a bit more independent. Anyway, Franco pushed and pushed. He asked her for funds. He said, 'I can't go on unless I sign with the distributor and get an advance, but for that I need money to pay for the preparatory work, the designers and so on.' But Maria told Zeffirelli that she wouldn't sign unless she could see some plans, some designs, something more tangible. Apparently, Aristo asked Maria how much Franco needed so as to get things going. Franco asked for thirty thousand dollars, which, at that time, was a lot of money. Aristo advanced the money unofficially and Maria made this clear to Franco. She said, 'Aristo is putting up the money, but I am responsible for this sum. So the minute you sign the contract, you have to give this money back.' But the project was unwieldy, everything was upside down," Rossellini said, refilling my wine glass. "And, seeing how things were going after a while, Maria decided not to do the film.

"From that day, Zeffirelli refused to give the money back. He said, 'Onassis is rich enough, he can afford it.' This is gospel truth! Can you believe it? He didn't pay! You can imagine how livid Maria was, and Onassis started to say, 'You see these friends of yours, these movie people; they are this and that and the other.' After all that, I don't know how she got the confidence to agree to do *Medea*.

"With an artist like Maria, you have to go slowly, be very very patient. That's why I had to wait so long for her to make up her mind."

Listening to Franco, my thoughts turned back to the summer of 1969, to Turkey and Grado. Knowing so much more about Maria now, I realize I had been oblivious to the magnitude of her insecurities. It is also clear to me how much courage it took for her to get through those months and I understand the sporadic behavior pattern that, at the time, mystified me. One moment she was warm and relied on my friendship; then, without warning, she would withdraw in an impenetrable reserve.

The stand-in's accident in the fire brought Maria and me closer.

We were two weeks into the shoot when that accident occurred. The understudy's burns were too serious for her to resume work. At such short notice it was difficult to find a suitable substitute, especially one willing to work in Turkey in midsummer. Pasolini and Rossellini decided to find someone locally, but the solution was not as easy as it had seemed at first. The possible candidates were the seamstress, the hairdresser and the costume assistant. But the seamstress was endowed with an overabundant pasta figure, the hairdresser was pocket-sized and the assistant to the costume designer was too busy to be spared. As I passed by the makeshift production office on my way to see Maria, I felt Pasolini's and Rossellini's eyes glued on me. Before I could protest, I found myself wearing a costume identical to Maria's and a very tight black wig that kept sliding back to reveal my fuzzy blond hair. From then on, I stood in for Maria whenever the scenes were far away enough for me not to be recognized. Hiking up those Turkish hills under the noonday sun is something I won't easily forget.

After a few weeks on location, when Maria and I (as twin Medeas endlessly waiting for the cameras) had gotten to know each other well, she admitted to me that she had been terrified of doing the *Medea* film. She said that before making up her mind, she had consulted many of her friends as well as Joëlle de Gravelaine, a respected Parisian astrologer.

During those first weeks in Turkey, what surprised everyone, aside from Maria's professionalism, was her *entente* with Pasolini. The predicted personality clash between Callas, the demanding prima donna, and Pasolini, the introverted poet, never took place. Their affinity was perfect on and off the set.

"I feel I've always known her," said Pasolini. "It's as if we'd been to school together."

They'd spend hours in conversation or sit silently, feeling the comfort of each other's presence. Something deeply metaphysical bound these two unlikely friends, and as time passed, Maria and Pier Paolo fell into a platonic love.

Pier Paolo gave Maria a ring: an ancient bronze coin set in silver. On one side, there were the worn profiles of a man and a woman and on the other, a victorious warrior. Maria ran over to show it to me between takes.

"Do you think this means he is in love with me?" she asked, childlike with excitement. "The other day he told me that, besides his mother, I am the only woman he has ever loved. He even said that if he could feel desire for a woman, it would be me. I think I can help him, Nadia, I can save him from self-destruction."

I remember Pasolini as a small, well-proportioned man with a muscular body that moved with the firm precision of a mountain climber's. He had a handsome, deeply lined Tartarlike face with sunken eyes and high cheekbones. Pier Paolo certainly was not a substitute for Aristo, but Maria's need for romantic illusion made her cling to him. She knew this could only be a friendship, but at times she purposely avoided facing that truth. When Maria, Arthur Coppotelli, the dialogue director, and I witnessed young peasant boys coming out of a rock cavern pulling up their trousers and counting the coins, followed by Pier Paolo, Maria pretended not to notice. On another occasion, she took her glasses off while Pier Paolo's roving eyes followed a thirteen-year-old waiter who was serving us dinner.

As a bystander, I still haven't figured out where Maria's and Pier Paolo's meeting ground was. I know she didn't share his interest in politics and she lectured him about being a member of the Communist party. She found most of his film work erotically self-indulgent and only read his poetry once she got to like him. Was she fascinated by his intellect or did she see herself as the woman whose mission it was to "save" him?

When I asked Giuseppe Gentile, the young athlete Pasolini had cast as Jason, what his reaction had been to Maria's relationship with Pasolini, Gentile surprised me by admitting that he had been slightly jealous of it.

"Since Maria and I had established such a pleasant rapport, I felt as if Pasolini was intruding on our friendship. But I kept my feelings to myself," the still-handsome, six-foot Jason told me during our meeting fifteen years later. "Maria and I got on very well. Our conversations were about everyday things. I spoke to her as I would to any woman. She was easy, natural, but I was aware that under her simplicity there existed artistic power and intuition. We often compared our training, the endless repetition artists and athletes submit to for the sake of perfection: the breathing, the self-discipline.

"Did I ever tell you about shooting the scene of the 'kiss'? For me, it's the scene of the film which remains most vivid in my mind. It happened during the second week of shooting. You may remember Pier Paolo had chased everyone away except the cameraman. It was a difficult scene for both of us because, somehow, our friendship didn't leave room for such intimacy. Anyway, just as Jason was supposed to kiss Medea, Maria would turn her head to one side and I to the other. Only then did I realize that Maria was shy and that she'd been as nervous about that scene as I had, if not more so. Although Pasolini took into consideration that this was our first film experience, he was a bit put out with both of us. He'd become used to Maria doing scenes in a couple of takes."

Dialogue in the film was sparse. Pasolini felt Maria's expressions and movements projected Medea more convincingly than words. Medea's static silence was very moving at times, but to me it was somewhat eerie to watch Maria, the "voice of the twentieth century," as Pasolini's silent *Medea*. A recorded tape exists of Maria as Medea singing a lullaby, as she rocks her children to sleep before killing them, but it wasn't used in the film. After seeing the rushes (with the soundtrack) Maria asked Pasolini to omit the lullaby. Everyone was very disappointed. The lullaby added a lot to the scene; it was gentle and beautiful. I only understood Maria's reasoning years later, when speaking with Sergio Segalini. "Callas," he said, "wanted to prove herself as a complete actress, not as a has-been singer. I also think she wanted to leave room for a planned comeback in a *Traviata,* to be directed by Visconti, at the Paris Opéra in 1970."

When word got around the valley that the great Callas was in their midst, the mayors of Goreme, Urgup and Nev-shehir insisted on paying their respects to the Diva. As her spokeswoman I explained to them that Madame Callas appreciated their courtesy, but her film schedule left little time for socializing. She asked to be excused: she had to save her energy for her work.

The mayors' obsessive insistence was augmented by the national press, who accused Callas of insulting the dignitaries of the region who'd offered her hospitality. Reluctantly, she accepted their visits and gifts: antique kilims, precious embroideries, a silver box, an antique jug. . . . The thick-whiskered gift bearers received an autographed picture of Callas and went off happy.

"There's something fishy behind all this, believe me!" Maria warned us.

But the Turks weren't the only ones who made demands on Maria's free time. There were also the foreign correspondents and television networks. While Matteo Spinola's office in Rome handpicked those who would interview Callas, I acted as a buffer once they arrived on location. Then of course, there were plenty of nonaccredited hangers-on who made their unexpected appearance around the set and spent hours waiting for Maria to come out of her hotel. They played cards and drank beer in the shaded parking lot or slept in their cars to the exotic lament of Turkish music.

One morning, I was leaving the hotel, dressed in my Medea costume, black wig and dark glasses, to rehearse a stand-in scene for Maria, when I was met by the group of "loitering journalists." *Click, click* went the cameras, and questions flew at me from all sides.

"Why did you choose to impersonate a woman who kills her children for the sake of teaching her lover a lesson?" one of them asked. I was trying to explain the case of mistaken identity when I heard Maria's voice behind me. We were wearing identical Medea costumes.

"Because *I am* Medea. I hate compromise. I like clarity in people and situations. Now please move on, and let me get to work."

Another member of the press, a photographer, somehow managed to talk or bribe his way into the Club Méditerranée Hotel, supposedly reserved solely for us. He ended up in the only vacant room, which happened to be the one next to mine. His first attempt to get into Maria's room failed, so he tried a less conventional route. When I opened my terrace door to get some night air, I found him clinging to the iron railing, suspended in midair, desperately trying to extract his foot from the ledge of Maria's bathroom window. I called the manager and I made a terrible scene. The next day, the local newspaper carried photographs of the dark Tigress Medea, and the blond Tigress who did her public relations.

Among the chosen reporters who had come to interview Callas in Turkey—from NBC, RAI, *Life* and *Look*—the one that stands out in my mind is the *Life* correspondent, to whom Maria seemed allergic. She did everything to avoid the woman.

"Keep that journalist away from me," she told me, "or I'll throttle her."

The woman had a piercing voice that she used overtime. The minute Maria finished a scene and sat down, guess who would come lurking from behind the hummocks in her white knee socks, khaki shorts and tropical helmet? Her insistence drove Maria mad, but Franco, Matteo and I convinced her that she should do the interview. We felt the article would be good exposure for Maria in America. Months later, out of the blue, Maria said, "I told you that woman was a waste of time!" It's true. The interview Maria finally gave her was never published in *Life*.

The only diversion on our day off was the bazaar in Nevshehir. Inhabited since prehistoric times, renowned for its rock-carved churches and dominated by the twelfth-century Seljuk citadel, this remote village did not have much to offer those in search of entertainment or tourist-type mementos. Besides the occasional kilim, the market provided Turkish muslin scarves, ornate shish-kebab skewers and the luscious gummy *lokum*, better known as Turkish delight. As we stopped to buy some *lokum*, a gypsy in brightly colored tatters rushed up to Maria and grabbed her hand. She looked at Maria's palm, then solemnly into her eyes, speaking Turkish all the while. Our local driver gestured the gypsy away. He pulled and shouted at her, but she wouldn't let go of Maria's hand.

"Leave her," Maria told the driver, who spoke some English. "I'd like to have my fortune read and you can translate. All right?" She nodded to the gypsy and smiled. The gypsy spoke, but the driver remained silent.

"What is she saying?" Maria asked.

"She is no good, madame. She knows nothing."

After a lot of prodding from Maria, the driver stammered

out, "She says you are going to die young, madame. But you will not suffer."

The color drained from Maria's face. For a moment she leaned against the candy stall. That evening at dinner she spoke at length of the power of the occult. She was distant, preoccupied. Knowing how impressionable she was, I worried about her.

The morning following our Nevshehir outing, I was jolted out of my sleep by a horrendously loud, tinny noise. In my stupor, I grabbed my pillow and was swinging it around the room trying to kill the unwelcome sound when I heard a stifled giggle behind the door. I opened it to find Maria and Bruna doubled up with laughter. Like Maria, I am a late riser, so at the market she had bought me a gigantic tin clock with a hammer alarm. Maria's silly prank relieved me, and convinced me she'd forgotten about the gypsy.

Our farewell to Turkey was not what we had expected. At the Ankara airport, our luggage was searched. When customs found the kilims and other antiques given by the mayors of the Anatolian villages, they confiscated them. Turkish antiquities, they said, could not leave the country. The gestures had been made, and now all the gifts were being returned to the owners. Maria's sense of righteousness was aroused. She was annoyed at having been duped. However, she managed a small personal victory. Pasolini had given her an antique sculpture he had bought at Uchisar. Not knowing how or where to pack the cumbersome object, she had put it at the bottom of the *"Wagon-Lit"* with Pixie and Djedda sitting on top of it. When a customs officer asked if he could look in the bag, Maria graciously agreed. "Of course," she said, "please do." He put his hand on the *"Wagon-Lit"* and it was instantly met by two growling poodles. When he made a second try,

Pixie's sharp teeth snapped shut on one of his pudgy fingers. We were beckoned to proceed to the aircraft. We had cleared customs.

A few days later, the international press reported they had been informed by Turkish authorities that Maria Callas had tried to export antiques worth $70,000. The Turkish authorities maintained that these "national treasures" would be destined to various museums in their country. Maria's prophecy had proved correct.

The heat in the north of Italy, where we were shooting next, was, unlike Turkey, humidly debilitating and the island near Grado was infested with mosquitoes. Despite the comforts of civilization, our stay in Grado proved harder than the Cappadocian experience.

As Maria's mastery of film acting developed, Pasolini added words to Medea's silent image. The dialogue didn't follow the Euripides *Medea* or the Apollonius Rhodius poem. Instead, Pasolini wanted his Medea detached from time and history so as to give him the freedom to invent costumes, settings and lines. His Medea was a sorceress-priestess of savage rituals brought out of the most remote past.

But the absence of a script confused Maria. "It wasn't easy for her," Franco Rossellini pointed out. "She was used to having the music and the libretto. Our *Medea* script was nonexistent. It was simply conversations and impressions Pier Paolo and I recorded while we were looking for locations."

Arthur Coppotelli agrees that the constant changes became a real problem for Maria. "She couldn't handle it," he says. "She couldn't remember dialogue. As we didn't use direct sound, I often hid behind her voluminous costume, shouting lines. Although English was not really her language, she'd also call me late at night to question the literary quality of the dialogue. She felt it should be more Shakespearean."

Every evening in her hotel suite, and driving to the set in the morning, she and I went over her part. I cued Maria, changing roles from Creon to Jason to the nurse as the script required. She was sometimes very frustrated. "I just cannot memorize lines without music. That's all there is to it, Nadia."

Once in front of the camera, she often muddled or changed things. Finally, it didn't matter that much, as her expressions and gestures were perfectly in character, and when the film was dubbed into Italian, Maria's and Arthur's efforts proved to be more than adequate.

To save Maria's energy, Pasolini asked me to stand in for her in a scene in which Medea is supposed to run back and forth in a trancelike state across the wasteland. The scene was shot from a considerable distance, and there was no dialogue, but when Maria found out that I was going to substitute for her in this scene, she had a fit. She insisted on doing it herself.

She was particularly tired that day. The five pounds of ceremonial jewelry she had worn throughout the film had exhausted her. In addition, her blood pressure was very low and she was suffering from a minor infection. She went through the scene a couple of times. Since Pier Paolo was satisfied with what he'd shot, he shouted, "Stop, Maria. *Va bene così. Grazie.*" Maria couldn't hear him, so she went on. Seeing that she was engrossed in the part, Pasolini kept the cameras rolling. She was doing a great job. She rushed forward, stopped, started off again, swayed, staggered, brought her hands to her face and fell. A moment passed, but Maria still lay motionless on the ground. She had fainted. A worried Pasolini and the entire crew rushed to her side.

The film proceeded according to schedule and we moved on to Rome to finish the last scenes in the studios of Cinecittà. A visible change had taken place in Maria since I'd met her in Rome four months earlier. She was now radiant and full of joie de vivre. She told everyone she loved her new career, wanted to do more films and she hated to see the *Medea* experience come to an end. One day she said, "We only have a few weeks left. Can I ask you to be *tanto cara* and help me pick out a present for the crew and staff? I hear it is customary for the star to give a souvenir at the end of the film. I don't feel like trailing in the stores and having people stare at me. And besides, you know Rome like your pocket. Would you do that for me, *cara?*"

Every day I arrived with a new suggestion and a price list, but Maria was always undecided. After a week of this unproductive exercise, I realized she had no intention of untying her purse strings. In fact, little by little, she dropped the subject and no one received the anticipated Callas token.

As soon as the press found out Maria was back at the Grand Hotel in Rome (again pampered by Rusconi), she was under siege. They all wanted to interview her, but she refused. Because of my years of public relations work in Rome, I knew most of the journalists who called, and when they realized that I was working with Callas, I was in trouble. They were terribly insistent. I remember one in particular, Adele Cambria, who tried to woo Maria with chocolates, flowers and telephone calls. But her attentions only exasperated Maria. Since a number of people had mistaken us for one another on the phone, Maria decided that I should pretend to be the diva next time Adele called. Maria briefed me, and we rehearsed the answers to Adele's written questionnaire. When Adele called, I was doing beautifully, until Maria sat herself opposite me, laughing, egging me on and making faces. I got such a fit of giggles that I broke down and admitted our silly scheme to Adele. Although she has a good sense of humor, Adele had put too much effort into getting the Callas interview to be amused. Maria granted her the interview as an apology.

As for the more famous side of Maria, her temper, she lost it only once with me during the time we worked together.

The driver, who always called for me before picking Maria up at the Grand Hotel and proceeding out to Cinecittà, was stuck in the usual Roman traffic jam. We were ten minutes late. As we approached the Grand, I could see Maria, her loose hair bobbing up and down as she paced the sidewalk like a panther in captivity. Her face was pale and set. Silent Bruna kept her distance from Maria and anxiously scrutinized every passing car.

Maria leapt into the car without saying good-morning. I started my speech of excuses but she turned on me. "There are no excuses, Nadia. You are late. I'm not interested why. You are either professional or you are not. If there is traffic, you leave an hour earlier." I sank into my corner of the seat and was trying to contain my hurt and anger when I heard Maria mention shoes. "I saw the most beautiful evening shoes in a shop on Via Condotti," she was saying in a cheerful voice. The storm had blown over. Her temper cooled as quickly as it flared.

After shooting had been completed, Maria stayed on to see the rushes. We saw them together, and as she watched herself on the screen, she commented on her performance. *"Oh, che brava la Callas!"* or *"Bella la Callas"* or "No. Not so good here." She spoke of herself as if she were watching someone totally unknown. At a certain moment, she turned in the darkened theater and looked up at the projection booth. "You see the two edges of that beam of light, Nadia? Maria the person and Callas the performer are like those two edges of light. But it is what that light projects on the screen that we really see. And even that is only an image."

14

Rome with Maria

After three months away from home, I had expected Maria to rush back to Paris the minute she'd finished her role in *Medea*. But every week, she prolonged her stay by another few days. "I'm enjoying myself," she announced, "and Rome is beautiful in the autumn. Paris can wait."

Since she no longer had to rise at dawn, she slipped back into her old nocturnal schedule. She stayed up half the night and then slept until one the following day. She reappeared just in time to join Pier Paolo, Franco or myself for a late lunch. It wasn't uncommon to find Pier Paolo and Maria having long, relaxed meals in some picturesque trattoria in old Rome or at the Escargot on the Appia Antica, which was one of Maria's favorite restaurants.

Maria had plenty of acquaintances in Rome's music and movie circles apart from the three of us, but she rarely made the effort to contact them. A number of American stars, some of whom she knew, were living and working in Rome in the late sixties. Elizabeth Taylor, Audrey Hepburn, Burt Lancaster, Carroll Baker and Clint Eastwood, for example, had all exchanged a Hollywood in crisis (and its artificial luster) for co-production work in the Italian movie capital, which was enjoying an era of elegance and good living. When Pier Paolo and Franco got tied up with the editing of *Medea,* I urged Maria to call some of these people, as I too needed time to organize my office and follow up on my future P.R. accounts, but she wouldn't listen. She insisted she preferred to be with me and my friends. "I like the group you've introduced me to and the stylish informality with which you live," she announced. "Anyway, the music and cinema people are part of my other life. I can see them anytime. I'm not in the mood for them now."

Maria's remark about the "stylish informality" of my life always made me smile. I lived in the heart of the city, between the Parliament and Piazza Navona, but that was before it was chic to have an apartment in the old town. Going home meant climbing five poorly kept flights past the apartments of modest Romans whose families had lived and died in the same building for at least three generations.

When I first moved in, doors opened a crack every time I went in or out. Curious eyes examined the mad *straniera* with suspicion—the "foreigner" who had *chosen* to live in an old building without an elevator. When I carried luggage up the five flights after a long trip or forgot to buy milk, I sometimes thought they were right to wonder about me. But I got used to the exercise, and the hike up the 102 steps was well worth it. The apartment was full of charm and sunshine, and the view from my terrace overlooking the church steeples and rooftops of Rome was something I marveled at every day.

The first time Maria visited me, her reaction was not unlike that of many other friends. Without a word, she went straight into the living room and sat down. When she'd recovered enough to speak, she whispered, "How do you get anyone to visit you? Those who make it up here more than once must be true friends. Do you keep an oxygen mask for the older generation?" Then she looked around and beamed. "What an adorable place! This is the perfect love nest to hide in. I think I'll make it up here again."

She returned often, for small dinners on the terrace with my friends. Sometimes someone would play the guitar or sing, and if Maria felt like it she joined in. She liked the odd mixture of nationalities and interests. She felt comfortable with the set designer and actors I'd worked with in Spoleto, with the diplomats and aristocrats that were part of my Roman life, and the lawyers, doctors and professor who were either married to Italians or were there on sabbaticals. I owe this hodge-podge style of entertaining to my parents, who throughout their life as diplomats were known for their parties. They threw the most unexpected and diverse people together and, believe me, it worked 99 percent of the time.

So I gamely gave a couple of cocktail parties to distract Maria and introduced her to people whom I hoped she might like to spend some of her leisure time with—while I worked. One evening, the much acclaimed hodgepodge system went awry. A Roman *nobil donna,* famous for her beauty, got into an argument with Maria. She took it upon herself to tell Maria she had no business being in the movies. "You should stick to singing," she said, only half-jesting. "You are selfish. Think of those, like myself, who have spent our good money to listen to you for years!" The remark didn't go over at all well with Maria, and for a moment I had visions of the Roman lady being pushed off the terrace. To save the evening from disaster,

I quickly exchanged the beauty for a dashing Austrian diplomat. The following day, Maria sent me a huge bouquet to thank me for the party. She regretted the incident caused by the arrogant woman, whom she added, "looked rather faded, didn't you think?"

But aside from the aforementioned lady, Maria was totally at ease with my friends, perhaps too much so. I remember when my good friend Franco Crespi, a professor in sociology, joined us for dinner one evening, her lightheartedness went a bit far. Franco was a dedicated Callas admirer and he had very much looked forward to meeting her. I seated them opposite each other, and they were engrossed in a conversation about opera when Maria suddenly pointed at Franco. "You know who he reminds me of?" she said, interrupting him. "I've got it! I've been trying to figure it out all evening. Dracula! Look at the way his teeth stick out on either side. Just like Dracula." I was long familiar with Maria's lack of tact, but my friends were a bit surprised.

In the country or at the seaside near Rome, Maria enjoyed finding out-of-the-way restaurants where she was seldom recognized. On these outings she usually wore a sweater and slacks, pulled her hair back in a ponytail and didn't bother with makeup. There was a place near the village of Sacrofano that she loved. The three wooden tables and benches under a trellis could hardly be called a restaurant, but the cackling guinea hens running through the vegetable garden and the toffee-colored mongrel endeared the place to Maria. What's more, the pasta and wine were homemade and the food was cooked over a crackling wood stove.

Marco and Andreana Patriarca first took us there. We lunched with Ferruccio Nuzzo, a bushy-haired poet-journalist-*cum*-actor who had played St. Matthew in Pasolini's *Gospel According to St. Matthew,* and Aldo Volpi, a colleague of Marco's. Of all my friends, Maria had a special fondness for Marco. She fell under the spell of the young lawyer's poetic nature and didn't object to his good looks either. They became close friends and often saw each other in Rome and Paris. She enjoyed Marco's unpretentious charm, his knowledge of music, and knew he liked her for what, not who, she was. Maria admitted to me, with a slight blush, that her interest in Marco went beyond his artistic and cerebral gifts.

"I wouldn't mind having a little fling with him," she said coyly, "but of course it's out of the question. There is 'La Andreana.' " "La Andreana" is Marco's beautiful wife, whom Maria admired and envied. In her eyes, Andreana had everything she lacked: a home, a loving husband, children and a title.

To escape hotel life, Maria spent many afternoons sunbathing or reading magazines on my terrace. We also went to the movies and shopped quite a bit. The latter was agony! I loathe shopping under any circumstances, unless I know exactly where I'm going and what I want. But with Maria it was excruciating. It was a true act of friendship on my part. Every shop we went into, Maria looked, touched, made loud remarks about the merchandise but didn't buy, and when everyone had recognized her, swept out grandly. Neither the attention lavished on her by the salesgirls nor the looks of the curious who pointed and whispered seemed to bother her. But I was miserable!

One clear autumn day, I picked up Maria in my tiny Fiat 500 and we headed for Villa Borghese, Rome's Central Park. Rusconi had asked the chef of the Grand to prepare a picnic for us. What a picnic! His gourmet meal was made even more special by the perfect weather. The park was bustling with activity in a last euphoric moment of outdoor living before the arrival of winter: children played and watched the Punch and Judy show; dogs tugged at their leashes; *carabinieri* bounced by on horseback. Lovers were intent on loving. A balloon vendor passed by.

"How about a balloon?" Maria asked.

"Why not?" I said.

Maria paid the man, and his glum expression was instantly changed into a joyous one. She handed me twenty-five balloons. The entire lot!

"I'll race you," said Maria. "I dare you! Give me a few balloons."

We divided the balloons and ran through the park like children on their last day of school, Maria's auburn mane racing after her in the wind. When we stopped to catch our breath, Maria said, "I have an idea! Why don't we go and have tea with Marco—at his office."

Curled up in my minuscule car, we made our way to Marco's law office on Via Bruxelles. Since the car was barely large enough for the two of us, Maria held the balloons out the window. Their cheerful colors totally obstructed my rear window.

We heard a siren, but Maria assured me it was not for us. "I can't see anyone," she said squinting. "Just drive on, Nadia."

A young policeman on a motorcycle signaled me to stop. He looked seventeen but might have been twenty-two. With a grave face, which I think he felt gave credibility to his status, he asked for my papers. I handed him my U.S. and French licenses, which he could not make head or tail of. Not wanting to lose face, he turned his attention to Maria. She too played dumb and answered in English, but after a few phrases unconsciously slipped into Italian.

The policeman was reassured; his dignity had been restored.

"Your papers, please, signora . . . and kindly tell your foreign friend to follow me to the police station."

Maria flashed her diva smile and with a doe-eyed look said very gently, "You wouldn't do that to Maria Callas, would you?"

"Yeah, sure, Maria Callas," said the young man. "I've heard that line before. Your papers, signora."

"You mean you don't believe me?" Maria replied with innocence.

"Listen, signora, if you are Maria Callas"—the impatient young officer reached through the open window for Maria's passport—"I'm Toto!" (a well-known Italian comic). He seemed visibly proud of his presence of mind. He opened the passport. His cheer vanished and his year-round Mediterranean tan went ashen. He returned the document without a word, stopped the oncoming traffic and waved us through a red light.

Marco's office was on the third floor. We tried to get into the elevator with the balloons, but they rebelled. For every eight we squeezed in, four popped out. Limp with laughter, we headed for the stairs. We'd reached the second landing when Maria froze. There was a look of disbelief in her eyes as she pointed to the nameplate on the door. It read *Giulietta Simionato*.

"*Dìo mìo*, I'm dished if she comes out now. She'll never understand this Callas. Come on, hurry!" Maria slipped out of her shoes and ran up the next flight, whispering as she went.

"We've come to have tea with you," Maria announced as Marco opened the door. He couldn't believe his eyes. "They are mad, quite mad," he repeated. "It's midafternoon and this is an office, not a tearoom. Where do you expect me to get cups from?" I reminded him, in case he'd forgotten, that his grandmother lived on the floor above. He sent his bewildered secretary for the tea and cakes.

Our tea party was in full swing when the doorbell rang. The secretary announced a very important client. "Disappear, please disappear!" Marco pleaded, pointing to the bathroom and closet doors. We scurried around for our balloons, which had floated to the ceiling. Unable to reach a couple, Maria got up on a chair just as the client came in. Marco went crimson. I'd never seen him lose his composure before. He gingerly attempted the introductions.

"This is . . . ah . . . Do you know . . . ah . . . Maria Callas and . . . her . . . my friend. . . ." We greeted the baffled gentleman politely, thanked Marco for a wonderful afternoon and left.

When I spoke with Marco recently, he said, "It was behind those balloons that I first saw the real face of Maria Callas. The way I will always remember her: laughing, childish, happy. . . . Two years after that, I was staying in a scruffy little hotel in Paris when a chauffeur-driven BMW delivered a bunch of colored balloons in memory of that afternoon."

Maria's return to Paris was not easy. After a period of productivity and a carefree stay in Rome she now had to face the void she had left behind. She called frequently to say how much she missed Rome and her new friends. "I'm already bored with the snobbishness of the grand Parisians. I long to see you. When are you coming? I want to talk to you about helping me with my autobiography." Ten days later, she called and repeated the question with greater urgency.

I had intended to visit my brother John and his family in Paris that autumn, so I decided to take a holiday and combine the two visits.

Maria and I saw each other daily during my stay, but still, when I got back to my brother's house, she might call two or three times "just to say hello"—calls that lasted anywhere from fifteen minutes to an hour. In fact, my nephews and nieces, who had been very excited that their aunt should receive calls from such a celebrity, soon got quite bored with it all. After the tenth call, they no longer came to my room to tell me I was wanted on the phone. Instead they shouted from the library, "It's for you! It's that 'chanteuse' friend of yours again!" When I told Maria how my eleven-year-old niece referred to her, she laughed and then said with genuine surprise, "But you mean to tell me she doesn't know who Maria Callas is?"

Over luncheons, teas and walks, Maria went on endlessly about Onassis and her work in the *Medea* film. She mentioned she'd had other film offers but didn't feel any of them were suited to her. Joseph Losey had shown an interest in working with her and that gave her confidence. She liked Losey but was unsure about the part he'd offered her. "Should I do the part of an aging figure in the entertainment world making a comeback? What do you think, Nadia? No, there is still time for that. I'm not *da buttar' via* [to be discarded] yet, am I?"

Such soul-searching was about as close as we ever got to any work on an autobiography. This was fine with me at the time, but I did wonder why, right then, she had become so obsessed with recruiting my help on the project. Now I see that, quite simply, she needed someone to talk to. Someone to whom she could replay her memories. She lacked a single intimate sounding board and that was a major problem when she considered writing her autobiography or even rethinking her life. I discovered later that I was not the only one she had asked for help on her "project." When we spoke of working on her book together, she would ask, "When can we start?

How much time can you spend with me? Why don't you rent your apartment and move to Paris for six months? We'll have a wonderful time together." I told her I would love to do it but there were practical details such as my work in Rome, survival in Paris, air fare and so on to be worked out. We planned and discussed, but when it came to the financial aspect of the project, the meeting was adjourned, the project postponed and off we went to the movies.

Maria loved thrillers and westerns. One time I remember she chose two new movies she wanted to see: *Easy Rider* and *Midnight Cowboy*. No amount of insistence on my part would persuade her that they were not westerns. We sat through the roar of motorcycles in *Easy Rider,* but she was so stubborn that she was unwilling to leave. "You'll see, Nadia, it will change, this is just a warm-up," she assured me. *Midnight Cowboy* was an even bigger failure. It shocked and confused her. She babbled throughout the film and asked questions in a loud voice while the spectators around us whispered their annoyance and asked for silence. This was an experience many of her friends endured at the movies with her. François Valéry and I compared notes.

"I frequently accompanied her to the movies," François recalled, "or on shopping trips in her neighborhood to fill the monotony of her afternoons. We once went to see a takeoff on a detective story which Maria, who sometimes lacked humor, took seriously. Fully immersed in the film, she participated by commenting aloud, crying out and sighing. At intermission she needed to replenish her energies: 'François,' she said, 'would you get me a Toblerone?' 'Of course, Maria.' A little while later, 'Could I also have an Eskimo?' 'Absolutely, Maria.' At the end of the film, I asked her if she had any preference as to where we should dine. 'Well, if you don't mind too much, I'd love to see the de Sica film playing next door.'

MARIA

"We arrived before the film began, during the commercials. 'Do you mind if I have an ice cream cone? They are better than the Eskimos.' 'Oh, please do!' I answered, wanting to be polite. At one in the morning, after the show was over, I repeated my question: 'Where shall we go for a bite?' 'Well, I'm not really hungry,' Maria answered, 'but if you'd like, you can come up to my place for an Alka-Seltzer!' "

Valéry remembers another occasion, a shopping outing at Jones, an elegant shop on the corner of Avenue Victor Hugo and the street that bears the name of his father, poet Paul Valéry. "She picked up the most useless objects," he told me, "looked at the price tags, then proceeded to bargain with the salesgirl, whom she knew. 'What kind of a discount can you give me?' Maria asked. Her oriental 'souk' mentality had surfaced, surprisingly out of place in the somewhat grand atmosphere. The manager offered us an orange juice. It was a modest gesture but a reminder of her former 'royal status.' 'François, isn't this the best juice you've ever tasted?' she said. She was touched by the attention, which perhaps, for a moment, made her feel less alone."

Those who sensed Maria's aloneness put up with her little idiosyncrasies. Just to go for a walk along the Paris boulevards with Maria was an exercise in patience. Her idea of a brisk, constitutional walk was to stop in front of every window display, no matter whether it was clothes, jewelry or vegetables, and if it happened to be the end of the month, she checked all the newspaper kiosks along the boulevard for the arrival of *Astro* magazine, to see what the following month held for Sagittarians. She was also keen on numerology. I think that, like her fellow countryman Pythagoras, she believed that "the world is built upon the power of numbers." According to her, most of the good things in her life had happened on dates that included her lucky numbers, three, six and nine.

For me, our luncheons and teas in her small salon on Avenue Georges Mandel will always be among my warmest memories of Maria. We sat on the carpeted floor, leaning against the couch, our feet under the coffee table, and enjoyed a relaxed lunch while we gossiped about the past and the future.

The past usually brought up the anger against her mother or Onassis. Rarely did she mention Meneghini, or touch on the glory of her career. She was preoccupied with the future. Onassis had let her know that he wanted to return to her. Whenever he called, she refused to speak with him. When he arrived on her doorstep laden with flowers, the servants had strict orders not to let him in. But Onassis, not being used to losing, continued his tactics of slow persuasion. "What would I do with that *old* man?" she said with disdain. "I don't want any part of him. I'm doing fine on my own. The last time he was in town he stood in the garden whistling and throwing stones at my windows. But I wouldn't let him in. I'm through with him."

As we waited for lunch one afternoon, Maria started lecturing me about the mismanagement of my life. "You shouldn't be working. You should find a rich man—a decent man, mind you—but rich, who will take care of you and give you the security you need. Time goes by very quickly, dear Nadia, and you are going to get stuck without a bean in your old age."

"Look who's talking," interrupted Bruna's high-pitched voice. She had come in unnoticed, our luncheon tray poised in midair. "Signora, you of all people, you who spent eight years with one of the richest men in the world, and what do you have to show for it? A car, a pair of earrings or two, and half a boat. Remember, you had to pay for the other half yourself."

"Well, that's true," Maria said weakly, "I haven't done too well, but there is no reason why my friends can't do better. Nadia must find someone who will give her love, a house, jewelry, security, the works." She turned and looked at me for a moment and added, "You are hopeless, you'll never do it. You are like me, you don't know how to make compromises; but learn, girl, learn before it's too late!"

She had worldly possessions on her mind that afternoon. As soon as Bruna left the room, she launched into a soliloquy on her financial situation. "I don't have a great deal, Meneghini took care of that, but I can get by comfortably." I looked around the room at the beautiful decor of Maria's Parisian apartment, its antique furniture, exquisite carpets and collector's porcelain. "Of course," she continued, "I have my mother and sister to take care of every month, that's a duty. But as I told you before, they are not going to get a penny out of me when I am gone, not a penny. They've had more than their share. When I'm gone," Maria repeated, "I don't want them or my ex-husband to get anything. I mean it. *Nothing*."

"Since you feel so strongly about it, Maria, and have no heirs, I hope you've made all this clear in your will."

"Oh, yes, and I've taken care of *la cara* Bruna and faithful Ferruccio. They deserve it. They've been with me for years and have stood by me through thick and thin. The rest I've put into a scholarship foundation to help promising young singers . . . and of course, I've remembered my friends."

It was the end of October, and to the distinct relief of my family, my visit was coming to a close. Maria's frequent phone calls, especially those after midnight, were disrupting the household. By the twenty-third, "la chanteuse's" agitation had reached its peak and the telephone calls were incessant.

"He's just phoned again, from New York. What could I do . . . I spoke with him. He wants to see me. Do you think I should?" Needless to say, she never needed to mention who "he" was.

Half an hour hadn't gone by before her next call. "When are you going back to Rome, Nadia? Can I come with you? I've got to get out of this city and find a place where he can't reach me. Could I hide in your apartment?" I could tell by her high-pitched tone that she was frenzied.

"Fine, Maria, come to Rome. You can stay with me for as long as you like. Get Bruna to pack for you while I take care of the reservations."

I changed my flight, broke my dinner date and warned the maid in Rome that we would arrive the following day.

Later that afternoon, I was given the current update on the Onassis situation.

"He's on his way to Paris. He wants to take me to Maxim's for dinner. What do I do now?" she said in a panic. "He says he'll find me wherever I go and will plague me until I give in. I can't believe he's doing this to me. What's wrong with men? They leave you, wrench your heart open and expect to be welcomed back with a brass band!"

But it was obvious she was dying to see him. After a long discussion, we concluded she should see him as soon as possible and rid herself of her growing anguish, but I insisted the meeting take place on her terms.

"Why don't you give a small dinner at your house?" I suggested. "You need to be surrounded by friends who will protect you and an ambience you feel comfortable in. You can't go to Maxim's! He's just publicity-crazy and wants the whole world to know that he's won you back."

"You are right," Maria agreed, "I couldn't go through that. It would kill me. I'll give a dinner at home, but promise you'll stay and help me out. I'm terrified. Maybe you and I can escape to Rome together after this is all over."

The gathering was limited to a handful of friends who had shared the euphoric Onassis-Callas years as well as their arguments and breakup. At the outset they had been "his" friends, but his cruel behavior had alienated them and their presence that evening was a sign of solidarity to "her." The guests were Hélène Rochas, Kim d'Astainville, Francesco Chiarini, François Valéry and Maria's dearest friend in Paris, Maggie van Zuylen.

I was the only one present who didn't know Onassis. Obviously, I was not well disposed toward him either.

Maria looked lovely in a white-and-gold caftan. Tense with anticipation, she had a glow I had seen only when she was in front of the camera. Her friends arrived punctually and did their best to minimize the importance of the evening so as to ease Maria's anxiety, although we all shared it. But she couldn't sit still. She fidgeted, ruined the flowers by rearranging them, cuddled the dogs and talked nonstop.

The conversation over drinks was about the new theater and opera season in Paris. The city's activities in arts made Rome look very provincial in comparison. I listened with interest while I watched Maria. She smiled and answered questions, but I knew she was totally absent. Half an hour passed. It was becoming apparent that Maria's anxiety was getting to all of us. Pauses grew longer and there were glances at the clock.

At the sound of the doorbell, everyone fell silent. Ferruccio, in livery and white gloves, opened the door of the *grand salon*. A short, stocky man in an ill-fitting double-breasted suit and red tie walked over to Maria and embraced her. She pulled away nervously and said, "Ferruccio, please get Monsieur a drink," and, turning back to him, she asked, "Did you have a pleasant trip? Aristo has just arrived from New York," she added unnecessarily, since everyone had been informed.

Onassis greeted his old friends warmly while they displayed a certain restraint. His dark intelligent eyes flashed behind thick-rimmed glasses, taking in the atmosphere around him in seconds. His presence pervaded the room.

He was the opposite of the word *handsome,* yet his magnetism and enveloping smile would have brought a number of movie stars down a peg or two. That evening I felt some of his attraction and began to understand Maria's fascination for him. I could see why this "little" man stood seven feet tall in the eyes of some. Even in casual company, he gave the impression that his strength lay in the fact that he had never bent to rules and conventions as he reached for the top. His rough ways and egocentric interest in captivating those around him were riveting.

During that evening, he acted as if he were dining in his own home. He was totally at ease, which I think annoyed his friends, who had expected a small sign of repentance, and while we sat stiffly in our evening clothes, Aristo shed his jacket and pulled his red tie down to half mast without even consulting the hostess. The surprise was general, but no one dared object.

After dinner, the men retired to the *petit salon* for their smoke and liqueurs. From the adjoining room, Onassis' voice dominated the conversation, as did the smell of his Havana cigar. "Maria," he shouted, "come in here a minute."

Maria jumped up. "Yes, Aristo, I'm coming, I'm coming," she said, rushing to his side. I was startled by her docility, but as the evening wore on and Maria relaxed, her words and manner were unmistakably those of a woman in love.

When the men joined us again, they found Maria show-ing us piles of photographs taken during the *Medea* film. There was talk of the extraordinary Turkish landscape, of the heat in Grado, of her fainting, of work in Cinecittà.

"Here I am with Pier Paolo," Maria pointed out to Onassis, "and that's the leading man. My Jason. Good-looking fellow, no? Oh, Nadia, do tell us about the hotel we stayed in! . . . And what about the fire scene when the stand-in got burned? . . ."

When my answers were too brief, I got a pleading look and a little kick under the table. I talked and talked, telling the well-worn anecdotes only because I knew what it meant to Maria. It was important to show how she had managed without Onassis, proving that she had not crumpled under his blows.

He moved next to her on the sofa and leafed through the photographs with detachment. An occasional comment or compliment came through a cloud of cigar smoke. We all observed how vulnerable Maria still was to every word Aristo uttered.

His hand found its way to Maria's lap and rested on her upper thigh. He took his cigar out of his mouth long enough to exclaim, "Ah, that feels good! It's great to feel Maria's big fat thighs again. I've really missed them. Jackie is nothing but a bag of bones."

Maria's expression was one of embarrassment and de-light, while the rest of us avoided each other's eyes and feigned amusement.

By the time our party left Maria's apartment, there was a crowd in front of 36 Avenue Georges Mandel. The press had followed Onassis from the airport and the news was out. Onassis and Callas were back together.

*

On January 9, 1970, at the gala premiere of *Medea,* a large crowd of admirers braved the cold to applaud Callas, the film actress, as she made her entrance at L'Opéra. The theater was brimming with celebrities, starting with Mme. Claude Pompidou, the wife of the president of the republic, and illustrious personalities such as the Aga Khan, Maurice Chevalier, Mrs. Sargent Shriver, wife of the American ambassador in Paris, actresses Nathalie Delon and Marie Bell, Marc Bohan of Dior, the Rothschilds, as well as ambassadors from eleven countries. One important person absent from the first-night audience was Aristotle Onassis.

The film was well received, but didn't inspire the ovations of the Divina's operatic performances. Maria's acting abilities were admired, but generally the audience felt there was something missing in this slow, static *Medea.*

Having seen all the rushes, I can't understand myself why Pasolini used so many unflattering shots of Maria. I believe some of the most beautiful material stayed on the cutting-room floor. I can't help but feel if Pasolini had devoted more time to the editing, the film might have launched Maria on a new career.

Princess Marina of Greece says she was "uncomfortable" with Maria's film *Medea.* "She had nothing to do with the genius of the stage Callas, who never disappointed me. The way she was directed, her role and behavior seemed very *petit bourgeois.* She reminded me of my Athenian aunts."

"Seeing her in Pasolini's film," adds composer Gian Carlo Menotti, "I wondered, can that be the great Callas? To me, she was not a great actress, but a magnetic personality. That, no one can take away from her."

15

Tragonissi Again

It was that summer, a year after we'd met, that Maria invited me to join her on Tragonissi.

The phone rang in the dead of night.

"Hello? *Pronto*. What's become of you, Nadia? You haven't given me your news for ages. *Che fai?*" She didn't have to identify herself; the hour of the call and the cocktail of languages left no doubt as to who it was.

"Listen, I'm off to Russia to be on the jury of the Tchai-kovsky competition. When I get back, I've been invited by Perry Embiricos to his island in Greece. He's an old friend and Callas fan. Anyway, he said I could bring a friend. Why don't you come with me? You need a rest. I'll call you in a week, but I want an affirmative answer, OK? *Ciao, cara*. We'll catch up on our news on the island."

She'd hung up and I hadn't had a chance to get a word

in. I dozed off thinking about Maria's invitation but didn't take it seriously. A nice gesture, I thought.

When she did call the following week, I really was surprised.

"Well? You are coming, aren't you?" a voice said. "Don't find excuses. I can already guess what you are going to tell me. You can't come because of your job and because you are broke. Right? You just tell your boss you are going on holiday with me. As for the ticket, there is a round-trip ticket in your name, waiting for you at Olympic Airways. See you at the Athens airport. *Ciao!*"

Before leaving Paris, a happy Maria told Naomi Barry of the *International Herald-Tribune* that she was going on holiday—"just swimming, snorkeling, nonsense. When I play, it is so nice to be a child."

On July 19, Maria and I were picked up in Athens and taken to Tragonissi by boat. The stone house, shaded by white awnings, was only a few yards from the sea. Around it, Perry Embiricos had created an oasis of lawns and cheerfully colored flower beds that were lovingly tended and watered daily with a supply brought in a "water boat" from the mainland.

Tragonissi's lushness stood out in surprising contrast to the barren islands surrounding it. In that private corner of the world, the days flowed lazily into each other, and at sunset Maria and I routinely joined our host for a walk around his floating Olympus. I loved that jasmine-scented stroll.

Sometimes we sat on the terrace and listened to recordings of Maria's period of glory. There was a solemn, religious quality about those sessions. A shadow of sadness came over Maria as she listened. She sat motionless, staring at the vague outlines of islands that had once been mountain ranges forming the landlock connecting Europe to Asia Minor. At the end of the record she was silent. On one occasion she was visibly moved. *"Brava,"* she said. "La Callas will never sing like that again."

Halfway through our stay, Pier Paolo Pasolini joined us on the island. At first, he had declined the invitation, maintaining that his political views and proletarian life-style could not co-exist with the unabashed opulence of the island. But it didn't take him long to adapt with visible relish to the comforts of our life.

Here too, Maria and Pier Paolo spent a lot of time together. They chatted on the beach while he sketched her. After folding a large piece of drawing paper into eight segments, he drew a profile of Maria on each square. Then he outlined the pencil marks with transparent glue, which gave the lines texture. In the center of each portrait, he placed a variety of flowers—geraniums, hibiscus, bleeding hearts, trumpet-vine flowers, and so on. Then he ceremoniously dipped his sun hat in the translucent sea water and, with the concentration of an alchemist, poured the fluid on the flowers and drawing. He stepped back to admire his handiwork, as I watched skeptically. "This is art in the making," he exclaimed, placing sand and stones on the painting. "Now it must dry in the sun for twenty-four hours. I shall make only three, and one will be for you."

Thinking back to that summer, a particularly delightful outing of our holiday comes to mind. On our way by motorboat to a nearby island, we encountered two fishermen pulling in their catch. A brief exchange between our host and the fishermen resulted in an unexpected lunch. The fish was stuffed with wild herbs gathered among the rocks by Maria. It was baked on a driftwood fire and was plunged back into the sea just before serving, to give it nature's seasoning.

Maria loved moments like these. "The kind of freedom I find in nature restores my psychological balance," she used to say.

On another occasion we visited Meligala, the village in the Peloponnese where George Kalogeropoulos came from, and where he and Litza had lived before going to America. Maria wanted to touch base with her origins, I think, in view of her recently acquired Greek citizenship, but we barely made it to the old Kalogeropoulos house. Well-wishing villagers trailed us, children tugged at Maria's clothes and women kissed her hand, crying. After years of life in the public eye, I thought Maria would be used to such demonstrations. But, although she was touched by the people's welcome, her reaction was one of irritation and claustrophobia.

After Pasolini's departure, Perry extended his hospitality another week. He tempted us to stay (we didn't need much encouragement) by offering us a spectacular sight-seeing tour of Greece by helicopter. What a trip! We flew over windswept ocher lands, olive groves and austere monasteries clinging to cliffsides, the bay of Piraeus, Corinth, Delphi . . . all the sights I had yearned to see! When Perry asked Maria if she wanted to visit Delphi, she replied, "No, thank you, I can see it from here, but I'd like to stop on the island of Skiathos and visit Mrs. Konialidis, Aristo's sister."

Having very much wanted to visit Delphi, I was quite put out with Maria, but then again, I wasn't the guest of honor. At any rate, unlike her Aegean sister islands, Skiathos is green and lush. While Maria was on her visit, I consoled myself on a breathtaking beach framed by pine-covered hills.

Tragonissi, Maria often remarked, was the ideal hideaway for someone of her notoriety. Distance and logistical problems ensured the island's privacy, or so we thought.

MARIA

We were sitting on the beach late one morning. As I recall, Maria was absently leafing through a magazine—she hardly ever read an entire article, and in the eight years that I knew her she traveled with *Nicholas and Alexandra,* in which she made little headway. Suddenly, Maria sprang out of her chaise longue shouting angrily in Greek.

"What in the world is wrong with you, Maria?" I asked, preoccupied.

"There's someone here. I feel a presence," she said. "There! Near that oleander bush."

I looked around. We were alone. There weren't even any fishing boats in sight.

A few minutes passed, then I saw a fleeting shadow and heard the rush of the falling stones. "Maria! Cover yourself!" I shouted. "There's a photographer!" My warning had come too late. The photographer had obviously been snapping away unobserved for some time. Maria screamed insults at the man. She hated being photographed in a bikini, and she was still terribly self-conscious about her heavy legs.

In trying to make a quick getaway, the photographer rolled down a cliff and splashed into the sea. "Serves him right," said Maria, watching the photographer extract himself and his equipment from the water.

Unfortunately, he was the first of a series of such unwelcome visitors who put a damper on the remainder of our stay. Maria was no longer relaxed. She didn't dare sunbathe in a two-piece suit or go for her long swims. She was always on the lookout for intruders.

Finally, a few days after my return to Rome, I heard that another uninvited visitor had appeared on the island that summer: Aristotle Onassis. He had come to wish Maria a happy name day—followed by the usual throng of paparazzi, who immortalized the kiss that Onassis placed on her lips under a beach umbrella.

We returned to Paris and Rome respectively and Maria and I kept in touch by mail and telephone. We met again at La Scala, on December 7, 1970, when Maria was invited by Ghiringhelli to inaugurate the theater's newly installed lighting system and be present at the opening performance of *I Vespri Siciliani*. The Milanese were looking forward to hearing Renata Scotto in the role of Elena, but at the end of the first act the Callas worshipers got out of hand. There were shouts of "We want Maria! We want Maria!" "You are the Scala." "*You* should be on that stage." The crowd faced the box in front of mine, which Maria shared with Wally Toscanini, and continued clapping, totally disregarding the artists taking curtain calls. This was repeated at the end of each act and at the close of the performance.

Although flattered, Maria felt the uproar was unfair to Scotto, and Scotto was rightly livid that Maria had upstaged her. "It is customary to applaud the artists onstage, not those sitting in the audience," was Scotto's pained reproach.

Although few will believe it, at the party given by Biki after the opening, which Scotto chose not to attend, Maria said to me, "Poor Scotto, that must have been awful for her. I know what it's like. You are up there giving your all, and someone comes along and messes you up! I feel badly that I came."

In the autumn of 1971, I received one of Maria's frequent calls. "I'm leaving for New York next week," Maria announced. "I don't really feel like going, but now that I've made the commitment, I have to. Wish me luck. I've accepted to teach a series of master classes at New York's Juilliard School of Music. I don't think teaching is going to be my thing, but I like working with the young, so I'll give it a try. As you know, I'm not wild about New York City. I do have friends, but I don't feel at home there. Why don't you come along? You can stay with me at the Plaza; there surely is space for both of us. After all, they owe it to me, I'm doing this free, you know. I'm not getting a penny." Unfortunately, I could not accept her invitation.

It is true she didn't get a fee; however, Maria's idea of "free" was a suite at the Plaza, a limousine waiting at the door, first-class travel arrangements, food, and fresh flowers in every room. Juilliard was not exactly getting a bargain by any standards. Maria was a bit frightened of her role as a teacher, but it was an excuse to fill in time until she was offered something more congenial. In her interview with the *International Herald-Tribune* that June, she said, "It will not exactly be teaching. I would like to try to pass on some of my experience to others. Opera is in crisis. I have been saying that since 1954. I do not want to let it die. I will be playing it by ear. Each singer is an individual, and must be treated differently. I want to show these young students about breathing and how you spare yourself. The voice is a human instrument. It can't last at all without technique. Yet the supreme art is to hide technique until all seems effortless. That requires work and tremendous discipline, sacrifice and risks. If you really want to serve music, you must live it day and night."

True, and beautifully said; yet those who knew her well, like Larry Kelly, had no doubt that an ulterior motive lay behind Maria's "altruistic" undertaking. "Maria thought of it in terms of herself and not in terms of the kids. As a human being she was extremely attractive, extremely careless and extremely selfish. The classes were really her way of presenting herself to an audience for the first time in six or seven years. She needed an audience's reaction, and with time the handful of people grew into a paying audience of a thousand. She told me, 'What I'm doing deserves an audience, because the audience wants to come. So why not charge them?' It was not the money that interested her, but the chance to prove she was capable of recapturing her audience."

"The master classes were fascinating because they were conducted by Maria Callas the singer, not Callas a pedagogical teacher," Vera Zorina, who was there, insisted. "They were constructive because you were aware of her extraordinary perception and knowledge despite the difficulty she had in imparting it to her students. She was not a revealing teacher."

John Ardoin agrees. "The Callas instinct and her personal technique were impossible to convey to someone else. The 26 students she had chosen out of the 350 she had auditioned were without a doubt extremely talented, but none was Callas. She could not improvise the necessary technique to fit each individual pupil. Unable to tell them *how* to do it, she would demonstrate how *she* would have done it. 'Just do it this way,' she'd say as if it were as simple as the ABC's. During these demonstrations, the attentive public was touched, for a few moving moments, by Callas's great musicality and temperament. She would start singing in a whisper, in an incidental sort of way, which, once she was assured of audience acceptance, turned into a Callas performance. She had started out by saying things like, 'Oh, I can't sing above A-flat' or 'We all have those problems with B-flat.'"

But those present, including music critic William Weaver, were fascinated by Maria's impromptu performances. "She sang the 'Veil Song' from *Don Carlos* in bits and pieces, interrupting occasionally to remind the mezzo-soprano, 'I would do it a bit like this . . . but you understand, I don't sing this part, it's not my role!' She would sing sections of it and then the student would follow. With corrections and repeats, Maria ended up singing the whole thing, as she did with a number of other arias.

"When another student, a dramatic soprano, launched into 'A Perfido,' she was soon interrupted by Maria. 'No dear, that's not the way. The words are right, the music is right, but you must keep in mind that this is someone who's been abandoned by her lover and is terribly unhappy. I think it's more like this.' Piece by piece she went through the entire aria in front of a very moved audience. On another occasion, she sang 'Zaccaria's Prophecy,' the bass aria from Verdi's *Nabucco,* to show an unimaginative singer how the aria should be sung, getting him to understand the feeling of the *whole* opera. And when, during a class, a student let out a shrill note while singing the 'Stride la Vampa' aria from *Trovatore,* Maria interrupted. 'What is this grating sound?' 'It is a cry of desperation!' answered the student. 'Young lady,' said Callas, 'it is not a cry of desperation, it is a *si bemol* [B flat] and that's the way Verdi wrote it. Please respect it.' "

Work and praise were essential to Maria, yet her period at Juilliard was extremely lonely despite the affectionate attention of Dr. Peter Mennin, the school's director. So when her old friends Tito and Tilde Gobbi arrived in New York, Maria clung to them for dear life and wouldn't leave their side. When the time came to part, after dining with them at the Plaza, Maria kept chatting, wishing the evening would not end. She told the Gobbis of her numerous plans and aspirations. "The way she spoke," Mrs. Gobbi told me, "she made it sound as if she were singing *Lucia* one night and *Lucrezia Borgia* the next. I said to her, 'Do you want to stick to such a demanding and difficult repertory?' 'Oh, Tilde, you and Tito understand why! This is *my* music. I must sing Bellini,

Donizetti, Rossini, Verdi. . . . This is my pride, I cannot give it up!' Everyone had left the restaurant, including the waiters. The maître d'hôtel hovered nearby, but Maria refused to acknowledge his presence and went right on with her chatter. Tito finally got up, saying it was time to go. It was late, and we were leaving for Europe the next day. Maria rose reluctantly and took forever to walk to the elevator with us. She was inside the elevator when she announced that she wasn't sleepy and didn't want to go to bed. 'Please buy me an ice cream,' she begged and stepped back into the lobby. She managed to stretch the ice cream for another half hour. When we finally saw her to her suite, she said, 'I'm so lonely. I haven't even got my little dogs. Will you call me when you get home?' She really was pathetic."

The letter I received from Maria dated July 21, 1972, gives her comments on her work at Juilliard and confirms it was around this time that Giuseppe di Stefano reappeared in her life. She wrote:

> I had lots of work this year at Juilliard and enjoyed it. I studied on my voice also—it went very well—only opera is going even more down the drain—the approach is none professional and less than mediocre—and I have been so spoiled—so to resume is really something I'm not looking forward to.
>
> Anyway, we shall see—If you want to write to me I'll be in San Remo c/o di Stefano 'till the 8th August—

Maria and I returned to Tragonissi in the summer of 1971. George and Daphne Embiricos, distant relatives of our host, invited us for a cruise of the Greek islands on board their magnificent ship, the *Astarte*. We floated in great comfort from the bustling port of Hydra, with its caïques and sponge boats, to the whitewashed houses of Mykonos.

On August 15, Maria's name day was celebrated on board the *Astarte* with ladles of Persian caviar and champagne that I could only feast my eyes on through my seasickness.

Daphne gave Maria an Indian necklace of hers that Maria had admired with persistence. Dear Daphne did not yet know of Maria's compulsion for collecting objects or presents from friends, that Maria was enticed by the idea of getting something she wanted free. Carla Mocenigo laughed when she told me of all the objects Maria had "extracted" from her mother over the years. "Maria would come to our palazzo in Venice and pick up a silver box on a table and say, 'What a lovely little box! Can I have a look? It really is charming. It's antique, isn't it? I'd love to have something like this, it's just beautiful.' Think of it, she even got away with a wall hanging with the Mocenigo crest on it! Maria played the game until her friends gave in to her, but no matter what the objects were—a lipstick, a perfume sample or a precious antique box—she held on to these mementos for years."

After dinner, Maria startled us all by offering to sing.

"Remember?" Daphne prodded me last year in her chalet near Lausanne. "She sang two bits from *Tristan und Isolde*. Her high notes were a bit hesitant, but the middle range held true to the 'Great Callas.' She was very relaxed. After she'd finished, she explained that Wagner was not really difficult to sing. Unfortunately, her lovely arias were followed by a concert with those poodles.

"Maria was a wonderful woman, simple and somewhat naïve. Years after that cruise, in '77 I think, she called me in Lausanne to ask me if she could come and spend ten days with us. I was delighted at the thought of seeing her again and suggested she come with a friend, if she felt like it. 'No,

Daphne, I'll come by myself. You know me, I'm a loner.' Her answer filled me with sadness. She told me she'd call back to confirm her dates, but never did."

We returned to the island to resume our deliciously self-indulgent way of life. But Maria's insistence on having company until she retired and her habit of getting up late made the household organization and meal schedules rather complex for our host. Routinely, after endlessly bidding each other good-night, there would be a knock on my door. "Can I come in?" Maria's voice would say shyly. "I brought you a magazine" or "I have something to ask you." Any excuse was enough. Once she was in the room, it was hard to get her out. Much as I loved Maria, some of those nightly talks were boringly repetitive. She sat on my bed and talked on and on about Onassis: his behavior, her love for him, her future with and without him. Sometimes the theme changed to her artistic future: her fear of returning to Paris. Would she go back to singing? Would she be offered more film parts? If so, what did I think she should do? Or she would ask me to compose answers to the love letters that Peter Mennin had started writing while she was at Juilliard. She'd say, "I don't know what to tell him. He's a nice man, but I don't feel about him the way he does about me. I don't want to get involved with another married man. So, you dictate and I'll write."

Back on Tragonissi, our threesome doubled with the arrival of Constantine and Anastasia Gratsos and a ravishing Chinese friend of Maria's, married to a prominent Jewish New Yorker in the garment trade. Constantine Gratsos was a long-time friend of Onassis and the trusted executor of his business interests in America.

In honor of his distinguished houseguest, Perry organized a spectacular party and asked a few of his friends from other islands to join us. There was a delicious buffet, champagne and music. Tragonissi seemed touched by magic in the glow of torchlights.

Maria had slightly overindulged in champagne that evening. She was giddy and in an amorous mood. She gazed with hazy abandon into the eyes of a handsome Greek guest, who, flattered by the Diva's attention, responded with the same fervor. Arms entwined, they raised their glasses in a toast "to beauty, to love, to happiness."

But Maria's uninhibited playfulness didn't go down well with our host. He was annoyed by the attention she showed the young Apollo. And later in the evening, matters only got worse when Maria, in a moment of misplaced gusto, made a disparaging remark about the Jews and their "way of doing business." The young Chinese girl understandably took offense. My heart sank when, instead of apologizing and dropping the subject, Maria increased the tension by arguing her point. I could have killed her.

At four in the morning, I was awakened by angry Greek voices. Maria, Perry and the Apollo were having a heated discussion in the patio near my window. I was curious to know what they were so upset about, but not understanding Greek, I went back to sleep.

The following morning, Maria joined me at the beach at ten-thirty, which for her was like rising at dawn. By her walk, I could tell she was nervous and ill humored. She came straight to the point.

"Listen, what did you say about the party last night? I'm told you made rude remarks about the food and didn't like the torches."

"There must be some misunderstanding. I praised the buffet, the lighting, the flowers!" I replied in surprise.

"That's what I thought," said Maria somberly. "I argued and stuck up for you last night, because I know it has nothing to do with you. I'm furious that you've been dragged into this. Perry is using you as an excuse because he doesn't have the guts to tell me he is upset with me—with my behavior last night. I don't like the fact that he put the blame on you, when I'm the culprit. Nadia, we are leaving."

Maria was firm. It was a matter of principle she said. We could no longer stay in a place where our presence had become undesirable. She asked Perry if he would make arrangements for the Criss Craft to take us to the mainland. We were told the motor was broken, we'd have to wait. Maria asked for a helicopter. There wouldn't be one available for two or three days.

There we were on a tight little island with no one speaking to us. The Chinese girl wouldn't have anything to do with Maria, and Anastasia Gratsos sided with her. As for Perry, he was monosyllabic.

After two days, which seemed endless, a helicopter came for us. We said good-bye with a mixture of sadness and relief. I sat in the backseat holding Pixie and Djedda, while Maria was in the front next to the pilot.

We were flying over a stretch of the Aegean when the door on Maria's side flew open. She showed surprise but was in no way alarmed, as she was securely tied in with a seatbelt. As for myself, my sense of adventure overruled my apprehension. The nervous one was the pilot. He kept repeating that everything was OK and that we should stay calm.

We cruised a bit, but there was nowhere to land. At last we came down on something that, in all that blueness, looked no larger than a pebble. The pilot skillfully balanced the machine long enough to bolt the door, and we took off again in the direction of Athens.

Maria and I were making our way through a crowd of disgruntled tourists in the chaos of the Athens airport when we were blinded by the flash of photographers. Just as I pulled her toward the transit lounge, an airport official came to our rescue—or so I thought. He whispered something to Maria. Her face changed suddenly, and she began to scream at him in Greek.

It turned out that our negligent pilot, afraid of losing his job, had reported to his superiors that Madame Callas had put our lives at risk by opening the helicopter door in flight.

16

The Last Test

One of Maria's last visits to Rome was in the fall of 1972. When I heard her voice on the phone, I was convinced she was calling from Paris. It was 12:30 P.M., her breakfast hour.

"Surprise!" she said. "I'm in Rome at the Grand. I came to spend some time with you and our *amici*. I'm so tired of my Parisian fogies. Let's call a few friends and gather at our restaurant in Campagnano. I need fresh air and jovial faces."

During the drive out to the country, she admitted the real reason for her sudden visit.

"I need to see a doctor, Nadia. Can you recommend a good one?" She avoided my glance. "I think I'm pregnant. It's Aristo's child, but at this point we are both too old. I'm scared and I can't count on his getting a divorce. I'll stay in Rome the time it takes to have the examinations and so on. . . ."

When I asked her if she had discussed her pregnancy with Onassis, she was inarticulate at first and then, as if to silence me, she remarked abruptly, "I think you forget that he's married and to whom he's married."

To avoid curious reporters I asked a doctor to come to the Grand Hotel to do the tests. Maria was understandably nervous while waiting for the results, but the tests were negative.

I was relieved she had that off her mind before starting her recording commitment for Philips, with the London Symphony Orchestra. But what puzzles me about this visit, now that I know more about what followed, is that after trusting my friendship sufficiently to share such an important secret with me, she never mentioned that she was recording with di Stefano, on whom she'd always had such a crush. From her letter in July, I knew she had visited "Pippo" and Maria di Stefano. Was it that, having always spoken of Onassis to me, she was too embarrassed to mention her interest in di Stefano? Or was there nothing more than friendship between them until they worked together in London? This is only speculation on my part, but I wonder if Maria's prima-donna-like behavior during the recording session did not stem from this budding affair with di Stefano, in addition to their professional competitiveness. It is difficult otherwise to justify the switch in Maria's professional behavior when I compare her impeccable work during *Medea* with what conductor Antonio de Almeida has told me about those trying recording sessions in London.

The duets they recorded (from *L'Elisir d'Amore, Don Carlos, Otello, La Forza del Destino, Vespri Siciliani* and *Aida*) remain in the Philips archives, since Callas never gave Philips the okay to release them. Maria's excuse was that she was "too loud." Conductor de Almeida does not agree with Maria's story. "She was against the recording from the start. She was artistically egotistical. She was using the recording as a warm-up for a farewell tour."

Cellist Pashanko Dimitroff, who was then with the London Symphony Orchestra, cringed as he recalled the endless waits within the cold walls of St. Giles's church. "The sessions were three hours each, but Callas arrived for the last twenty minutes. She sang a little, then spent the remaining time in the control room arguing with di Stefano."

"I never knew when we would be recording," adds de Almeida. "The orchestra had to be ready at all times. The problem was not with the recording but with two nervous, aging singers. When one was in top voice, the other might not be. To help Callas before we began, we flew a coach to Paris. It was so strange. When she was working at home she always asked Bruna, the maid, how she sounded. She never asked the coach or myself, who were there for that purpose and were the experts. She obviously preferred not to hear the truth, as she was painfully aware of her vocal problems. Not being able to do it alone, she had di Stefano share the agony. What intrigued me about the two artists was their totally different understanding of the situation and themselves. Maria suffered but di Stefano was completely oblivious of his short-comings. He was a very nice guy, but a great voice was just thrown away on wine, women and song. Such a shame."

While in London, on December 4, two days after a happy celebration of her forty-ninth birthday, Maria learned of her father's death. She called to tell me of her sorrow, which I understood only too well, having lost my father five months earlier. In true Maria fashion, she found release for her pain through anger. At this time it was directed against Alexandra Papajohn. Somehow Maria blamed the death of her eighty-six-year-old father on the kind, devoted woman who had shared his life and cared for him for thirty years. "When that woman married my father," Maria said, her voice filled with emotion, "she cut off the last link I had with my family."

"Maria was constantly at war with herself and the universe," Tilde Gobbi once reminded me. This was the beginning of a period in which her "gods" seemed to be at war with Maria as well. They were sparing her no grief. That same year she suffered the loss of her great friend Maggie van Zuylen.

And then in January 1973, Alexander Onassis was killed during a test run in his father's Piaggio. The crash was so violent that Alexander's remains, found near Athens airport, were barely recognizable. Onassis believed it had not been an accident but sabotage. With his son's death, Onassis buried his future hopes. Even Maria couldn't help alleviate his miseries.

"He no longer hears me," she said to me one day. "He's obsessed with Alexander's death and he keeps talking about tracking down those who killed him, although I'm certain it was an accident. Aristo has changed, Nadia. He really is an old man now."

The tables had turned; he was now leaning on her, and I think that frightened her. When he left her, he had stripped her of her self-confidence and inflicted so much pain that she could expose herself to no more. The fear of trusting him drove her to consider other men. It seemed as if the more he needed her, the more she doubted him.

At the time I wondered if that fear and her longing to prove to herself she still had a place in opera weren't the dominant factors that led her to agree to co-direct *I Vespri Siciliani* with di Stefano that April.

Was her instinct no longer guiding her? Maria, who had repeatedly insisted that professionalism could not be improvised, now planned to direct a full-scale production of a major operatic company, having had absolutely no previous experience.

Friends warned her. Visconti tried to dissuade her, reminding her (gently, I hope) that her artistic stature could be vulnerable to such hazardous exposure.

The production of *I Vespri Siciliani* was to inaugurate Turin's recently completed Teatro Regio, replacing the one that had burned in 1936. This important event evoked a great deal of interest and publicity before casting had even been completed.

"I was already under contract to sing when rumors reached me that the production might be directed by Maria Callas," said Raina Kabaivanska, when we met in Lausanne, before her opening in *Tosca,* at the Théâtre Beaulieu. "It seemed incredible! The final choice proved even more astonishing: Maria Callas, Giuseppe di Stefano, with Maestro Gianandrea Gavazzeni conducting. It was an unprecedented publicity coup!

"In my mind," Kabaivanska continued, "there is no doubt why Callas accepted to direct *Vespri*. She did it for di Stefano, out of love. I couldn't understand this love, but it's not for me to judge. We will never know how much he really loved her, but his seduction was very convincing. He gave her the courage to confront a new phase in her career."

A look at Callas's life and career makes it clear that she never sang totally of her own will; I believe she couldn't have done it on her own. First she sang prodded by her mother, then urged by Meneghini. In 1962, when faced with a vocal crisis, she turned to impresario Michel Glotz and conductor Georges Prêtre for the courage she needed to return to the stage. Finally, she accepted the concert tour in the seventies for love of di Stefano. Music in itself was never enough.

"Di Stefano is the last man in Maria's life on whose support she depended and at whose will she performed," John Ardoin remarked as we discussed the Turin Callas–di Stefano venture. "After a tremendously successful career, di Stefano managed to alienate himself from the operatic world. When *I Vespri Siciliani* came up, he saw it as a financially tempting offer and a spectacular publicity campaign for his return. With the name of Maria Callas in tow, it was his chance to surface again."

Evidently she thought they would surface together. When she first got to Turin, she was confident and excited by the novelty of her work, but soon her mood changed.

I never made it to Turin for *Vespri,* as I had planned, but feel as if I had been there through Maria's lengthy telephone conversations during that time. I followed her anguish during rehearsal and listened to her mixed feelings about di Stefano's interest in her. She always spoke of "how in love he is with me" but never clearly stated her love for him. At least not to me. Nonetheless, it was obvious Maria was flattered by di Stefano's attentions, especially after such a long wait.

"Pippo is going through a very oppressive period," she said. "His beautiful daughter has a brain tumor. Pippo has tremendous medical bills hanging over him, poor man, and he's done some unwise deals in real estate."

Some nights her conversation was distant and her thoughts uneven. Perhaps she was tired and frightened by the monumental artistic undertaking; or perhaps di Stefano was present while she spoke. One evening she said, "I'm not sure what I'm doing here, Nadia, but I guess it's normal to feel insecure in a new job." Obviously she wanted to do the best job possible, but was dissatisfied with the project as a whole. A few days later rumor had it that Callas was going to quit and be replaced by Virginia Puecher. Then Callas made an about-face and decided to stay.

Instead, Maestro Gavazzeni resigned, and this was only the beginning of a series of difficulties during the preparatory phase of the venture. Pressure was put on Callas by an important recording company to drop Kabaivanska in favor of a rising young star backed by them, but Maria refused to comply.

"I only found that out much later," said Raina. "Callas stood up for me. She said, 'Kabaivanska is under contract. Contracts are to be respected. She will do the role.' Then other problems came up. During a rehearsal, Maestro Vittorio Gui, who had replaced Gavazzeni, collapsed on the podium. I rushed to his side, as did other colleagues. When Maria reached the old maestro, she turned to me and said in a reprimanding voice, 'Raina, what is wrong with you, what's got into you?' 'Can't you see?' I answered. 'He's unwell. I'm very worried.' 'We are going to go on with the show anyway!' Maria snapped back. I was shocked by her seeming lack of concern, but I realized she was right; it was a professional requirement. Such are the rules of life. We had our differences during the time we worked together, perhaps because of the similarity in our characters. I, too, always say what I think. That is why I understood and loved her. It is not easy to have a character like ours; it makes life more difficult in certain ways.

"As for the directing, di Stefano had designated himself as the mastermind of the production while Maria supervised the outcome. The truth of the matter is that neither of them knew what to do. Di Stefano was of the opinion that the singers and conductor were the real directors of the opera, since in his stage experience he had only been concerned with his own performance and his own voice. All at once he had to consider sets, costumes, relationships, the orchestra and the conductor. Occasionally, he would give the chorus vague instructions, but the singers were completely left to their own devices.

"A good deal of the time Callas watched di Stefano; then, all at once, she'd leap out of her seat and rush onstage to show Gianni Raimondi or Liliana Cosi how to raise an arm or hold a prop. Callas somehow expected us to *know* what we were meant to be doing, as *she* had always known. I had looked forward to being guided by her experience, but dramatically she showed me nothing, and she was right. The worst thing an artist can do in creating a role is try to imitate another person's style. I truly believe," said Kabaivanska with regret, "that Callas could have done a magnificent directing job had she been helped by a professional, but with di Stefano it just couldn't work."

The outcome was boring performances torn apart by the critics. But Maria's pride and her sense of loyalty toward di Stefano and the artists could not accept that. After the opening night she gave a press conference to defend their positions.

"I think," says Kabaivanska, "she suffered a lot. Looking back on that period, I'm filled with remorse. I didn't understand her need for help and company. I should have extended a hand to the woman, to Maria. After each performance, Maria came to my dressing room with the same question. 'Where are you going to eat tonight? What are your plans? Can I join you?' I didn't pay enough attention to her. I was surrounded by friends and admirers, who, by the way, were also Callas admirers, but they kept their distance after seeing *I Vespri Siciliani*. Those who had so venerated Callas, the great artist, couldn't understand her fiasco and were devoid of pity when she needed it most.

"But as I said, we did have our differences. She asked me to come to her apartment one day and proceeded to make remarks about the way I was singing. You must understand that by then I was already a formed and affirmed artist. 'Why are you singing *scuro*?' Callas said. 'You must open up and sing *chiaro*.' I sang in my own way, but it resembled the old way Callas used to sing. Her accusations really upset me. I was livid and I let her have it. 'Wait a minute,' I said. '*You* sang *scuro* all your life, and now you revoke it all? Your entire career? 'Yes, because I was wrong. I did it wrong all my life,' Maria answered in her impulsive way. You see," Raina explained, "in the desperation of her voice loss, she clung to di Stefano, who was giving her singing lessons in the hope of retrieving what she'd once had. But di Stefano sang without technique, using only his natural God-given voice. He sang *aperto*. In her admiration she bent to his singing methods. She repudiated twenty years of work, her own extraordinary way of singing, the way real bel canto must be sung."

A fiery exchange between the singers resulted in a twenty-four-hour silence in which not so much as a look was exchanged.

" 'Listen, Raina,' my husband finally said. 'You must get on your knees in front of this woman, send her a big bunch of roses and make up.'

"When Maria arrived at rehearsal the following evening, she was like a child," Raina continued. "She rushed up to me and hugged me. She had tears in her eyes. 'You're adorable,' she said. 'Thank you so very much. Come to see me tonight after work, I'll show you how one should sing.'

"It was an amazing experience. That evening Callas sang *Vespri* in its entirety, giving me invaluable musical advice. I suddenly understood what the real Callas was all about. She was instinct, musical instinct. She had that incredible quality that allowed you to *see* the characters' faces while you listened to her recordings. She painted the characters through her voice. When I asked her about her very personal way of phrasing, she modestly attributed her knowledge to Serafin, but those are things one doesn't learn. There is only one truth, and Callas had understood it: read the music. She knew how to read the composer's intentions.

"She wanted to help me, but most of all it was the human contact that was important to her. I believe the lack of that warmth brought about her premature death."

Callas was invited to repeat the Juilliard classes, but she was restless and dissatisfied. The failure of *I Vespri Siciliani* still rankled. She felt artistically rejected, but could not call it quits.

"I want another year. I don't care what happens after that, but I want another year," she said to John Ardoin.

Work distracted her. It was an escape from solitude, a chance to leave behind the melancholy of her daily life: the hairdresser, shopping, walks with Pixie and Djedda and the TV that was always on.

She still needed to believe she could make her comeback if and when she wanted, on her own terms. At least that is what she thought she was doing when di Stefano persuaded her to join him on an extensive concert tour.

Maria had originally agreed to begin the tour with two concerts with di Stefano in Japan. "Perhaps Japan seemed protective in its remoteness," John reminded me. "She was undone when Larry Kelly told her he and some of the most important U.S. critics would be present at those concerts. The news startled and depressed her. 'Larry,' she had said sadly, 'you didn't have to tell me that.'"

Before leaving, Onassis begged her to abandon the tour. "He speaks to me of divorce the way he used to speak of marriage," she confided to Mary Mead Carter. "I'd be a fool to believe him until I hold the signed paper in my hand."

"To me," says Mary Mead Carter, "*that* was the Greek tragedy. Again and again Aristo implored her to marry him. He was serious this time. He had started divorce proceedings, but Maria wanted black-and-white as proof. She was not a woman who forgot or forgave easily. So she went off with that horrid little man, Giuseppe di Stefano, believing that the tour was her salvation as an artist and a woman."

That "ill-fated" tour, as the press was later to refer to their new undertaking, started in Hamburg on October 26, 1973, with the octogenarian Ivor Newton as accompanist. The tour was to cover eight countries in seven months.

The reviews were not good, but audiences were enthusiastic wherever they performed. Surprisingly, the spectators were mostly young people who had not been exposed to the great Callas, except through her recordings. In addition to the negative reviews, the tour was riddled with tension caused by their individual fears and di Stefano's emotional problems. The rapid advancement of his daughter's illness and the occasional appearance of di Stefano's wife Maria during their travels didn't make their already precarious co-existence any easier. Combat had always been part of Callas's life. "If you live, you struggle," she had said, but her determination didn't always win out. In New York, seized by fear, she took enough sleeping pills to knock her out for forty-eight hours so as to skip the concert the following evening.

I happened to be in London when the two concerts at the Royal Festival Hall were scheduled. I gave Maria a call the day before her November 26 concert and suggested that we meet for a late lunch. She was her friendly self, but for the first time since I'd known her, she said she couldn't find time for a meeting. She chatted for half an hour, skipping from one subject to the other, explaining that "I have to have a manicure, get my hair done, and most of all, not speak. I have to save my voice for tomorrow night. I'll leave two tickets in your name. Make sure you come backstage to see me afterwards."

It was evident that she was terrified and unable to concentrate on anything that was not associated with the upcoming event. I asked my friend Henry Pleasants, music critic of the *International Herald-Tribune* and a Callas admirer, to accompany me.

The hall was packed to capacity and permeated with restless expectation. When the house lights finally dimmed, Maria's appearance onstage was met with deafening applause before she'd even sung a note. She looked ravishing in a flowing chiffon gown designed by the faithful Biki. Di Stefano seemed distracted and resembled an overweight penguin in his white tie and tails. The choice of solos and duets that evening was from Massenet, Bizet, Boito, Verdi, Puccini, Donizetti, Gounod and Mascagni. The audience reaction was poignantly enthusiastic, in spite of a lot of uneven moments when neither Callas nor di Stefano had the necessary control in the high register. Henry Pleasants cringed and shook his head while I agonized for Maria throughout the performance. I remembered what Bruna had said to me in Turkey: "I pray every night that the Signora stop singing." I was witnessing an emotional moment in musical history, but one I could have done without.

We didn't go backstage that evening. There was no point in embarrassing Maria or Henry. As for myself, I was at a loss for words and respected Maria too much to lie to her. The following day I sent her flowers to thank her for the tickets, but we didn't get to see each other during the week between her concerts.

I went alone to the December 2 concert, which was on Maria's fiftieth birthday. The hall was so heavily oversold that four rows of chairs had to be placed in a semicircle onstage. The seat Maria had given me in the front row was perfectly placed to follow both singers. Maria looked beautiful. She seemed joyous and less strained than during her previous performance. An occasional back-kick with her foot in her cherry red evening dress was the only indication of her nervous state.

She caught sight of me as she returned to the stage for the interminable ovation. "Hello, Nadia," she said with a wink and a broad smile. Flowers rained from all directions; people waved programs, shouted bravos, and others rushed to the stage to clutch her hand or touch her dress. Maria was blissful. She was La Divina again. During a lull in the applause, Giuseppe di Stefano burst into "Happy Birthday." The crowd went wild. They shouted their good wishes, and some of the young and agile ones even leapt on the stage. Maria's eyes were moist, as were those of many in the audience. It was wonderful to see her so happy!

Backstage, her friends and di Stefano's joined in a champagne toast. Maria was visibly moved, as we all were.

"Oh, there you are, I've been looking for you," Maria said, addressing a pale, slim English girl. "I want to introduce you to some of my friends. Nadia, this is—the friend I've often talked about. The one who writes me those lovely long letters, which is more than I can say for you, *cara!*"

I felt myself blushing, not at Maria's teasing accusations but at the realization that this was the girl whose weekly ten- and twelve-page letters I had read aloud to Maria in Greece and in Paris, while Maria readied herself to go out or endlessly filed her nails. Maria loved receiving these handwritten letters whose pages were filled with details of daily occurrences: a minor disagreement at the office, a smoked trout for dinner, a walk in Regent's Park, or shopping at Marks and Spencer. I think she was attracted by the balanced regularity of the girl's life, which was in total contrast with the uncertainty of her own.

By the time the concert tour reached America, Maria's artistic and emotional fears had built to uncontrollable proportions. She called her agent, Sander Gorlinsky, and told him she wanted to cancel the rest of the tour. Pippo was impossible to work with, she said. (Personally I think that the presence of her colleague's wife and her own good friend, Maria di Stefano, certainly added to the tension and caused Callas to examine her conscience.) Gorlinsky reminded her there was no way she could quit because the contract for both of them was under Maria's name. So she went on, despite the agonizing fear and the increasing lovers' tiffs.

"They fought quite a lot," publicity agent Sheila Porter told me. In Boston, di Stefano walked out just before a concert. To fill in the program, Sol Hurok, the U.S. tour manager, flew in Vasso Devetzi, a concert pianist whom Maria knew, and who happened to be in New York at the time. "But having to sing alone," says Sheila Porter, "became a problem. She suddenly had a word block. The tension caused her memory to play tricks on her. I had worked with her on the London *Tosca* and had found her illuminating, but I was faced with a very different Maria in Boston. She had no problem with the music, but couldn't remember words or the order things came in. When di Stefano was with her, she didn't seem to have that problem, but when she was on her own, she used cue cards all the time. It was sad to see the change. I adored the woman and would have moved heaven and earth for her. She was wonderful to work with. The only time I can remember her being really upset during that tour was when she picked up her little dogs from an East Side grooming salon, where we'd dropped them off, and found one of them with a lavender bow around its neck. She nearly hit the ceiling." In Italy, lavender represents the ultimate of bad luck in the theater. No one associated with the performing arts in Italy would step inside a theater wearing lavender.

"She looked ten years younger than her actual age," John Ardoin pointed out, "and would not recognize that her strength and voice were much older. The only time she ever kidded herself artistically was during that last tour."

By the end of their tour, her liaison with di Stefano had soured. In an effort to recapture some of its initial freshness, they briefly hid away in a friend's villa, in the south of France, but that too turned out to be futile. "This time the fracture was permanent," the owners of the villa told me. "Di Stefano's departure left behind a lonely, disenchanted woman and a demoralized artist."

By the time Maria had permanently broken off with di Stefano and got back to Paris, it was nearly too late to make amends with Onassis. His health was gradually deteriorating, and during Maria's absence and seeming lack of interest he had given in to his illness.

She called me in Rome after the letdown with di Stefano but spoke mostly of Onassis. "He's going downhill," she said, "and he has serious business worries. She's probably spending too much. All she knows how to do is spend, spend, spend. Clothes, antiques, jewelry, everything!" I was always amused by the anonymous "she" Maria used when speaking of Jackie Kennedy Onassis.

"She" may have added to Onassis' problems, but the crux of the matter was that Olympic Airways, one of his most cherished business interests (perhaps because of Alexander's great love of airplanes), was disintegrating despite his personal participation. The final blow came in January 1975, when he was obliged to turn over his airline to the Greek government. After that, Onassis showed little desire to live.

When I asked Maria how things were with Pippo, whom I'd met briefly in London, she sighed, "He's just like the rest of them. I don't feel like talking about it, but it's over. You know the expression 'A good man is hard to come by'? Well, need I say more?" I knew no more questions should be asked.

A few weeks after losing Olympic Airlines, Onassis had to undergo an urgent gallbladder operation, from which he was never to recover. Instead of flying back to New York for the operation, he decided to have the surgery at the American Hospital in Paris.

Because of his marriage, Maria had to stand in the wings and look on helplessly, frustrated by the impossibility of visiting or comforting him in the last days of his life. She had to be satisfied with the daily reports transmitted through the pianist, Vasso Devetzi, whose mother was ill in the same hospital at the time. Only once, a few weeks before Onassis' death, did Maria manage to sneak into the hospital for a short visit unobserved by the press.

As I was coming home to my apartment in Rome one day in March of that year, the concierge handed me a telegram. She crossed herself. "I hope it's not bad news," she said. For her, telegrams either announced births or deaths. The telegram was from Maria. It read: COME JOIN ME IN PALM BEACH. HAVE RENTED A HOUSE. OFFER YOU ROOM, BOARD AND CHATS BY THE POOL. LOVE MARIA.

I called Palm Beach. I was lucky; she had just arrived. "Please come, Nadia. My godfather Leo is coming and John Coveney, who is very fond of you."

"I'll see if I can work it out," I said, "but what about Aristo? Is he better?"

"No, he's in a semiconscious state, from what I've been told, but I had to get away. Away from Paris. It's killing me to stand by and not be able to be with him now that he really needs me. I can do nothing. You understand that, don't you? Now he is in the hands of God."

A week later, on March 15, I read in the paper that Onassis had died in Paris.

When I spoke with Maria again, she was trying hard to be courageous, but I could tell the effort was immense.

"Nothing matters much anymore," she said, "because nothing will ever be the same again . . . without him."

After his death, she went through the motions of pursuing her career, of planning ahead. She was hanging on to the only point of reference she still had—the image of self: the image of Callas.

Three other deaths followed the same year: those of her mentor, Visconti; di Stefano's daughter, for whom she had a deep fondness; and Pier Paolo Pasolini, the great friend who had written poems for her. On a November night, in a squalid shantytown near the beach of Ostia, Pasolini was brutally murdered. "He was a friend on whom I could always rely without ever being disillusioned," Maria said. "If another Pasolini existed, I did not know him."

She still kept up with François Valéry, Hélène Rochas, Prince Michael of Greece and her faithful group of Milanese friends as well as pianist Vasso Devetzi, who helped her practice her voice; but her outings became less frequent. Nonetheless, she hadn't "retired" or given up artistically. On May 14, 1975, two months after Aristo's death, she wrote me:

I'm fine—working very hard—I have Japan *Tosca* in November. God willing!

I've made no summer projects. Of course I would need two or three weeks of *mare* and no *fotografie*. Where do I find that!

(She later cancelled the *Tosca* and di Stefano persuaded Montserrat Caballé to sing it with him.)

Reading her letter I remember thinking, Maria, what courage you have. After all you've been through, you've managed to pull yourself together again and march on. *Brava!*

I always marveled at Maria's will to go on. I recently reminisced about that with her friend Sir John Tooley, general director of the Royal Opera House. Sir John stressed the events of the winter of 1975–76. He told me he had invited Maria to make her comeback at Covent Garden. "I chose the role of Santuzza in Mascagni's *Cavalleria Rusticana* because I felt it reasonably comfortable for her voice, and therefore would not display its weaknesses. For some time, the idea appealed to Maria, as did her prospective leading man, Placido Domingo. But later, she had a change of heart. She called me and said, 'Santuzza is not really a role for me to make my return to Covent Garden in. I think I need a more glamorous role like Tosca.'

"I went along with her wishes. I sent a repetiteur to work with her in Paris. She started to prepare *Tosca,* but little by little, the familiar excuses surfaced—her low blood pressure, a cold, the flu. You see, she pushed herself beyond her capabilities. During the years she spent with Onassis and those of her semiretirement, she made the mistake of insisting on singing the roles that had made her legendary. However, she never took into account that there were long gaps between her performances. Every performance became a first night for her, which put her in a terrible state of nerves. Instead of switching to parts she could have sustained vocally, she continued her battle to maintain prima-donna status by insisting on *Norma* and *Traviata*. Torn between singing and giving it up, she endured an inner conflict tantamount to a private hell."

She still worked on her voice, but eventually the practice periods became less frequent. Other friends, such as Franco Manino and Massimo Bogianckino, offered her work that she either declined or postponed.

Prince Michael remembers that at a dinner party, on one of her infrequent outings, Maria was engrossed in conversation with Dame Margot Fonteyn.

"My life is a nightmare, Maria," Dame Margot said. "In my profession, for a dancer, I am old, yet I have to go on dancing so as to pay for my husband's medical care. I'm so tired. At times I must push myself to get out onstage. I have the impression it's endless! The more I dance, the more debts I seem to have!"

Maria looked at her with compassion and said, "For all your miseries, I envy you!"

Sir John Tooley often visited Maria during the last two years of her life and remembers her as "an enormously warm person, equally an incredibly lonely one in her latter days. In going in to greet her, one sensed the exchange of pleasure, because it was the meeting of friends and therefore a happy occasion. I found it incredibly difficult to get out of the flat a number of times. She clung to her friends and guests simply because she had nothing to do. As I was leaving, Maria would bombard me with questions, so as to keep me for a moment longer. 'What are you doing these days? Where are you going tonight? What! You are going to the opera? Opera is dead, why go! Who is singing? Oh, no! What a waste of time. They are no good! Who is conducting? For heaven's sake! You are not serious. You can't go hear him! Why don't you stay and chat and then we'll go out for dinner?' "

Maria now turned down the grand social occasions that "Callas" used to attend. She no longer wished for the fanfare she had been attracted by during the Onassis period. She spent a lot of time in her apartment.

I remember my astonishment at finding her at home alone one New Year's Eve. I was in Rome seeing in the New Year quietly with a friend when Maria came up in the conversation. I decided to call her but didn't expect to find her at home. I was going to leave my message of good wishes with Bruna or Ferruccio, when Maria answered. "What are you doing at home, by yourself on New Year's Eve, Maria?" I asked.

"No one dares ask me out on New Year's Eve. I guess they feel they'd have to take me to some fancy ball. Silly people. All I want is someone to take me to the movies. Never mind, I have Pixie and Djedda and my TV."

She now spent most of her day watching television. It had turned into an obsession. Whoever went to visit her had to put up with her TV mania. John Ardoin remembers the first time he called on her in Paris. "After a while she picked up the remote control and started to watch television. I must be boring her terribly, I thought. She's obviously telling me she wants to be alone. So I got up to leave. 'Where are you going?' she said. 'No, no, don't leave. Sit down.' She clicked off the TV. We'd talk a few minutes, and she'd turn it on again. On, off. On, off.

"After Paris I went to Vienna, where Leonard Bernstein was conducting *Fidelio*. When I went to see him backstage, I told him I'd just seen Callas in Paris. 'That woman,' Bernstein said good-naturedly. 'I'm never going to see her again! I'm so angry with her. While I sat talking with her, she picked up the remote control and turned on the television. On, off. On, off.' I burst out laughing."

The endless watching of TV programs, the switching from one program to another, was not just a pastime, I am convinced. It was a means of searching for answers in her own life through the dramas and joys of others, of trying to connect, unconsciously examining her options. Did she have any left or was she trapped in her own legend?

She had been given an extraordinary voice, which she had learned to live with but never understood. She knew the effect it had on people but couldn't understand why she was no longer its total mistress. The well-oiled machine was breaking down and it terrified her. When she wasn't watching TV, she listened to her records over and over again. I think, in those moments, Maria wondered if Callas, like the public, hadn't betrayed her too.

Ironically, the ones most faithful to her were the press and gossip columnists, who wouldn't allow her rest from the myth. During a holiday in northeastern Greece she wrote me:

> . . . of course the photographers bothered me, but the Governor of Salonika was with us—and if there were photos taken it was without my knowing. They are beasts! All dressed, they are not interested, but in a bathing suit, ah, that's what they want— am I fat—am I thin—who is with me! etc. . . . Naturally I was with plain friends, but what will they invent? What are your plans? My love life is *null*—but very peaceful.
>
> —We shall talk when we see each other but please write lots of details.
>
> Love Maria

Weeks later, Maria woke me in the middle of the night. *"Dormivi?"*—Were you asleep? The quality of surprise in her voice as she put her question made me feel as if I were the one committing the irrational act in choosing the night for sleep. She seemed progressively unaware of time. I was annoyed at being awakened and told her so. "Take a sleeping pill after we've finished our chat," she said. After nearly an hour's talk about her difficulty in coping with Onassis' death and what she called "Pippo's rough, ungentlemanly ways," I was deeply worried about her and frustrated by the distance that separated us. She barely alluded to her work. I did not press her. Loneliness predominated in her voice. She was weary. She yawned. "Good-night, *cara*. See you soon." A monotonous, hollow tone replaced Maria's voice. I stared at the receiver. Now I was wide awake and had a number of questions I wanted answered. I started to dial her number in Paris when my eye fell on the clock. It was four in the morning, and I had no sleeping pills.

Of course, Maria's other friends were still there, although she saw little of them.

"A few months after the death of Onassis," Prince Michael recalled, "we were at a dinner party and the conversation came around to Onassis and Maria. A guest attacked Maria and, since Maria wasn't there to defend herself, I had to speak up. It was shameful to attack her like that. I told them that Maria loved Onassis; she was probably the only woman who really ever had loved him. She couldn't have cared less about his money; she was totally uninterested!"

Two weeks later, around midnight, the telephone rang at Michael and Marina's house. Marina answered. A strange voice said in Greek, "Marina, good evening, it's Maria speaking."

"The voice was totally unfamiliar. I couldn't make out who it was," said Marina. "I didn't think of Callas right away, as I hadn't seen her for quite some time. We had repeatedly invited her to lunch or dinner *en famille* over the last six months, but Maria had told me she was very busy or she had found a last-minute excuse and hadn't shown up. 'It's me, Maria,' the dark voice repeated. 'I heard about what you did for me the other night and I'm calling to thank you. You stood up for me; you behaved like true friends. I'll never forget that. I'm very touched . . . such circumstances reveal one's friends, those that really matter.' She spoke with me for about half an hour and then repeated the same speech all over again to Michael. It was the last time we were to hear from her. But the night she died, we found ourselves in a strange co-incidence involving Maria. We heard the news as we were preparing to join some friends for dinner. To our surprise, Christina Onassis, whom we rarely saw, was among the group. She went up to Michael and, without hiding her emotion, asked, 'I know you were great friends of Maria's. What was she like? Tell me, what kind of a person was she?' "

Later, Christina asked similar questions of Hélène Rochas. "Tell me, Hélène. You knew my father and Maria well. Do you really think Maria loved my father?"

"Yes, she loved your father deeply," Hélène said. "He was her great love."

"It's a pity they didn't make their life together," Christina mused. "They were two people who spoke the same language."

17

Death

When I answered the telephone in my Rome apartment on September 16, 1977, I expected to hear my travel agent's voice confirming my flight to Paris. I was going to spend ten days there visiting family and friends, Maria among them.

The caller was my friend Franco Crespi, the sociology professor. "Have you heard?" he said. "Isn't it awful! I can't believe she's gone. I'm so sad for you. . . ." I didn't understand. "Maria is gone, Nadia." I didn't react. "Maria is dead. Listen to the radio," Franco repeated patiently.

"That's not possible. I'm off to Paris to see her. . . . I spoke with her last week. Maria can't be dead."

Although I didn't believe it, my fingers groped for the radio dial.

"The voice of the century is silenced forever," said a voice out of the dark box. "Maria Callas, the greatest soprano of our time, died today in her Paris apartment." I was only half listening. "No, it's not true! It's not possible," I shouted back at the radio announcer. Then there were other voices, excerpts of old interviews: Visconti, de Hidalgo, Zeffirelli and other colleagues. They reviewed her memorable interpretation of operatic roles, they lauded Callas, the *prima donna assoluta del bel canto,* but none mentioned Maria, Maria the human being.

The music world had lost a nightingale, but what about the sensitive woman with the volcanic personality? What about my friend? The everyday Maria, full of doubts, passion and laughter? I was overcome, both by disbelief and frustration, and then I remembered what she had said to me: "I don't want to suffer. I'll go with a sigh of relief because I know I've done my work well. I mistrust the fickleness of glory but I'm not afraid of death." Maria had gone the way she had hoped, without suffering and at the height of her renown: a death almost on her own terms.

I dialed Maria's number in Paris. It was busy. Of course it's busy, what did you expect? I said to myself. In need of solace, I called Franco Rossellini. *"Il signore* has left for Paris," the housekeeper said. Franco later told me that after speaking with Bruna he had dropped everything and flown to Paris.

"When I got to 36 Avenue Georges Mandel," he said, "I found Sander Gorlinsky, Maria's agent, and her old friend, Manolo Boromeo, locked inside the apartment. Late that evening, the pianist Vasso Devetzi arrived from Athens, where she was giving a concert. Bruna told me Devetzi had been close to Maria during the last years, but until then, I must tell you, no one . . . none of Maria's friends, had ever heard of her. Then Franco Zeffirelli called, he wanted to come, and to know when the funeral was going to be, but Bruna told me to dissuade him. She said La Signora would turn over in her grave if he stepped into the house. Finally, he didn't come; he had a funeral mass said for Maria in London."

This information surprised me since I knew Zeffirelli had given contradictory accounts to other friends. He claimed he had been responsible for laying Maria out on her deathbed and had brought in ice to preserve her body during the four days it stayed at the Paris apartment.

Carla Nani Mocenigo was among the few friends Bruna and Ferruccio allowed into the apartment. "In spite of their pain, the servants were wonderfully professional," said Carla. "They firmly turned away the curious, the Callas leeches and the press. Do you realize how much money they could have made? The press offered us all huge sums to get them inside the apartment to take Maria's picture on her deathbed. They certainly were barking up the wrong tree! Can you imagine *any friend* of Maria's doing that? I must say, Maria looked beautiful on her deathbed. She looked as if she had fallen asleep and hadn't had time to comb her long hair back into a chignon."

As Maria had predicted, now that she was gone, everyone loved and claimed her. Suddenly she had masses of "good friends." If Maria watched her funeral from behind a column, as she had said she would, even she must have been astonished by the diversity and number of her new friends—two thousand of them! Government officials, delegates of the music and film worlds, stars, personalities and members of society. Maria's mother wasn't there—an attack of diabetes had kept her in Athens—but Jackie had been sent to represent the family. Meneghini wasn't present either. He was suffering from a heart condition that left him unable to travel.

The crowd filled the Greek Orthodox church on Rue Georges Bizet, while reporters pushed the mourners and each other helter-skelter in an effort to get the exclusive shot of

Princess Grace and other celebrities. Even Maria's coffin was pushed out of the way.

The mood on September 20, in the tiny Greek Orthodox church of St. Andrea in Rome, was very different. There was no show, no photographers.

That morning I had stopped at the Orthodox church— my Fiat 500 laden with pink roses and white carnations—to ask the priest in charge if a service could be arranged for four-thirty that afternoon. I wanted it to coincide with the funeral service held in Paris. "A service this afternoon? Why all the haste?" the priest inquired. "Who is it to be held for?" It seemed rather an unusual request so late in the day, coming from one who wasn't even a parishioner. "Oh, by the way," I said, purposely avoiding his last question, "I would like the service to be sung. Could you get a couple of choir members to answer your chants?"

"I'm afraid it's too late for that. Midafternoon is a bad time in Rome; that is when office work resumes." He smiled. "If you want, I can sing a little." He stroked his long dark beard. "I don't have much of a voice, but I can sort of hum along. I'll do my best. Tell me, who is the servant of God who has gone to his reward?"

"It is Maria Anna Kalogeropoulos. She loved music. I know she would love it if you sang. Father, would you allow me to put lots of flowers around the chapel? She wanted a very festive service, nothing gloomy." The priest assured me that the sexton would take care of the flower arrangements, but I wanted to do that myself. Maria would have hated the customary hedgehog flower arrangements used at funerals.

"Did this Kalogeropoulos lady live in Rome? I do not remember hearing her name, but then she may not have been a churchgoer. Did she have a family?" The priest asked. "A profession?"

"She was an opera singer," I replied. "Her stage name was Maria Callas."

The priest turned crimson, and his commanding assurance disintegrated. "Maria Callas! You want *me* to sing for Maria Callas? Oh, I cannot do that. No, no, please."

It took a bit of coaxing to get him to agree, but in the end, the service was beautiful. The priest's wavering voice gave it an individualistic touch that would have amused Maria.

The small group of friends I had summoned a few hours earlier included Giulietta Simionato, costume designer Piero Tosi, Marco Patriarca, Matteo Spinola, Giuseppe Gentile, Franco Crespi, Teresa (Maria's hairdresser during *Medea*) and a few of her other Roman *amici*. Among those gathered was an unfamiliar figure too engrossed in his grief to notice anything around him. His tattered full-length coat and uncontrolled sobbing made him very conspicuous. We all wondered who Maria's mysterious admirer was, since the commemorative service had not been announced in the press.

After the ceremony, we spoke of the fun we'd shared with Maria and the plans we'd made together. Marco Patriarca had spoken with Maria a few days earlier and had found her in an excellent mood, charged with optimism by a letter she had received from a pupil in London. She promised that she would soon be back in Rome to see her old friends, who she said were very important to her now. She wanted Marco to take her to Fregene for a fish dinner and a walk on the beach "so that we can discuss the matter of the world and of the human heart." As we chatted, I watched the man in the gray coat leave the church, clearly still filled with his grief.

I decided to go ahead with my trip to Paris and, upon arrival, made an appointment to meet Bruna the following day.

I walked along Avenue Georges Mandel, leaving the Musée de l'Homme and the Eiffel Tower behind me. Along the familiar route, I looked for a sign that would convince me that something had changed radically, but the handsome buildings and manicured gardens were as they'd always been.

I reached the third-floor landing of number 36 and rang the doorbell. After a long pause, I heard Bruna's shuffled footsteps behind the door.

"*Qui est là?*" asked a small voice.

"Bruna, *sono io,* Nadia," I answered.

Locks and bolts were turned and I was admitted into the entrance hall. Bruna looked older and lifeless. In her arms she cradled a trembling Pixie, whose cataract-covered eyes blankly searched my face for recognition. When I patted her, a high-pitched bark shook her little body, and she wouldn't let me hug Bruna until she'd licked my hand and ascertained who I was.

We stood in the bare entrance talking. After a few moments Bruna sat down on the black-and-white marble floor and motioned me to join her.

"I'm sorry I can't offer you a chair," she said, "but I can't take you in there. . . ." She pointed to the *grand salon.* "The *signora* doesn't want anyone to go in there." At the time I didn't ask who had barred access to the apartment. I wanted to hear about Maria.

"She did *not* suffer," Bruna began. "Thank God for her, it went very quickly. I had gone in with the orange juice, as usual, and to open the curtains. She said good-morning, and I went back to the kitchen to get the hot coffee. When I returned, I found la Signora slumped on the floor near the bathroom propped up against the small chest of drawers. When I asked her what was wrong, she said she was on her way to the bathroom when she had been seized with a dizzy spell and had fallen. She was all right, she said, and tried to get up. As she did so, she fell again and her color changed. I rushed to call Ferruccio, and together we managed to lift her onto the bed. She was breathing with difficulty and her complexion had turned a terrible color, her lips were blue.

"I ran to the phone to call la Signora's doctor, but the line was busy; the American Hospital was busy too. La Signora asked for some coffee, so Ferruccio took over the telephoning while I spooned coffee into her mouth. After a few spoonfuls, she said she'd had enough, that she felt better. For a few minutes, she looked comfortable. The telephone lines at the doctor's office as well as the American Hospital were still busy, so Ferruccio called his own doctor and asked him to come immediately. By the time the doctor had made his way through the heavy traffic, la Signora had passed away."

I asked Bruna if Maria had complained of any health ailments the days or weeks before her death. I remembered that the previous week when I called a second time, Maria had not come to the phone. She had a cold and a sore throat that she couldn't shake off. "Apart from the lingering cold, she seemed in good health," Bruna assured me. "The night before her death she complained of a sharp pain in her lower and middle back. She asked me to massage her back. She said it helped and told me to call a masseuse for her the following day." Bruna had difficulty finishing her sentence; she was weeping, and Pixie imitated her with a whimper.

"It's so depressing here now," Bruna stammered, looking at the empty hall and blank walls. "I'd like to go back to my village in Italy, but we don't know how long we'll be locked in here. I think it depends on the settlement of the estate. It may take a long time because la Signora Callas did not leave a will."

No will? Strange, I thought. I wonder what happened to the will Maria told me she had written a few years back that benefited the servants. Maybe she forgot to sign it? That hardly seemed possible; she was so neat and precise by nature. I didn't mention it to Bruna, since it really wasn't my business, but the question stayed with me.

A few weeks later I heard that Meneghini had come up with a will dated May 23, 1954, which he and Maria had made out before leaving on a concert tour. It stated that in case of the death of one of the two parties everything should go to the survivor. Although the couple had been granted an Italian divorce a number of years before Maria's death, the document produced by Meneghini was found valid.

As soon as Meneghini's health permitted, he went to Paris to have the will probated and to clarify a number of unanswered questions surrounding Maria's death. He also hoped to obtain permission to move Maria's ashes to the burial site he had chosen long ago for his wife and himself in Sirmione. Shortly before his own death, Meneghini expressed some of his feelings and questioned the circumstances of his ex-wife's death in a taped interview he gave Fiorella Mariani (whom I've known and worked with over the years) for a TV documentary she was preparing on Maria Callas. Fiorella finally didn't use Meneghini's interview and passed it on to me when she learned of my book project.

"Suddenly, she was gone," Meneghini told Fiorella, "and the world did not know the real reason for her sudden death, nor was there the possibility to investigate because Mr. and Mrs. Devetzi, these illustrious unknowns, gave the order to have her cremated. [Meneghini was convinced that Vasso Devetzi was married to her companion.] They determined the physical end of the great Callas. How dare they? I am the only guardian of the life of Maria Callas. And think, in their haste to have her cremated, these people didn't even have the good sense or foresight to take an imprint of her hand or have a death mask made as a remembrance."

There were other matters that troubled the old man, but his complaints fell on deaf ears. By the time he reached Paris, many people had been through the apartment, and papers and personal items seemed to be missing.

"Why the mystery, the silence around Maria's death?" Meneghini, among others, suspected that Maria had died of some kind of poisoning.

"While there is a corpse, there is still a possibility of establishing the cause of death. This woman, Maria," he said to Fiorella, "was afflicted with a number of ailments; insomnia, fatigue, nerves. . . . In other words, she was a woman who was unwell. She took drugs to alleviate these ailments, that is evident, but it was not suicide as many have suggested. I exclude that. I found out one thing," Meneghini continued, "these drugs come from the United States. They were brought in from America. For instance, Mandrax. I inquired here about Mandrax and I was told that it is a powerful poison and its use is prohibited in Italy.

"I spent all of 1978 in Paris," Meneghini recounted, "and I went regularly to the cemetery to pray and place flowers to my wife's memory. Then I found someone had played a horrible joke on me. My wife's ashes weren't behind the stone inscription. The day after Christmas 1978, the urn with Maria's ashes had disappeared and was found again the following day thrown aside in the cemetery grounds. Afterwards, someone had taken them away and placed them in a bank vault. Why? I asked the mother, the sister and Devetzi to give me an explanation. They knew nothing, they said. They were mute. Ashes belong in a church or a cemetery, perhaps in some cases in the family's home, but never in a bank.

"Why the great hurry to cremate her half an hour after the arrival of the body at the crematorium? Why hadn't they waited until the following day as is customary?"

"It was all a buffoonery! Maria's ashes were left in the depths of a Parisian bank until June 3, 1979, and then her earthly remains were scattered over the Aegean by a high-ranking official of the Greek government, but he hadn't considered the direction of the wind. The ashes flew back on board the vessel, and some went on Devetzi, and she said, 'The wind brings back the ashes, it's a gesture; it's Maria's last embrace.' Well, I would have liked to reply, 'Shame on you. That's not Maria's last embrace nor was it intended for you or for anyone else. Her last embrace was intended for me! She had written she wanted to return to Sirmione.'"

I heard about the auction of the contents of Maria's apartment through John Ardoin, who had been present on that hot, airless day in June. It wasn't quite clear who had decided to auction Maria's belongings, but among the bidders at the Georges V Hôtel were a handful of Maria's old friends as well as Meneghini.

"I walked in and the first thing I saw was the bed," said John. "The bed I had sat on many afternoons, the bed she had died on . . . and then the piano. This is awful, I thought. How she would hate people walking through here, picking up her things and looking at them." But John wasn't the only one who was outraged. John reported, "In the middle of the sale Meneghini cried out, 'This auction is a disgrace. We are insulting the memory of a great artist. This should never have been allowed!'"

Ardoin went on, "Meneghini spent lavishly that day. He bought back most of the paintings he had given Maria during their marriage, Maria's bed and the glorious eighteenth-cen-

tury silk carpet that was in her Paris living room. He intended
to add these to Maria's belongings in the museum he had
planned in her memory at Sirmione. Christina Onassis was
there too. She bought a big ceramic elephant.

"Those who believe in the occult may well have felt
another presence during the auction," John added, smiling.
"One of the locked glass doors leading out to the garden patio
burst open with immense force. It knocked over a chest of
drawers, broke its marble top and caused a painting to crash
to the floor. Later, as people were bidding on a scalloped
silver tray with a mirror inset, there was a sound as sharp as
a rifle shot. The mirror cracked down the middle and fell to
the ground."

Meneghini was very dejected by his ineffectual investi-
gations during his time in Paris. He returned to his villa on
Lake Garda to vegetate in anonymity. Loneliness and health
problems made him rely more and more on Emma Brutti, his
housekeeper. She was already in his service during Maria's
time, and after her mistress left, she slowly assumed the role
that had been vacated. After Meneghini suffered a stroke,
Emma Brutti accompanied him everywhere, even to the com-
memoration La Scala held in 1982 for Maria.

Carla Nani Mocenigo could hardly hide her irritation
when she told me about that event. "I was sickened by the
superficiality and hypocrisy of the affair. Half the audience
claimed to be great friends of Maria's, which believe me was
totally untrue; but what tipped the scales for me that evening
was my meeting with Meneghini, whom I hadn't seen or
spoken to since 1959. He asked me to come to his box. As I
came in, I saw Emma Brutti sitting in the semidarkness. Anyway, he asked me what Maria was like on her deathbed. I told
him, 'She was very beautiful.' Like a fool, I was touched by
Meneghini's interest, and then it dawned on me why he had

asked to see me. 'Carla,' he said, 'while you were in Paris, did you see any of Maria's jewelry? What about that lovely wall hanging with your family crest? Did you see that? Did you ask where it was?' I couldn't believe my ears. The jewels? The tapestry? 'Titta,' I said, 'I don't believe what you are saying! I went to Paris to pay my respects to Maria, the friend I loved, and you ask me if I saw the jewels and the tapestry? Why would I have seen or asked about them under the circumstances?' "

"Who knows where all those things ended up? It was like a thriller; objects and people kept disappearing," Giulietta Simionato told me during our meeting in Milan. "When I saw Meneghini, he told me he'd salvaged a jewelry case on which there was the inscription *jewels belonging to my husband Battista*. He was thrilled. 'You see,' he told me, 'she set them aside, which is proof of her love for me.'. . . . But Maria's papers and most of her belongings had been removed before he got to Paris. Even Maria's ashes disappeared for a while. Who assures me that the ashes that were scattered on the Aegean were Maria's? They could have been those of a donkey for all we know. . . . I asked Battista if I could buy one of Maria's rings as a remembrance, but he died before we could get together to make arrangements. After his death, although he left a clearly detailed will, to avoid discussions, everything— furniture, paintings, jewelry—vanished into thin air. Emma Brutti got what she was supposed to get, but as for the rest, no one knows what happened to it. When Signora Brutti was questioned, she said, 'I have no idea, I know absolutely nothing.' "

The mysteries surrounding Maria's death intrigued and frustrated me. But I think what annoyed me most was that Maria's private papers were not available to me or to any other writer.

Not only would they have been a great help to me, but scores and other musical materials that would have been invaluable to future voice students also seemed to have vanished.

Since two attempts at meeting with Vasso Devetzi, the president of the Maria Callas Foundation, had not been successful, I wrote to Bruna. But my letters were unanswered, and my attempts failed to reach Ferruccio and Consuelo (Maria's cook) through a contact in Milan. Their silence surprised me and seemed unwarranted after so many years of friendship. I couldn't understand it.

To whom should I turn next? Maria's mother had passed away in 1982, and at that point Jackie had yet to be found. The only alternative was Meneghini's housekeeper, Emma Brutti, whom I was told had settled with her husband and grandchildren on the outskirts of Sirmione. I had been warned she was reluctant to give interviews, and if she did, her financial demands were high.

I set out for the resort town on Lake Garda, hoping luck would be with me, as I had neither Emma Brutti's address nor her telephone number.

I chose a café-bar Valeria Pedemonte had recommended, and over a Campari soda I went about my inquiries. At the name of Emma Brutti, the card players and customers stopped their conversation and in a matter of minutes were vividly participating in mine. I'd found the local gazette! "She deserved it," said the owner's daughter from behind the bar. "Remember, after Callas left, everybody dropped Meneghini. Brutti is the only person who stuck by him."

"Yeah, yeah, and she was also seen out at parties with Meneghini wearing jewels the old man had given Callas."

"But you must admit, she took beautiful care of him," said the owner. "If she hadn't been around, he would have died ten years earlier. She did inherit a lot—nobody knows how much, for sure—but she inherited problems too. She's been robbed. I guess they were after the unpublished tapes and letters, and now Meneghini's nephews are fighting Brutti in court for part of his fortune."

"She's a sourpuss, but you've got to give the ol' girl her due. With Meneghini dead, she still goes on with the yearly commemorative service for Maria, the way he used to do."

"How should I approach her?" I asked.

"Go without calling. All she can do is boot you out," was the general consensus.

Emma and I never met. "Emma is at her sister's death-bed," her husband told me when I got to their house. He thought she would be gone at least another week.

Before leaving, I walked to the outskirts of the town to have a look at the villa where Maria and Battista had spent so many happy years. When I reached the house, perched on a hill overlooking the lake, I had a shock. The place was totally abandoned. I climbed over the rusty iron railing surrounding the grounds and walked through the overgrowth to a ruined aviary, which, judging from the trampled grass, had recently served as a lover's hideout. The stone banisters on the terrace were crumbling and the first-floor windows were boarded up, while the broken ones in the attic exposed the interior to the elements. Over the front door a shredded green canvas flapped in the wind.

Meneghini's closing words on Fiorella's tape came back to me. "By some mysterious fate," he had said, "that which belonged to this great woman has crumbled. The house in Verona was torn down, the house in Milan was torn down, the apartment in Paris had its unhappy end, the villa in Sirmione, the pool, the park . . . ravaged."

MARIA

*

Jackie Kalogeropoulos Stathopoulos's duplex apartment in Athens is a few minutes' drive from where Jackie and Maria used to live during the war.

"We've just moved in," said Jackie. "Sorry it's so dusty, but the dry climate here is a menace and good help is hard to find. Come and sit down, Nadia," she said, beckoning me to the dark green, cut-velvet sofa.

The far wall of the spacious living room was taken up by an artificial garden, from which stuffed pheasants, a life-size porcelain Afghan and a Dalmatian peered out of a wilderness of ivy, palm trees and artificial flowers.

"How do you like our garden?" Jackie asked.

"It's very cheerful," I said.

"Since the terrace will not be ready until spring, I've brought nature indoors. Do you recognize these curtains, Nadia?" said Jackie, stroking the red velvet curtains by the terrace windows. "They are from Mary's Paris apartment, remember?"

For someone who had barely moved in, Jackie had the place in shipshape order. Porcelain-framed photographs of Litza, Maria and Jackie decked the walls, tables and mantel.

Following my initial excitement at meeting Jackie at the Atheneum restaurant, I gradually became aware that she had wanted to meet me too. The invitation to her home after our dinner together made me understand that she had her own story to tell.

Now, as she served me a drink in her living room, Jackie said, "Well now, in front of Dr. Marchand and my husband, I want to say that I have accepted to talk with you because I know you were really a good friend of Mary's. For me, you understand, it is difficult to speak of these memories.

"One month or more before Mary died, I received a telephone call. I didn't recognize the voice. It said, 'Here is Maria' and I said, 'Maria who?' and she said, 'Hey, don't you recognize my voice? Maria, your sister.' Think of it, after so many years, she remembered me. I don't know why. . . . She called many times after that, always late at night, and we spoke and laughed for hours about our youth in New York and Athens. Mary would say, 'Remember this, remember that.' She said we should see each other the next time she came to Athens, but she said she did not wish to meet our mother.

"They notified me here one afternoon that my sister died. A friend of Miss Devetzi notified me. I thought that they are joking. I said, 'Who died?' 'Your sister, unfortunately, died at one o'clock.' I couldn't believe it. When I believed it afterwards, of course, I cried. My passport had expired, so friends helped me to get one quickly because I had to leave. Instead of Sunday, the funeral took place on Tuesday. I got to Paris four days after Maria died. They had her corpse in her home four days, until her cremation. My mother heard it over the television. At six o'clock, she always opens the television. They said, 'We have some news to say about the famous singer, Maria Callas, who died today. . . .' It was a terrible shock for Mother. She phoned me immediately. 'Your sister died!' she was crying. I said, 'I know. I'm sorry, Mother. I didn't want to tell you.' From then on, Mother lost her health. It was a terrible thing for her. She adored Maria. From then on it was from hospital to hospital with her diabetes, and in the last year and a half she was paralyzed. I sold the apartment here in Athens and with our furniture we moved to Paris, but we only stayed six months. The climate was not good for Mother.

"I went to Paris and saw my sister's corpse in her bedroom. It was awful, a great pain for me. There I met Miss Devetzi. She told me she was a close friend of my sister's. She took care of the funeral, everything. Mother stayed in Athens. She was too sick.

"When I arrived I found everything had been decided by Miss Devetzi. I was a stranger in Paris. I did not know how to move around in the city and I don't speak French. I was uninformed about my sister's matters."

"Was there an autopsy, Jackie?" I asked.

"No. The doctor came for her death. I was not there then, but he said it was the heart."

"Didn't you ask for an autopsy?"

"I didn't ask for anything. Then she was cremated immediately after the funeral. In the beginning, Miss Devetzi knew more about Maria's affairs than I did, so she helped me and Meneghini. She was always present at all the legal inquiries of the division of Maria's will."

"You mean, Meneghini's old will?" asked Dr. Marchand. "The will Maria told Nadia about was never found, was it?"

"No, as far as I know, there was no other will. But maybe papers were removed from the apartment before I got to Paris. Oh, I want to ask you, Nadia, about the cremation. Vasso decided about the cremation, but there was nothing in writing about it. Do you think that was really my sister's wish?"

"Yes, Jackie. That I am certain of. She told me so on two occasions."

"And what happened about the servants in all of this? Were they or were they not in Meneghini's will?" Dr. Marchand asked.

"No, they were not, and at first Meneghini did not want to give the servants anything, but Mother and I insisted. They had been so faithful to my sister. After six months' litigation Mary's estate was divided between my mother and Meneghini, and he agreed to share with us the very comfortable sum we gave them. You see, Bruna and Ferruccio were not paid very much salary during all those years with Maria and they didn't get any social security. I saw Bruna always in the same patched dress when she was not in her uniform. After Mary's funeral, I took her shopping and bought her a suit, blouse, cashmere sweater and shoes, and when Bruna left for Italy, that is the outfit she was wearing.

"But what about all the contents of the apartment, all Maria's beautiful furniture, carpets, paintings. . . ? Who decided to auction them?"

"That was Miss Devetzi's decision. I wanted to keep some things of my sister's, but Vasso said it was better to auction and then divide the money with Meneghini. I wanted to get a Greek lawyer, because, as I said, I do not know the French law, but Miss Devetzi said to me, 'A Greek lawyer? Don't bring a Greek lawyer into all this.'

"We divided with the late Meneghini Mary's clothes and other belongings. Mary had so many clothes, it was like a shop! Two hundred blouses, 250 cashmere sweaters, many many shoes, negligees, gloves . . . beautiful things, still with the label and the price tag on them. I ended up with many, many parcels. I had my share stored in Paris until I could bring them to Athens. When I went back to pick them up, there were only seven left. Things just disappeared, Nadia."

"You asked about Maria's ashes earlier," said her husband, who had been extremely quiet. "Well, it is Devetzi who decided that they should be put in the bank vault."

Isn't it incredible? I thought. Maria's fate always ends up in the hands of others.

In one of Maria's last telephone conversations with her sister, Jackie remembered, "She was feeling very ill and quite alone. She told me about all her illnesses. . . . Maybe they were worse because of all the pills. Who knows? But obviously the pills caused a strain on her heart. Maybe a timely cardiologist's control some weeks before her death would have saved her life, but perhaps Mary didn't want to take care of herself. What could become of a heart so exhausted from fighting during a life with almost all people—even with herself?" Jackie concluded as we left each other that evening in Athens.

Questions, more questions! That's what I had started out with, and unwillingly I have to accept that many are still unanswered. Mystery will probably always surround the Callas legend. In death, as in life, Maria remains center-stage, surrounded by controversy. The woman and the artist's genius still stand trial, as if part of the "destiny" she so often referred to.

"I belong to the givers," she had said. "I want to give a little happiness even if I haven't had much for myself. Music has enriched my life and, hopefully—through me, a little—the public's. If anyone left an opera house feeling more happy and at peace, I achieved my purpose."

Perhaps she knew that through music we would finally understand and find her.

"To us she seemed a tragic character. But the question is, was she really aware of this?" asked Prince Michael. "Was she conscious of this or did we build up tragedy from what we knew of her life, her career, and then the end?"

see you we *will* talk — we have
lots to say, & laugh about —
I did lots of work
this year at Juilliard and
enjoyed it. I studied on my
voice also — it went very